LOVE AND JOY

AN OTTER BLUFF ROMANCE

LINDA SEED

Linda Seed

This is a work of fiction. Any characters, organizations, places, or events portrayed in this novel are either products of the author's imagination or are used fictitiously.

LOVE AND JOY

ISBN: 978-1-7343453-6-0

The author is available for book signings, book club discussions, conferences, and other appearances.

Linda Seed may be contacted via e-mail at linda@lindaseed.com or on Facebook at www.facebook.com/LindaSeedAuthor. Learn more about Linda Seed's novels at www.lindaseed.com.

Cover design by Kari March.

Created with Vellum

BY LINDA SEED

The Main Street Merchants

Moonstone Beach

Cambria Sky

Nearly Wild

Fire and Glass

The Delaneys of Cambria

A Long, Cool Rain

The Promise of Lightning

Loving the Storm

Searching for Sunshine

The Russo Sisters

Saving Sofia

First Crush

Fixer-Upper

Loving Benny

Otter Bluff

The Icing on the Cake

Christmas in Cambria

Love and Joy

SIGN UP TO GET A FREE LINDA SEED STARTER LIBRARY

Sign up for Linda's twice-monthly newsletter and get her free ebook starter library: three full-length romances and a bonus short story available only to newsletter subscribers. Your information will never be shared or sold, and you can unsubscribe at any time.

To subscribe and get your free ebooks, go to the following address:
https://claims.prolificworks.com/free/hDF1LvnI

CHAPTER 1

Joy Maxwell needed a new angle, because what she was doing wasn't working anymore.

Last year at VidCon, the line of fans waiting for selfies or an autograph had stretched for fifty yards. This year, she'd had to send someone out to round up people to wait in line for her. It had cost five dollars a head, but it would cost her more than that if people thought she was losing her audience.

Which, let's face it, she was.

You could only do so many hair and makeup tutorials, so many videos featuring the unboxing of purses or jewelry. You could only review so many moisturizing face masks before people got bored.

And when they got bored, they watched someone else.

Joy thought about it as she pounded away on the treadmill at her gym, a layer of sweat glistening on her skin. She'd done four miles, and she had one to go. The scale in the locker room had shown her up a pound, so she turned up the speed and increased the incline for the last mile.

Amber Pittman—her best friend, who occupied the treadmill next to her—was jogging at a much more sedate pace. Amber could afford to do that—it wasn't her ass that was scrutinized on Instagram for signs of spread or, God forbid, Photoshopping.

"Slow down. You're trying to stay in shape, not kill yourself." Amber slowed from a jog to a walk.

"Can't. Extra pound." Joy would have spoken in complete sentences, but she was breathing too hard to manage it. Her running shoes—free in exchange for an endorsement—pounded against the track.

"You've got to be kidding me." Amber scowled at her. "I'm looking at almost every square inch of your body right now, and you are not carrying an extra pound."

Joy's Puma running shorts and sports bra—free in exchange for product placement—left little to the imagination, and there was certainly no place for her to hide any extra weight. Still, if Amber saw the extra pound somewhere around Joy's thighs or midsection, she wouldn't say it.

The only thing to do was beat the pound into submission.

"Did you eat this morning?" Amber asked.

Joy nodded, sending her blond ponytail bobbing. She was too out of breath to answer verbally.

"Bullshit. Or if you did eat, it was two egg whites and an apple."

One egg white and an apple, actually, but she wasn't about to admit it and have Amber launch into one of her lectures about how Joy wasn't taking care of herself.

She hit the five-mile mark and reduced the speed to cool down. Sweat streamed down her forehead and into her eyes, and she mopped her face with a towel, then dried the back of her neck and the portion of her chest that peeked out through the sports bra.

On the wall-mounted TV over the treadmills, a show about tiny houses was playing silently as captions ran across the bottom of the screen. A couple in sneakers, jeans, and T-shirts talked about their transition to tiny living.

"That place couldn't even hold my shoe collection." Joy wrinkled her nose at the screen.

"You moving into two hundred square feet?" Amber laughed. "I'd pay to see that."

Joy turned off the treadmill, took a swig of water from her insulated bottle (free with an online review), and looked at her friend. "You would?"

"God, yes. The comic potential is endless."

It planted a seed in Joy's mind—a seed that was potentially much more fertile than anything the TV couple had in their permaculture garden.

"It's a good idea," Joy told Amber when they were both showered, blow-dried, and dressed and were heading out of the gym and into the sun-blasted parking lot. "The tiny house thing, I mean."

"What idea?" Amber hefted her gym bag and squinted at Joy in the sunlight.

"Your idea. That I move into a tiny house."

Amber stopped in the middle of the parking lot and turned to face Joy. "My idea?"

"Yes. You said you'd pay to see me move into two hundred square feet. If you would, maybe other people would, too."

Amber laughed. "Now, wait. I didn't—"

"Why not? I move into a tiny house for a period of time—say, six months or a year. It could be a blog, a series of YouTube videos, plus a big presence on Instagram. Then when it's over, I could write a book."

Amber stared at her. "Holy shit. You're serious."

"I need something new. A fresh idea. The stuff I'm doing is getting old. You've got to admit that."

Not to mention the fact that, with her decreased revenue, Joy wouldn't be able to afford the mortgage on her condo in Santa Monica for much longer. She'd been able to manage just fine when she was a top influencer, but now that her fortunes were falling, she was going to have to downsize.

What if she downsized more than she'd planned?

If she sold the condo and rented a tiny house, she could fortify her savings account and save a couple thousand a month at the same time as she was reinventing her media persona.

It could be a win-win.

Joy walked a little farther toward her car, with Amber at her side, as she thought about it. Then she stopped short and spun toward her friend. "And not just the tiny house, either. I need to do the whole deal. Off the grid, sustainable everything. Maybe even some organic farming. It's gotta be a whole lifestyle thing if I want it to get attention."

Amber pointed one finger at Joy. "You wouldn't last a week."

Joy grinned. "That's where the drama comes in."

Amber stared at Joy. Then she shook her head and laughed. "It could work. Tiny houses are a big trend right now, and when you add in the fish-out-of-water angle … Hell yes, I'd watch it."

~

NIX LANDRY still hadn't gotten used to the feeling of being one infinitesimally small person adrift in far too much space.

That's what happened, he supposed, when you moved from 250 square feet into a three-bedroom ranch-style house with two bathrooms, a great room, and an open floor-plan kitchen with five times the counter space he was used to.

He was accustomed to waking up in a sleeping loft with ceilings so low he had to crawl to the ladder to get downstairs. Now, he woke every morning in a bedroom so big his bed might as well have been a raft adrift on the ocean.

The house wasn't even that big by most people's standards, but compared to what Nix was used to, it was gargantuan.

Why in God's name did anyone need this much space? He could see it, maybe, if you had a family—a wife and three or four kids. But Nix was alone, and it seemed like so much wasted housing.

Well, he wasn't here for his own amusement, and he wasn't here permanently. He was at Otter Bluff to do a job, and once he'd done it, he could go back to his own place off Santa Rosa Creek Road.

It would be a while before that happened—the house needed a lot of work. The kitchen had been remodeled recently, so that was fine, but all three bedrooms and both bathrooms needed complete updating. Not to mention that he had to do something about the erosion on the ocean side of the property.

All that, and he still had to find a renter to stay in his own house while he was here at Otter Bluff.

He hadn't been up more than half an hour when Evan called him.

Nix was out on the back deck, sitting in an Adirondack chair with a mug of coffee and watching the waves crash against the bluff, when his cell phone rang.

"Why are you calling me so early?" Nix didn't mean for it to come out as irritably as it did, but hell, it wasn't even seven a.m.

"What's the problem? You were up."

"How do you know I was up?"

"Because you're always up at the crack of dawn. It's one of your quirks. Don't lie and tell me I'm wrong."

Okay, so maybe he was right. Nix and Evan Bridges had gone to high school together, and after that, they'd shared rent on a two-bedroom apartment for a couple of years until they'd both moved on to other things. Maybe it was true that Nix had a pattern of early rising. That didn't mean he wanted to talk to someone at this hour.

"Maybe you're not wrong," he admitted. "But still ..."

"I have a meeting in ten minutes, and I wanted to check in before then. How do things look?"

Evan had bought Otter Bluff as an income property after Lisa Barlow, the former owner and an internationally famous artist, had decided she didn't have the time or interest to deal with it anymore.

The house, which sat at the edge of the Pacific Ocean in one of Cambria's most sought-after neighborhoods, had been a vacation rental for years, but the outdated interior had kept rental prices lower than they were for comparable houses in town.

That's where Nix came in. Evan, in an effort to save money on the renovations, had suggested that Nix move into the house and do the redesign himself. He could live rent-free during the project, bring in some income renting his own place, earn a reasonable fee for his work—much less than Evan would have had to pay a professional contractor—and have the satisfaction of helping out a friend.

That was how Evan had pitched it, anyway.

So here Nix was, trying to figure out where to start.

"Well, you've seen it," he began, trying to sort out in his mind what the highest priorities might be in the renovation. "The bathrooms look like hell, you need all new flooring, the bedrooms still have popcorn ceilings, you probably ought to replace all the windows with double-pane, and that's just off the top of my head. But the first thing you've gotta do is put in a retaining wall to stop the erosion at the bluff. You're gonna need a professional for that, because I'm in over my head on that one."

Nix had built his own tiny house, a project that had been one of the most fulfilling things he'd ever done. But he wasn't a professional, and he didn't want to be held responsible if Otter Bluff one day crashed into the ocean in a mess of drywall and two-by-fours.

"Yeah, okay. I knew that was coming. If you can coordinate it for me, I'd appreciate it."

"Sure." Nix took a sip of his coffee and inhaled the ocean air. "Are you sure you trust me with all of this? I'm really more of a hobbyist. A licensed contractor would be—"

"I can't afford a licensed contractor."

"Oh, hell. Yes, you can." Evan could afford ten licensed contractors, each of them with a team of personal assistants and a fleet of chauffeured limos. He was just a cheap bastard.

"Well, maybe. But I'd prefer not to pay one. You still want to do this?"

The truth was, Nix was excited about the job. He loved this stuff—loved houses and building and painting and all of the other things that came with taking a place that was tired and outdated and making it new again.

He had to do his share of bitching about it, though, just to keep Evan in line.

"Yeah, yeah. I said I would, and I will."

"All right, then. Be sure to invoice me for the supplies."

"You'd better believe I will. And Evan?"

"Yeah?"

"This is a hell of a view I'm looking at. Are you sure you don't want to move here yourself when I'm done?"

Evan laughed. "I don't have time to look at a view. You enjoy it, though."

Nix hung up thinking that he would, in fact, enjoy it as long as he was here. Drinking your morning coffee with the ocean breeze in your face and the sound of barking sea lions in your ears was exhilarating.

If Evan was too much of a workaholic to come down from the Bay Area every once in a while, then Nix sure as hell would take advantage of everything his friend was missing.

CHAPTER 2

Joy didn't jump into the tiny house idea right away. It needed thought. The whole concept needed time to percolate.

The plan—if she could call it a plan this early—had tons of potential. Tiny houses were hot right now, so she had that working in her favor. Plus, everyone loved to see someone else do something they themselves wanted to do but didn't have the nerve for.

If it went well, Joy might even have fun. And if it didn't go well, that would only benefit the blog and eventual book.

On top of all that, she had to go somewhere. Her income was dropping, her savings account was dwindling, and her condo cost three thousand dollars per month.

She had to downsize, but if people saw her doing it, they'd assume she was on her way out. The tiny house idea had the benefit of hiding her failure behind a facade of intention and planning. People wouldn't see her move as a setback if she could convince them she'd chosen it.

"Are you really going to do the tiny house thing?" Amber asked on the phone one afternoon while Joy was setting up the lighting for an unboxing video. She'd be revealing a Prada purse that she couldn't afford and that she'd be returning shortly after shooting the video.

Joy cocked her head and propped one fist on her hip as she considered it. "You know, I really think I might."

"You have to. It'd be so cool. And make sure it's located somewhere close enough that I can come and visit."

Joy had already given some thought to the location, and she'd drawn a few conclusions: she needed somewhere picturesque for Instagram and somewhere as different from Los Angeles as possible to maximize the fish-out-of-water angle. At the same time, she wanted to be within a reasonable driving distance from L.A. to be near her best friend—and of course, Nordstrom.

"I don't want to pay the mortgage any longer than I have to, so if I'm going to do it, I'll have to pull it together soon."

"This is exciting!" Amber's voice rose into a squeak of enthusiasm. "I'll come over tonight and we can find you a place to rent."

"I'm still not sure," Joy said. "I'm still not one hundred percent on this."

"That's okay. We'll just look. Maybe if you see what's out there, it'll help you decide."

Joy paused with her hand on a light stand she'd been adjusting. "We'll just look."

She was pretty sure she'd be doing more than just looking, though. The more she thought about it, the more she was leaning toward doing it. She had nothing to lose but her sky-high mortgage payment.

~

THE PLAN WAS for Nix to stay at Otter Bluff for six months. He'd be working on the renovations in his spare time while he held down a full-time job, so it was likely to take that long.

The six-month timeline made sense for a few reasons: one, the remodel easily could take that long if Evan were using a licensed contractor, considering that contractors were so in demand in Cambria that a client usually had to wait months for work to begin. Two, the defined period of time would allow Nix to rent out his place on a six-month lease, which would be easier than trying to find someone to rent month-to-month. And three, the fifteen to twenty thousand dollars Evan would lose in potential rent on Otter Bluff over that period still came to much less than he'd be paying for a contractor if he'd decided to go that route.

The day Nix moved to Otter Bluff, he'd taken interior and exterior photos of his tiny house on Santa Rosa Creek Road, making sure to emphasize the natural beauty of the location. Then he'd posted an ad on Craigslist and a few of the tiny house rental sites offering the place for twelve hundred dollars a month—a price that would be hard to find anywhere else in Cambria.

He'd gotten a few inquiries in the week since he'd posted the ad, and he'd even shown the place twice. But one of the applicants had a bad credit history and the other had balked when he'd seen the composting toilet. Some people were squeamish about a lack of standard plumbing.

He found a couple of additional websites where he could post the ad, polished it up a bit with a new, more glowing description of the place, then posted it.

If he couldn't get it rented, then he wasn't going to come out of this project as well-positioned financially as he'd hoped. And that had been a big reason for doing this in the first place. Friendship with Evan was one thing, but the possibility of pocketing an extra seven thousand dollars over the course of the lease—plus what Evan was paying him to do the renovation—was an attractive incentive.

He created a flyer on his computer, printed it, and took it to work with him so he could post it on the bulletin board at the store. He carefully cut tabs along the bottom so interested parties could tear off his phone number.

Nix was stocking organic romaine at the small Main Street market where he worked when Louise, the assistant manager and Nix's friend, came up and nudged him.

"Somebody's tearing off a tab." Louise nodded toward the bulletin board. "Maybe you'll get your renter."

Nix looked over and saw the tab-tearer: an elderly woman with newly styled silver hair, full makeup, and expensive clothes. His shoulders slumped and he shook his head.

"Nope. You think that lady over there is going to climb up a ladder to go to bed?"

"Probably not, when you put it that way." Louise appraised the woman. "Probably shouldn't even try. She's gonna fall and break something."

"Maybe it's for somebody else. A relative. A grown kid who's been sleeping on her sofa."

"Yeah, maybe."

It wasn't, though, and Nix knew it. He dismissed the thought and focused on stacking the lettuce in an inviting fashion—an abundance of wholesome green goodness.

JOY AND AMBER met at Joy's place for wine and pizza. Well, Amber was eating pizza. Joy was making do with a salad drizzled with fat-free dressing.

"Are you sure you don't want some pizza?" Amber held out a slice to her. "It's good."

"Remember the extra pound?" Joy had endured days of running, stair-climbing, carb-cutting, and spin classes, and that damned pound was still there.

"Can't you just Photoshop the pound?" Amber asked, not unreasonably. "I mean, that's what everyone else does, isn't it?"

"Sure. I can Photoshop the pound. But if I let the pound stay, it's going to invite friends, Amber. And I can't Photoshop the pound *and its friends*. And anyway, this salad is fine."

"Bullshit. That salad tastes like disappointment and despair."

"How do you know?"

"I've eaten salad before. Believe me, I know."

Joy sighed and wished she could be as casual about her food choices as Amber was. Amber had a regular job at an insurance office, which meant she didn't have to live in front of a camera. If she gained five pounds, who would care? Amber had sweet curves that were only enhanced by the occasional slice of pizza.

Joy, on the other hand, made her living looking attractive in clothes—and sometimes without them, as when she modeled bikinis or underwear on Instagram or in YouTube videos. The pound would be noticed and remarked upon if she couldn't get rid of it.

That's where things had started to go wrong with her career, after all.

About a year ago, Joy and Amber had taken a girls' vacation together in Las Vegas. They'd gambled and shopped, and they'd enjoyed a few too many cocktails at glitzy bars in enormous hotels.

But more than that, they ate.

As any visitor to the Las Vegas Strip could attest, one of the pleasures of Vegas was the food—the endless buffets, the high-end restaurants, the room service.

For once in her adult life, Joy had indulged. And after a week of hedonism, she'd come home carrying an extra five pounds.

So what, she'd thought at the time. It was only five pounds. But the Internet was a cruel place, and the five pounds had been analyzed, critiqued, and made into a spectacularly cruel meme that would probably follow her for the rest of her life.

It wouldn't have been so bad if she hadn't timed her vacation to fall right before a lingerie photo shoot.

That was a mistake she would never make again.

Another mistake she didn't intend to make again was to think of five pounds—or even one—as no big deal.

The five pounds had started a decline in her viewership—and, therefore, her advertising income—that she hadn't been able to recover from. If a period of time crammed into a tiny house with a shower the size of a phone booth could turn things around, she had no choice but to do it.

When they were finished eating, Joy and Amber took out their laptops and began searching for the perfect place where Joy could revive her career.

"Portland's big for tiny houses." Amber scanned her laptop screen.

She was sitting on Joy's sofa with her feet propped up on the coffee table, her laptop balanced on her knees. To her right, a wall of windows looked out onto the Los Angeles nightscape.

"Oregon or Maine?" Joy asked.

"Oregon."

Joy wrinkled her nose. "Doesn't matter. Both of them are too far. I want to get out of L.A., but I still want to be close enough to visit my old life from time to time."

"*Hmm.*" Amber clicked a few keys. "San Diego?"

Joy tilted her head to the side, considering it. "Not different enough. I need a real change of scenery to make this work. A whole new lifestyle along with the tiny house. I need somewhere rural. Someplace in the middle of nowhere."

"But within driving distance of L.A.," Amber said.

"Exactly."

They searched in companionable silence for a while before Amber sat up straight in triumph. "I've got it." She spun her laptop around so Joy, who was sitting next to her on the sofa, could see.

"Cambria?" Joy squinted at the screen.

"Yep. It's perfect."

"Where is it?"

Amber pulled up a new window, typed information into Google Maps, and spun the laptop toward Joy again. "See? It's just south of Big Sur, right on the coast. Small town, lots of historic buildings, a quaint-looking Main Street. And the coastline. God, just imagine the photo shoots you can do there."

"Huh." At first glance, it looked good. "Okay, show me the house."

Amber brought a slide show of the property up on her screen and passed the laptop to Joy.

From the outside, the house looked like a rectangular box with a peaked roof, the whole thing on wheels. The house was covered in wooden shingles, and it had a miniature porch on one end. Windows dotted the sides.

The inside was constructed of blond wood, with a sitting area at one end, kitchen and bathroom at the other, and a ladder leading to a sleeping loft above the sofa.

"It's cute, don't you think?" Amber said. "It looks like a cozy cabin in the woods."

"It can't be more than, what? Three hundred square feet?" Joy said.

"Two fifty. Look, there's a washer-dryer unit tucked in next to the bathroom. And, oh, wow. There's an outdoor tub."

"An outdoor tub?" Joy wrinkled her brow. "You mean a hot tub."

"No. I mean a bathtub. Look." She pulled up the photo. "Can you imagine taking a bath under the stars? Jeez, that's like heaven."

"Maybe you should be the one to move there," Joy said.

"I'm not the one who needs a book deal," Amber said pointedly. "You are."

Joy scrolled through the photos of the house, which was nestled under a towering sycamore tree; the land, all rolling grassy hills dotted with oaks and pines; the organic garden off to the side of the house, exactly the way Joy had imagined; and the picturesque creek that ran through the property.

She needed to do a certain amount of suffering if this plan was going to work.

But maybe she wouldn't be suffering quite as much as she'd thought.

CHAPTER 3

Nix got the e-mail inquiring about the tiny house while he was on his break at the market. He was sitting in the back room with a veggie wrap and an iced tea, looking at his phone, when he saw it.

The inquiry was ordinary enough—was the house still available? How soon could an approved renter move in?—but things got really interesting when he Googled the name of the woman asking about his house.

He always Googled them; he'd have been an idiot not to. Usually, he found something on LinkedIn about their work history, or a Facebook profile showing their inordinate love of cats. This time, though, what he found made him put down his wrap and focus completely on his screen.

The first hit for Joy Maxwell was an Instagram photo of her standing on a balcony wearing nothing but a red bikini, a cityscape behind her and her shiny blond hair flowing in the breeze.

He didn't realize he was staring slack-jawed at the photo until Louise commented on it.

"What's so fascinating?" She paused on her way through the break room as she headed toward the employee restroom. "You're staring at that phone like you expect it to start spitting diamonds."

He blinked a few times as he came back to his surroundings. "Oh. Somebody wrote to me asking about the house."

"Okay …"

"Here she is." He turned the phone around so Louise could see.

"Oh. Shit." Louise whistled appreciatively. "Are you still gonna take her credit history? If it were me, it'd be an automatic yes as long as she brings the bikini."

"I won't tell your wife you said that."

Louise, a woman in her late twenties with spiky black hair and a nose ring, smirked at him.

~

JOY MADE an appointment to talk on the phone with the tiny house's owner the next day. If she'd been closer, she'd have driven up to Cambria and looked at the place in person. But she'd already put her condo on the market, and her Realtor said it would show better empty, so Joy wanted to lock things down sooner rather than later.

The phone call was routine enough until they got to the part about Joy's employment.

"I'm an influencer," she told him, as though that were an actual job.

"An influencer," he repeated.

"Yes."

"Who, exactly, do you influence? And about what?"

She launched into an explanation of what she did for a living: through various means including social media, YouTube, and her personal blog, Joy promoted products and the lifestyle that came with them.

"So you advertise things," he said.

"Sort of. But it's not just paid ads. It's product placements, reviews, videos of me using things and unboxing things. It's all out there on the web if you want to see it."

"Why would people want to watch you use things?" Nix asked.

It was a fair question.

"Look. I can show you my tax returns. I can show you bank statements. I can pay the rent, and I have references. I can get you in touch with the bank that has my mortgage—they'll tell you I've never missed a payment."

"It's first and last up front, plus a security deposit equal to one month's rent."

"I can do that." Hell, all of that combined was barely more than one month's mortgage payment at her current place.

NIX WASN'T sure why he'd given her a hard time about her work, asking her what an influencer was and why anyone would want to watch her do the influencing.

He went on the Internet as often as the next person. He went on Instagram. He knew what she did and how it worked and why.

It was all so absurd, though, that he'd wanted to hear her justify it. He'd wanted to hear her defend what she did as a real job, a real career.

In short, he'd kind of been an asshole to her.

He felt bad about that, because he wasn't an asshole in general. At least, he tried not to be.

He also had found himself giving her a ration of crap because he was wary of his own impulse to give her the house, no questions asked, just because of how she looked. He'd been pushing back against his own caveman urge to grab the pretty girl by the hair and drag her home with him.

Nix was a rational guy who was more evolved than that. So he looked at the financial documents she e-mailed to him, checked her credit, followed up on her references.

Then he called her back and offered her a six-month lease.

"Really? That's awesome. When can I move in?" She sounded so excited he almost forgot to ask the question that was really on his mind.

"Look, Joy. Are you sure this is for you? I checked you out online. You're into a certain kind of lifestyle, and the house—"

"It's exactly right for what I need," she told him. "Is the first of the month okay?"

~

ONCE SHE'D SENT him the up-front money and electronically signed the lease, Joy had a lot of work to do. She had to pack up her condo, hire movers, and prioritize her belongings, deciding what to take with her to the tiny house and what to put into storage with her furniture and other large items.

She had to arrange for a post office box—the tiny house didn't get mail service—and have her mail forwarded there, cancel her gym membership, and write her first blog post about the move.

She had to have the condo professionally cleaned so it would show well to house-hunters.

And she also had to tell her mother she was leaving.

She dreaded that last part, so she saved it until the last minute.

~

"MOM? ARE YOU HOME?" Joy poked her head in the front door—which had been unlocked in spite of all of Joy's admonitions—on the day before she was scheduled to leave for Cambria.

"Joy? Honey?" Delores Maxwell emerged from the hallway leading to the kitchen with a dishrag in her hand. "Oh! Did I know you were coming? I don't remember anything, but you know how I am these days. My mind's like a sieve."

"You're fine." Joy came into the house, closing the door behind her, and gave her mother a stiff and perfunctory embrace. "I just thought I'd pop by."

"If I'd known you were coming, I'd have planned dinner. We can go out, though. There's a new French place I've been wanting to try...."

"You don't have to plan anything, Mom. Just relax."

Joy followed her mother into the kitchen, where Delores had been in the middle of cleaning out the refrigerator. Plastic containers, milk cartons, and condiment jars littered the counter, and the refrigerator stood open. The sink was full of soapy water Delores had been using to scrub the shelves.

"I'll just put all this back," Delores said.

"Don't let me stop you from doing what you were doing," Joy told her. "Just pretend I'm not here."

"Well ... all right." Delores dipped the dishrag in the sudsy water, wrung it out, then stuck her head in the refrigerator, wiping down shelves and walls and scrubbing at stray bits of ketchup and milk residue that had accumulated since the last time she'd done the task. "To what do I owe the honor of your presence?"

Joy's first impulse was to be defensive at her mother's sarcasm. Why couldn't a daughter just make an impromptu visit without it being a big thing?

But when she considered it, she had to admit her mother had a point. Joy hadn't been to visit in more than a month, even though her mother's house in Manhattan Beach was less than twenty miles from Joy's condo.

"Actually," Joy began, "there's something I wanted to talk to you about." She was sitting at a new kitchen table Delores had bought to replace the one where Joy had eaten chicken nuggets and macaroni and cheese as a toddler, the table where she'd labored over math homework and school art projects. The old tabletop—probably in some thrift store now—still had the scratch she'd made when she'd accidentally dropped a ceramic bowl full of mashed potatoes on it in ninth grade.

"I thought so," Delores said. "If there wasn't something, you wouldn't be here."

"Mom, that's not fair." But it was fair. It was.

"Either way, you'd better come out with it." Delores emerged from the refrigerator, put the rag in the sink, and washed her hands. Then she came to the table and sat across from Joy, the contents of the refrigerator still lined up on the countertop.

"You can go ahead and finish first. I didn't mean to—"

"Go ahead and tell me, Joy. No sense putting it off, whatever it is."

Delores looked like an older version of Joy: trim figure, brown eyes, blond hair. The two women had the same finely sculpted cheekbones, the same refined nose. Like Joy, Delores had always had an eye for fashion, and even while cleaning out the refrigerator, she was dressed in an upscale ensemble that would look appropriate at a society luncheon. Her face was carefully made up to hide the fine lines that had formed around her eyes and mouth over the past few years.

"It's just ... I'm starting a new project, and I'm really excited." Joy tried to put the best possible spin on it. "It's going to combine social media and blog posts, and I'm hoping to get a book deal out of it. It's a new direction for my career, and I wanted to tell you about it."

"Your career," Delores repeated, and the way she pronounced the word suggested that she disagreed with its appropriateness in relation to what Joy did for a living.

"Yes. My career."

"Is this new direction going to get you an agent? Is it going to get you auditions? Because otherwise—"

Ah, now Joy remembered why she didn't visit more often. Her mother had decided early on that Joy was going to be a star, and to her, being popular on YouTube didn't qualify, regardless of the impressive income Joy had made at the height of her popularity. "I don't want auditions, Mom," she said. "I'm not an actress."

"After all of the money I spent on acting classes, you could at least make more of an effort. You're not getting any younger." Delores got up from the table, took a glass out of a cabinet, and poured herself some sparkling water from a bottle on the counter. She didn't offer any to Joy.

"Mom. If you want someone in this family to be a big TV star, maybe you should go out on auditions yourself. That way, you could have what you want and you can stop being ashamed of me."

Delores sat back down, looking tired. She pressed two fingertips to her forehead and sighed. "I'm not ashamed of you, Joy. I just think you could be doing so much more with your career. You're so beautiful. And your figure—"

Of course the conversation had come back to what really mattered to Delores—how Joy looked. The pattern had started early, when Delores had entered Joy in her first beauty pageant at age five. Since then, nothing else had mattered. Not Joy's interests, or her intelligence, or her own ambitions. Only the question of whether she photographed well and how effectively she could grab male attention.

She could have pointed all of that out, but she hadn't come here to anger her mother. She'd come to give her the news.

"I'm moving," she said. "I'm … I'm leaving L.A. and going to Cambria."

Delores looked at her daughter blankly. "Where's that?"

"It's on the Central Coast, near Big Sur. About a three-hour drive north of Santa Barbara, so I can still come down for weekends or holidays or—"

Joy stopped talking as she saw the stricken look on her mother's face. She watched as Delores composed her features and got up from the table to put her water glass into the sink.

"How do you expect to build a career in the industry if you're living in the middle of the wilderness?"

"I don't, Mom. That's what I've been telling you. I'm going to move into a tiny house and then blog about minimalism. I'm hoping to write a book."

Delores fixed Joy with a withering glare. "I will never understand why you set your sights so low. I had such high hopes for you and your career, and you settled for an Instagram presence and a YouTube channel."

"My Instagram presence and YouTube channel bought me a $750,000 condo, Mom."

"Which you're giving up. I suspect that's because you can't afford it any longer. Am I wrong?"

The fact that Delores was right stung more than Joy wanted to admit.

"I didn't come here to debate it. I came here to tell you I'm doing it," she said.

Delores turned her back on her daughter and started putting things back into the refrigerator. "That's fine, Joy."

But it wasn't fine—that much was clear from how her mother was avoiding eye contact.

"Mom, it's close enough that I can visit."

"But you won't."

Joy opened her mouth to protest, then closed it without saying anything. She could insist that she would call, that she would come down to take her mother to lunch or to enjoy Delores's home cooking. But that would have been a lie, and they both knew it.

"I know I haven't been around much, but … I've been busy," Joy tried. It felt as lame and meaningless as it must have sounded.

Delores stood at the sink, her back to her daughter. "You know, I don't see what difference it makes if you're here or there or on the moon. You're not interested in the things I want for you, and none of that is going to change."

Joy couldn't argue with that, because it was true.

CHAPTER 4

The visit with her mother had been awkward and painful, but it was done now, and Joy felt the relief of that as she loaded her things into her car and started the drive toward Cambria.

She'd packed light—she only had two suitcases full of clothes and six boxes of random belongings. She'd managed to fit all of it into her SUV without having to pull a trailer behind her or tie anything to the luggage rack.

Narrowing things down had been hard, but she was proud that she'd managed it. The rest of her things were being brought to a storage unit in Cambria.

She'd initially thought to store her belongings in Los Angeles, because it would be much cheaper if the movers didn't have to travel so far to deliver everything. But what if she needed something? What if she discovered that some indispensable item was locked up in storage a five-hour drive south? This way, she'd be able to retrieve anything she needed.

Joy left midmorning, after the rush-hour traffic had thinned. Leaving at ten a.m. also meant she'd been able to have a goodbye breakfast at a local diner with Amber. They'd both cried, but that was silly. Amber would visit. They'd already planned their first sleepover for the end of the month.

She blasted music as she drove up Highway 101 past Thousand Oaks and into Ventura beneath a clear blue sky. The temperature was cool but pleasant—typical of April in California—and Joy felt a sense of adventure and possibility.

Yes, the tiny house was going to be an adjustment. But surely she was up to the challenge.

At least, she hoped she was.

~

NIX SPENT the morning getting the house ready for Joy Maxwell's arrival.

He'd already moved all of his belongings to Otter Bluff, so today he focused his efforts on cleaning the place from top to bottom. He mopped the floors, scrubbed the toilet, scoured the shower floors and walls, polished the stainless steel kitchen sink, and even cleaned the inside of the oven—something he hadn't done before because he rarely used it.

He cleaned the windows, then swept the front porch and placed the outdoor furniture in an attractive arrangement.

All of that would have been standard procedure for a landlord preparing to rent a property, but for Nix, it was so much more. He'd built this place with his own two hands, his own sweat and labor. He was proud of what he'd done, and he wanted Joy Maxwell to like it. He wanted her to see in the place what he did.

Knowing what he knew about her, though, there was a good chance she wouldn't appreciate what he'd built here. Anybody with a clothing and shoe collection like hers would find it a significant adjustment moving into Nix's house.

His concerns proved valid when Joy arrived later that afternoon.

~

JOY WAS DISMAYED, first of all, when she realized she'd have to access the house via a dirt road. Her SUV was less than a year old, and she hadn't anticipated getting it coated in dust on a daily basis.

Not only that, but what would happen when it rained? Was she destined to get stuck in a bog of mud on her way to the grocery store or the post office?

She bumped her way along the road—if you could call it that—and emerged into the clearing where the house stood, a giant tree of some sort towering over it.

Joy had to admit it was pretty—the land with its tall grass and stands of trees, the painfully blue sky overhead—and she tried to focus on that as she parked next to the house and got out of her car.

The man standing on the front porch waiting for her was tall and athletically built, with thick, dark hair that almost reached his shoulders. He needed a shave, and he was wearing worn jeans, torn at the knees, a pair of sandals, and a T-shirt that looked like it had been laundered at least a hundred times. He was leaning against the doorway of the house, his arms crossed over his chest, already smiling at her before she even got out of her car.

The smile made something flutter inside her chest, and she wished he would stop it so she could focus.

"Hi," she called up to him as she made her way up the steps to the porch. "I'm Joy."

"Nix." He reached out to shake her hand.

His full name had been on the rental agreement, so she knew Nix was short for Phoenix. Looking at him, she had to figure his parents were hippies. Were those Birkenstocks on his feet? Yes, she concluded as she looked down while trying to seem like she wasn't looking. They were. Definitely hippies.

He wore the look well, though. His faded jeans fit his body like they'd been made for him, and the hair—well, the hair was simply glorious. She repressed the urge to touch it.

"You ready for a tour of the place?" He was still holding her hand, and the contact made her cheeks hot. She resisted the desire to stare at his eyes, which were a shade of blue so light they reminded her of a cloudy midday sky.

"Um … sure. I can't wait."

SEEING two hundred and fifty square feet in online photos was one thing. Actually standing in the space was another.

The place was tidy, well-designed, and cozy. But, my God, she could practically stretch out her arms and touch both opposing walls at the same time. And she would have to climb a ladder into the sleeping loft and crawl to her bed every night. She'd known that after looking at the photos, but the pictures hadn't been the same as standing here staring reality in the face.

"Everything okay?" Nix asked as she looked around the house in thinly disguised horror.

"Um … yes. Of course. Absolutely."

The stove only had two burners. Two burners! And the clothes closet—which was, inexplicably, in the kitchen—looked like it wouldn't hold more than five or six hanging items. Once she hung up the outfit she was wearing, she'd have room for a coat, maybe, and not much else.

"This isn't much space for clothes." She tried to make it sound like a casual, neutral observation instead of like the complaint it was.

"Well, there's storage under the sofa." He led her into the sitting area, where he pulled up a sofa cushion to reveal a space underneath. "And there's more under the bed."

They went up into the loft—where they both had to crawl to the bed—and he showed her that the mattress lifted on some sort of hydraulic mechanism, allowing her to store shoes, folded clothing, or anything else under there.

"Oh. That's … great." She tried to sound like she meant it.

She thought she was doing a fairly good job of hiding her dismay —until she saw the composting toilet.

"You store the sawdust here"—he pulled out a drawer full of the stuff, along with a plastic scoop—"and you just use it to cover your waste after you use the toilet. It vents to the outside, so it shouldn't smell if you keep the lid closed."

"I cover it with *sawdust?*" Surely humans weren't meant to do such a thing. "And then what do I do with it? You know, when it's full?"

"You just take out the liner, tie it closed, and throw it in the trash. Easy."

"Easy," she repeated, more to herself than to him. "And ... *why* doesn't it flush? Not that I'm complaining, it's just ..."

"Because this place is off the grid." He gave her a half smile that might have been mocking her. "No power, water, or sewer service. You get your power from the solar panels on the roof, and your water comes from the tank outside. Not only is it eco-friendly, it's low-cost. When I'm living here, I've got no rent and no utility bills."

"You live here usually? I mean ... full time?"

"Sure. Right now I've got a place in town, but I've lived here for the past year, ever since I built the place."

The fact that he'd built it himself meant she had to do a better job of hiding her bad attitude. Though she suspected from the look on his face that it might be too late.

~

NIX LEANED his shoulder against the wall, crossed his arms over his chest, and regarded his new tenant. They were outside, where they'd gone so he could show her the water tank and the solar panels. Now, he was wondering if all of this had been a waste of time.

He should have known it would be. The woman he'd seen online had not been someone who would appreciate eco-friendly off-grid living in a minimalist environment.

"Look. I know you've already signed the lease, but I'll let you out of it if you want." If she was miserable here and he held her to the lease, it would only cause heartache and suffering—for him, whenever she called to complain about something.

"What? No. It's … it's perfect. For what I need, I mean. It's just right."

He was skeptical, and he squinted at her in the sunlight. "And what's that?" he asked.

"What's what?"

"What you need. What is that, exactly?"

She seemed to weigh her answer. She ran a hand through her hair, and the strands shimmered as though she'd had gold woven in there. Which she might have, given her high-maintenance beauty rituals.

"I need to downsize," she said. "And I need a break from L.A."

"Well, this is downsizing, all right." He'd seen her condo on YouTube—the place looked like one of the Kardashians lived there. "And it's not L.A."

"Exactly. Now … the solar power. Does it go out a lot, or is it pretty reliable?"

~

NIX HAD a distinct feeling that his house was a mismatch for this overly pampered, overly groomed blond. That impression was only strengthened when he helped her bring her things into the house.

Two big suitcases and six large boxes. By the time they'd brought all of it inside, every bit of floor space was taken and there was nowhere to stand.

"You're gonna want to put some of your stuff in storage," Nix said mildly, trying not to sound judgmental.

"But … I already did. I already put most of my stuff in a unit in town. This is just the essentials."

She'd opened one big box to reveal it was entirely filled with shoes. Nix himself had exactly three pairs of shoes: the sandals he was wearing, one pair of athletic shoes, and one pair of dress shoes. He hadn't worn the dress shoes in months.

He picked up a four-inch spike-heeled pump from the box and held it up. "This is essential?"

She snatched the shoe from him. "For my mental health, yes."

"Okay." He nodded. "This is Cambria, though. Not much call for four-inch heels when you're walking on the beach or hanging out with the cows."

Up on the hill above her, several black cows grazed and mooed.

"Are you my landlord or my fashion adviser?" She was starting to sound testy.

"Landlord," he said. "You're right. Your shoes are your business."

"But?" She arched one eyebrow at him, which he found fascinating. He'd never understood why some people could do that and others couldn't.

"But, I'm just thinking this place doesn't seem like you. Not exactly a match made in heaven."

"Well, that's kind of the point," she said.

"What do you mean?"

She hesitated. "I mean, the way I was living wasn't working for me anymore. I needed something new."

CHAPTER 5

"So, are you there yet? How's the new place?"

Joy was just starting to unpack when Amber called. She paused amid open boxes and random items of clothing to update her friend.

"Small," Joy said.

"Well, that's why they call it a tiny house. Because it's … you know. Tiny."

Joy didn't say anything.

"Is everything okay?" Amber asked.

Joy sighed. She would have sunk down onto the sofa if it weren't entirely covered in her belongings. "Yes. I guess so. I mean … sure." She shoved a pile of jeans aside to make a space to sit, then settled in on a tiny cleared spot of cushion.

"Okay. What's wrong? What's the problem?"

How to explain? How could Joy convey to Amber the depth of her certainty that she'd made a horrible mistake? Changing her lifestyle was one thing, but this? This was barely more than camping.

"I'm just not sure what I've gotten myself into, that's all. I mean, you should see this place."

"I have seen it. We looked at it online together, remember?"

"Yes, but in person, it's even smaller. I have to crawl to bed, and Amber? I have to shit on sawdust."

"I don't even know what that means."

"It means, this place doesn't have a regular toilet. It's off the grid. Which means no flushing. Ergo, the sawdust."

Amber burst into laughter.

"What's so funny?" Joy demanded.

"I'm just imagining it, that's all. You, your shoe collection, and the sawdust."

"My shoe collection! That's another thing. He mocked my shoes."

"Who did?"

"The landlord. He held up one of my Louboutins and said I wouldn't have much call for it out here in the middle of nowhere. Which I won't, I suppose, but the asshole was *smirking*!"

"Oh, boy. He dared to diss your shoes. Did you hand him his ass?"

She wanted to say yes, but in fact, she hadn't handed him his ass so much as she'd enjoyed looking at it. Nix Landry, she had to admit, wasn't hard on the eyes. That hair? God. Joy had nice hair, but she'd have paid thousands to have his, with its rich color and its glorious waves. And his eyes were … magnetic. Even as he was mocking her shoes, she'd felt this curious urge to get lost in those eyes.

"Joy?" Amber brought her back from her reverie. "Are you there?"

"Yeah. I'm here."

"So, the landlord's a jerk. Is that going to be a problem, do you think?"

"Oh … probably not. The bigger issue is that there's no place to put my things. I brought the bare minimum, Amber! The absolute bare minimum! And it looks like half of it is going to have to go. Shit. The ad said there was plenty of storage space. Maybe that's true if you have three outfits, four books, and a coffee mug. But I have *things*! How am I supposed to live without my things?"

"You know," Amber said, "what you've described is the perfect scenario."

"How? How is it perfect?" Joy threw her free hand into the air in exasperation.

"Your project wouldn't amount to much if it were a seamless transition, would it? *Wild* wouldn't have been a very interesting book if Cheryl Strayed had been prepared and had a good time. 'I had a nice walk.' The end."

Joy allowed herself a wry smile. "I guess."

She knew Amber was right. This was supposed to be a fish-out-of-water story, wasn't it? It wouldn't be of much value if Joy had been moving into an environment similar to the one she'd left.

"It's just ... I feel like I've failed, Amber. And this? All of this? It's evidence of my failure."

"You didn't move to the tiny house because you couldn't afford your condo anymore," Amber said.

"I didn't?"

"No, you didn't. You moved there for an adventure, so you could write a blog and build it into a book deal. That's why you're there, and the place sounds absolutely perfect for that purpose. So everything is going swimmingly."

What would Joy do without Amber? How would she ever cope without her friend within close reach?

"I miss you already," Joy said.

"I miss you, too. But I can't wait to see the place. I can't wait to take a crap on sawdust."

"That makes one of us."

~

ONCE NIX GOT Joy settled in the house, he went back to the market for the closing shift. He clocked in, tied an apron around his waist, pinned on his name tag, and began stacking bags of organic quinoa on the shelves.

"So, how's the renter?"

Nix looked up from where he was kneeling on the floor to see Louise looming over him, her pierced eyebrows high in expectation.

"A disaster, probably."

"Really? Do tell."

He paused with a bag of quinoa in his hand. “Blond. Manicured. A big fan of four-inch heels. She won’t last a month.”

Louise let out a boisterous laugh. “At least you can ruthlessly judge and berate her while you’re waiting for her to flame out.”

“Yeah, there’s that.”

He didn’t really want her to flame out, though. When he’d built the house, he’d felt something special in it—something with the ability to soothe souls and unite restless people with the land. That’s what the place had done for him, anyway. And he sensed in Joy the need for a soothed soul.

It wasn’t Nix’s job to fix anyone, and it wasn’t his house’s job to do that, either. But was it so wrong that he kind of hoped it would work out that way?

“She didn’t like the place.” He didn’t mean to sulk, but Joy’s obvious distaste over the house he’d built had hurt his feelings.

“Are you kidding? That place is amazing. I’d live there in a heartbeat.”

He could tell she meant it, and that mollified him somewhat.

“I hope it wasn’t a mistake to rent it out,” he said. “That house … It’s more than just a house to me.”

“I know it is. Well, you can always kick her out on her ass if she doesn’t come around.”

He couldn’t, really—there was a lease—but that hardly seemed like the point.

“She’s even prettier in person than she is on Instagram,” he said, though the observation was irrelevant and probably sexist.

“Oh ho!” Louise clapped in delight. “Are you smitten, then? Are you enchanted, Nix?”

He wouldn’t say that. But he could admit that the way Joy Maxwell looked would make dealing with any bullshit from her a little bit easier.

~

IT DIDN’T TAKE LONG for Joy to unpack.

The house had come with kitchen essentials—dishes, pots, and pans—linens, and furnishings, such as they were. That meant all she had to do was put away her clothes, books, laptop, and random personal items, and she was done.

The hard part was deciding what to keep in the house and what to box up and put back in the SUV so she could take it to the storage unit.

Sadly, she had to admit Nix had been right about the shoes—four-inch heels weren't exactly appropriate for her current surroundings. She kept one pair of Louboutins—who knew? She might at some point end up at an upscale restaurant—and regretfully returned the rest to the box she'd brought them in. She supplemented those with a pair of running shoes and a practical pair of low-heeled boots, and that was all she had room for on the floor of the minuscule clothes closet.

The situation with her clothes was even more dire.

She decided which items got priority for the tiny hanger space as though she were triaging accident victims. Long-sleeved white silk shirt? Yes. Wool Valentino fit-and-flare dress? Sadly, no. Little black Escada sheath dress? Probably impractical, but she couldn't bring herself to put it in storage, so yes. Quilted Moncler coat? She was probably going to need that.

Once the closet space was full, she folded her more practical items—jeans, T-shirts, sweaters—and placed them in the storage space beneath the sofa. Underthings, pajamas, swimsuits, and other miscellaneous items went into a covered basket on a shelf in the living area.

She arranged her books on the same shelf, keeping the four she had room for and returning the rest to their box. Then she arranged her laptop, journal, pens and pencils, and other work-related items on a tiny built-in desk just off the kitchen.

When she was done, the SUV was nearly as full of boxes as it had been when she'd arrived. She loaded one of her suitcases—now empty—into the car as well, as she didn't expect to need it, and put the other in the space under the bed in case she needed to flee to civilization.

With all of that taken care of, it was time to go to work. She made a video of the house, highlighting the most interesting—and in this case, interesting meant horrifying—features.

She spent a good deal of time on the composting toilet—naturally —and the outdoor bathtub, emphasizing the concept that she had somehow left the twenty-first century and found herself in some rugged earlier time without traditional plumbing.

And, okay, she hammed it up a little in the video. If she was slightly unsettled by the plumbing situation, she portrayed herself as mortified. If she found the tight space a bit challenging, she played it in the video as though she had committed to living inside a hamster cage.

She rewatched it, edited it, and then uploaded it to YouTube. Then she wrote an accompanying blog post and published it to her site.

She also needed to post a photo to Instagram—something incorporating the outdoor tub, maybe—but that could wait until tomorrow. She'd accomplished a lot today, and she congratulated herself on it as she stripped off her clothes and stepped under the hot spray in the tiny shower.

Maybe she'd have to try that outdoor tub sooner rather than later.

CHAPTER 6

Nix had the day off from the market the following day, so he applied himself to the job of renovating the master bathroom at Otter Bluff.

He needed to replace everything: the vanity, the toilet, the tub and shower enclosure, and of course, the flooring. Then the room would need new lighting, a coat of paint, and some decorative towel racks, and he'd be done.

Easy.

He'd need some help with the demo, though—he was only one person, and carrying a bathtub out of the house and into the Dumpster he'd arranged for was more than he could manage on his own.

Louise's brother needed work, so Nix had arranged to hire him for the day at Evan's expense. Together, they removed the bathtub, carried it outside, and heaved it over the side of the Dumpster with a satisfying crash. Then they did the same with the vanity—a horrific relic of the seventies with a pink faux marble countertop—and the toilet, which they might have kept, he guessed, if he hadn't planned to upgrade to a more water-efficient model.

They also took down the ugly light fixture and trashed that, and they worked together to pry up the old linoleum flooring.

At the end of the day, Nix felt sore and tired, but in a good way—in a way that gave him the satisfaction of hard work done well. He paid Leon, then offered him a cold beer to celebrate the end of the workday.

They were both sweaty, dusty, and tired as they settled into the Adirondack chairs on the back patio, each with a cold beer in his hand, the waves crashing against the bluffs below the house. Nix had kept his hair tied back while he worked to keep it out of his way, but now it was loose and ruffling in the ocean breeze.

"So. Lou tells me you rented out your place." Leon looked out at the water. A sailboat near the horizon headed south toward Morro Bay.

"I did." Nix nodded and took a deep swig of beer.

"Wish you'd told me. I'd have taken it."

Nix took a moment to savor the idea of Leon in a tiny house. The guy was six foot three and went at least 220 pounds. The shower would fit him like an ACE bandage. Still, he'd have paid the rent on time—if he didn't, his sister would kick his ass.

"Wish I had," Nix said mildly as he looked out at the water. "I'm not sure about the renter." He told Leon the relevant details about Joy Maxwell, ranging from her shoe collection to her online profile. "I mean, if she's interested in the Central Coast, she should be down at the Four Seasons in Santa Barbara."

"Huh. Why isn't she?"

"The mysteries of women elude me," Nix said.

He'd never uttered a truer sentiment.

THE MYSTERY of this particular woman—at least, the one regarding her choice of living arrangements—became clear to Nix later that night as he relaxed on the Otter Bluff sofa with his laptop open in front of him.

When he Googled Joy Maxwell, thinking to check out her

YouTube channel, he found a video she'd just posted along with a link to her blog.

He played the video out of curiosity—then almost dropped the laptop onto the floor as he realized what he was seeing.

It was his house—and she was making fun of it.

There she was, leading the viewer on a tour of the home Nix had built with his own sweat, his own love and determination. In each space, she offered commentary about the absurdity of tiny houses in general and his own in particular, portraying his home as only slightly better than, say, a medieval dungeon or a Turkish prison.

There she was with her perky nose and her silky hair, making faces at the camera to indicate her distaste.

Because Nix was, apparently, a masochist, he moved on to the blog when the video was done. She made the same points there, for the most part, except that the blog allowed her to go into more detail. She contrasted the condo she'd come from—a spacious two-bedroom in Santa Monica—with the place where she now found herself. Barely more than a cardboard box on the side of the road, to hear her tell it.

Nix was so outraged he couldn't stay seated, so he put his laptop aside and stood up, running his hands through his hair. Then he sat down again. Then he stood up.

Shit. Shit. Could he still throw her out? Not likely. There was nothing in the lease agreement that said she couldn't slander his house on social media.

He could offer to let her out of the lease, though. He could even suggest it in strong terms.

Which was exactly what he did moments later when he had her on the phone.

"I saw your YouTube video," he said after a perfunctory hello. "And I read your blog. I guess you should have come up to take a look at the place before you signed the lease. It's fine, though. I'll let you out of it. You can have your up-front money back, and I'll prorate the rent. Let's just pretend the whole thing never happened. And if you could take down the video and the blog, that would be great."

He was trying to sound reasonable, but it was a challenge to keep the anger out of his voice.

"Take them down?" she said. "But … I've already gotten more views than for my last four videos combined."

"That's nice, I guess. But it's insulting, and it's humiliating. I'm hoping to develop a career designing tiny houses, and seeing you trash-talk the one I built isn't going to help."

"Oh. I didn't realize—"

"So, anyway. It's not for you. I get it. When can you pack up and go?"

"There must be some mistake," she said. "I'm not leaving. The place is perfect."

The cognitive dissonance made Nix's head hurt. He rubbed his eyes with his free hand and tried again. "It's perfect?"

"Yes. It is."

"But the whole video was about how much you hated it."

"I explained what I was doing on my blog. You said you read it."

Nix was starting to think he was missing an important piece of information. "I read it, yeah. It was all about the horrors of the composting toilet and the lack of closet space."

"Not that one. The one before it."

He sat on the sofa, opened his laptop again, and called up her blog. He found the post about the house, then navigated his way to the one preceding it. He skimmed it while she waited.

"Wait," he said when he was done. "This is some kind of stunt, then?"

"Not a stunt. A … a concept. A project. I'm thinking of calling it *Downsized*. Or maybe *From Tony to Tiny*. I kind of like that last one, personally."

"You're writing a memoir." Suddenly, things were becoming clearer.

"Yes, but not just that. It's a whole multimedia project. YouTube, the blog, social media. Pinterest. Then the eventual book." She sounded damned proud of herself.

"What, like *Orange Is the New Black* but without the jumpsuits?"

She laughed. "That's funny."

He didn't feel much humor in it, himself.

"Big-city girl moves to the country and goes minimalist, with entertaining results. Well, hopefully the results will be entertaining," she said.

He didn't answer.

"What, you don't like it?" she asked.

Objectively, he could admit that the idea had merit. But that didn't mean he wasn't offended.

"That's all fine," he said. "I mean, I can see how it might work. But it's based on you ridiculing my place, something I spent countless hours of work building. It means something to me, and you're just ... you're pretending it's the Amityville Horror house. Only smaller."

"Oh, come on." She sounded as exasperated as he felt. "It's business. It's entertainment. It's not personal."

"Except, you know what? It kind of is."

JOY GOT off the phone feeling profoundly misunderstood. Was he really so sensitive that he couldn't see she was creating a product? Couldn't he see she was acting? Well, mostly. She really had been horrified by the composting toilet and the size of the shower.

Fortunately, he didn't have to like what she was doing. He wasn't her target audience, and anyway, they'd both signed the lease. It wasn't like he could kick her out if he didn't enjoy her videos.

That night, Amber called to check in and to tell Joy she'd seen the first video—the one giving a tour of the tiny house.

"Oh my God, it was great. The look on your face when you showed the outdoor tub! And that thing about the Beverly Hillbillies in reverse? It was funny, Joy. I think you're onto something here."

"I hope so." Now that Amber was recounting all that Joy had said on the video, Joy started to feel bad about it. She started to see what had upset Nix.

"You don't sound too upbeat about it," Amber said. "Your views are up. That's good, right?"

"Yeah, it's good."

"So what's the problem?"

"There's no problem," Joy insisted. She was sitting on the sofa in the living area of the tiny house, and she was so close to the kitchen she could practically reach out and touch the refrigerator.

"Bullshit," Amber said. "I've known you since we were in middle school. I know your voices. There's something wrong."

"It's just ... he saw the video. The landlord."

Amber giggled. "That must have been awkward."

"It was. Especially since he built the place."

"Oh." Amber wasn't laughing anymore.

"Was I an ass?" Joy asked. "In the video, and on my blog. Did I come off as some entitled princess?"

"Well, yes," Amber said. "But that was kind of the point, wasn't it? Entitled princess goes minimalist? Riches to rags?"

"I guess."

Yes, that had been the point, and she'd played it up for effect. So why did she feel like crap?

"Is he hot?" Amber asked.

"Who?"

"The landlord. Is he smoking, fiercely hot, and that's why you're worried about what he thinks of you?"

"No. No, of course not." But she couldn't help thinking of the way his hair caught the sun, falling to his shoulders in thick waves. She couldn't help thinking of his eyes, as pale blue as a gas-fueled flame.

"Really." Amber sounded as though she didn't believe her. Of course Amber knew her well enough to spot the lie.

"Okay. I admit, he's ... not unattractive."

"And what about the ring finger? I know you checked."

"Bare," Joy admitted.

"Excellent. Are you going to make a move?"

Joy scowled. "Of course not. He's my landlord. And anyway, I don't think he's too happy with me right now."

She got up from the sofa and walked around the tiny house, getting a feel for the place as she talked to Amber. In the kitchen, at eye level to the right of the window above the sink, a small wooden shelf held a trio of spice jars—basil, oregano, and thyme. But the herbs weren't what caught her eye. The shelf had been stained and varnished into a warm hue the color of butterscotch. On the edge of the shelf, a trio of tiny frolicking dolphins had been carved into the wood.

Had Nix done that? She imagined him shaping the dolphins, carefully committing them to the wood, then lovingly staining the shelf and polishing it until it gleamed.

And she'd mocked him and this place.

God, she really was an ass.

CHAPTER 7

Over the next few weeks, Nix applied himself to the task of putting the bathroom at Otter Bluff back together.

He selected, purchased, and installed a water-saving toilet. When the tub he'd ordered came, he hired Leon to come over and help him carry it into the house and install it. Nix wasn't a plumber, but he'd taught himself a lot when he'd built the tiny house. What he didn't know, he learned from a YouTube tutorial.

Then he and Leon installed the vanity, which he'd bought at The Home Depot. That had been tricky, since it was bigger than the one he'd taken out, and that required re-centering the thing on the wall—which meant he needed to move the plumbing for the sink a foot to the left.

That took longer than he'd expected, and he'd had to hire Leon for an extra day to get it done. Which would have been easy enough except for the fact that Leon, like Nix, had a regular full-time job, and it turned into quite a task to find a day they both had available.

When they finally managed it, there was a certain amount of swearing, false starts, errors that required correcting, and more swearing before the new vanity was installed.

He'd barely gotten it done before his tenant called to complain that the stovetop wasn't working.

GIVEN that their relationship had gotten off to a rocky start, Joy had been hesitant to call Nix about the stove. But it was his job to maintain the appliances—it was right there in the contract. What was she supposed to do? Just refrain from cooking in an effort to avoid an awkward conversation with him?

She worked up her nerve and called late in the afternoon, after she'd written a blog post, gone shopping for groceries, and taken a walk on Nix's land, which really was gorgeous.

"Nix?" She sounded tentative even to herself when he answered the phone. "This is Joy. Joy Maxwell. Your tenant."

"I remember who you are."

And, yeah, he did sound irritated. He sounded as though he would have preferred to hear from anyone—up to and including an IRS tax auditor—rather than her.

"Well, I'm calling because the stove isn't working."

"It's not?"

"Uh ... no. I tried to turn it on, and ... nothing."

He sighed heavily, and she heard the weight of it through the phone.

"I wondered if you could ... you know. Come out here and take a look."

"I can get out there tomorrow. Early, before I go to work. Say, seven a.m.?"

"See, the thing is, I was wondering if you could come now."

"Now?"

"Yes. Please. I want to cook dinner, and I can't." His irritation with her was contagious, apparently, because she delivered this last bit as though she were scolding a cranky toddler.

"Joy ..."

"It's in the contract. I have it right in front of me. It says you'll maintain the appliances. And the stove is an appliance, Mr. Landry."

"Mr. Landry? What the hell is that? Mr. Landry is my grandfather."

"Fine. Nix. Will you come? Please?"

This time the sigh was replaced by a grunt. "Give me half an hour."

NIX SHOWED up at the tiny house after dark, freshly showered and fully annoyed. If the stove really was broken, that was irritating as hell because it was one more thing to deal with on top of the renovations at Otter Bluff. And if it wasn't broken, that was even worse, because it meant his tenant was finding petty things to complain about.

If she'd been nice—if she'd loved the house as much as he did, or really even a fraction as much—he'd have been gracious about the stove. He'd have seen it as an essential part of his job as landlord, and he'd have wanted to set things right for her. As it was, though, he just wanted her out—even if that wasn't actually going to happen.

"I'm here," he said when she answered the door. "Let me just take a look at the stove so I can get out of your hair." He sounded petulant. He knew that. But he couldn't get her insults about his beloved home out of his head. She'd mocked him. She didn't deserve his courtesy.

She led him into the house and to the kitchen, where she turned the knob to start one of the two burners on the miniature stove. Nothing happened.

"See? Nothing," she said.

He reached over and clicked the knob himself a few times, as though she somehow wasn't doing it right.

"Did you check the propane?" he asked.

She looked at him blankly. "Propane?"

Well, at least the fix wasn't going to take long.

He turned, went outside, and walked to the side of the house, where the propane tanks were kept.

Yep, the tank was empty. It was a wonder she hadn't called him about a lack of hot water, too.

Fortunately, he kept a spare. He switched the supply indicator over to the full tank and opened the valve. Then he closed the valve on the empty tank.

While he was working, Joy came outside and stood behind him. A light he'd set up specifically for this purpose illuminated the area where he worked.

"You have to refill the empty propane tank every few weeks," he told her, not looking at her as he finished the job.

"*I* have to?" She emphasized the *I*, as though it should have been literally anyone else.

"Well, no." He straightened and turned to face her. "You don't have to do it. You don't have to do anything, unless you enjoy hot water and a working stove."

"But … I thought … usually you just pay the gas bill, and there's gas."

"I told you the house is off the grid."

"You did say that. But …"

"What did you think *off the grid* means?"

She was looking at him wide-eyed, as though she'd been caught in some misdeed. In fact, her only misdeed was ignorance, but that was enough to set him off.

"I thought it meant the electricity. And, you know. The water."

And, okay, maybe that was his fault. When he'd given her a tour of the place, he'd pointed out the solar electricity system and the water tank, but he might have forgotten to explain about the propane.

He softened his voice and forced himself to be more polite than he had been. He gestured toward the empty tank. "If you take this and get it refilled, you'll be ready when the other one is empty. You'll want to do that, because you don't want to suddenly run out of hot water just when you need it."

She looked doubtful. "And how do I do that?"

"Do what?"

"Get it refilled. I mean … where do I take it? Who does that?"

He sighed and ran a hand through his hair, reminding himself that a girl from an upscale condo in Los Angeles likely had never had to deal with propane.

"You just take the tank down to the hardware store and they'll switch it out for you—they'll take this tank and give you a full one. You see how I've got this hooked up? You put it here, tighten this bar—it holds the tank in place—then you screw on the hose. Make sure it's tight. Then you just open the valve, like this." He demonstrated for her benefit. "Then you push the supply indicator over toward the full tank. Like this. See how this one over here is on red? It means it's empty. And this one's on green."

"Which means it's full," she said.

"Right." He showed her how to remove the empty tank, then carried it to her car and put it in the trunk so she wouldn't have to.

"Okay." She nodded.

"Simple. And now your stove should work again." He put his hands on his hips and regarded her. "You think you can handle that?"

"Yes. Though you might have shown me all of this when I moved in. Then you wouldn't be standing here annoyed with me because I didn't know."

It was a fair point. "I'm not annoyed," he lied.

"Really. Are you telling me you always glare at people like this?"

Was he glaring? He supposed he was. He took a deep breath, let it out, and told himself to stop the glare.

"Only when people make fun of my house on YouTube. Which I guess you're going to do again now that you've discovered I don't have a gas line."

"I told you, it's business. It's entertainment. It's—"

"Yeah. I suppose it's all of those things. You know what else it is? It's kinda mean. Good night. Happy cooking." He went to his car and got in before she could say anything else.

ONCE NIX WAS GONE, Joy was equal parts angry and embarrassed. The anger: how was she supposed to know about the propane when he hadn't bothered to tell her? And the embarrassment: she really had hurt his feelings, apparently, with her blog and her video.

Was this what it was going to be like for the next several months? Was he going to glare at her and treat her like crap every time she had to interact with him?

That would be a shame, because she wasn't what he thought she was. She was a nice person. Something he'd never find out if he didn't give her a chance.

Except, she hadn't seemed like a nice person in the video or on the blog. She could see that. And after the care he'd taken building the house, and that darling dolphin shelf in the kitchen ...

She was going to blog and do a video about the propane situation, of course. That kind of thing was her job. But maybe she could make it more about her own ignorance toward off-grid living rather than the primitive conditions here.

They were both true, weren't they? The conditions really were more basic than what she was used to, but she really had been naïve.

It was a fair approach, and maybe it would go a little way toward softening up her landlord.

That hair, God. It had been loose tonight, all thick and wavy and luscious.

Hair like that was wasted on a man.

Or, considering how much Joy enjoyed seeing it on Nix, maybe it wasn't.

CHAPTER 8

When Joy had imagined coming to live in the tiny house, she'd had fantasies of turning into a hemp-wearing, granola-eating woman of the earth. She'd thought she might even take up organic gardening, an idea that was certainly possible given the fact that Nix had a vegetable garden in raised beds a short distance up a dirt path from the house.

But imagining organic gardening was one thing—doing it was another.

Nix had never mentioned whether he expected her to maintain the garden, so she wondered whether he was upset with her when she came outside one day and saw him in a pair of gardening gloves, working in the planting beds.

Uncertain whether to expect annoyance, friendliness, or something in between, she put on a sturdy pair of shoes and a jacket and walked up the path to meet him.

Nix was pulling weeds from the soil and depositing them in a bucket. He must have heard her shoes crunching on the dirt, but he didn't look up as she approached.

"Hey," she said.

He glanced at her and she offered a tentative wave.

"Hello." He focused on his work, pulling a weed and smoothing the soil with his other hand.

"I didn't know whether I was supposed to … do anything with this." She gestured toward the planting beds.

"Of course not. I wouldn't want you to mess up your manicure." He probably intended to insult her, but she *did* have a nice manicure, and gardening *would* probably ruin it.

"That was supposed to be rude. Right?" she asked. "I can't really tell."

He looked up at her with a half grin. "If you couldn't tell, then I have to work on my sarcasm."

"Very funny." She crossed her arms over her chest and cocked one hip in a stance of irritable defiance.

He offered a reluctant smile then turned his focus back to his work. "No, I don't expect you to garden. Though you can if you want to. I kind of neglected things out here when I moved into town, so I thought I'd better get back to it." He was kneeling on the ground, wearing faded jeans and a T-shirt that bore some sort of slogan that had mostly peeled off over the years. His hair was tied back to keep it out of his way.

"What are you growing?" she asked.

"Nothing yet. But once I get these beds weeded, I'm going to be planting beets, carrots, spinach, and Swiss chard."

"Huh. All organic, I suppose."

He gave her a side-eyed glance. "Oh, that's right. You made fun of organic gardening in your first blog post, when you came up with the idea to come out here."

She felt a blush rise to her cheeks. Okay, yes, maybe he was right. Maybe she had. "Look. About that—"

"You don't have to explain or defend yourself," he said, interrupting her. "Though you might want to look into the benefits of organic gardening before you judge it. I'm thinking your opinions aren't built on a foundation of good, solid research, am I right?"

She scowled. "You know, Nix, I can admit that the video I did about the house was … rude. And insulting. And I apologize for that.

But if you insist on being unpleasant to me every time we speak, this is going to be a long six months for both of us."

~

DAMN IT, she was right.

He really was falling into a habit of rudeness toward her, and it wasn't useful or productive. And if she could manage to apologize for the video, then maybe he could come a little bit her way, too.

He looked at her from where he was kneeling and shaded his eyes with one gloved hand. "Seems to me that when you were writing about organic gardening, you said you might be interested in trying it."

She blinked as though she was surprised he remembered anything other than the parts that had offended him.

"Yes. I did."

"I'll tell you what. I'm going to leave that bed over there empty." He pointed with his free hand. "If you want to plant something, you're free to use it. I've got a few books on organic gardening I can lend you. If you want."

He'd have bet that on Joy's mental list of things she wanted to try at some point in her life, organic gardening ranked somewhere between coal mining and sewer maintenance. Still, to her credit, she nodded and smiled politely.

"Okay, thank you. Maybe I will."

Another olive branch from Nix: "How did things go with the propane?"

"Fine. I got the tank refilled and ready to go. That sucker was heavy."

The tanks really were heavy, especially when they were full. If he hadn't been so focused on acting like an ass, he'd have thought of that and would have offered to help her with it.

"Next time you need one refilled, let me know and I'll take it in. They really are a lot to lift."

"Thank you."

"No sweat." He turned back toward his gardening feeling optimistic that he and Joy might be able to forge some kind of amicable relationship that would make her time at the house easier to manage for both of them.

WELL, that had gone better than she'd expected.

Joy walked back to the house feeling better about things between herself and Nix. And she really should try organic gardening, if only because it would make some interesting entries for her blog—something for the whole city-girl transformation narrative. She didn't have to like it, and she didn't have to be successful at it. She only had to try it and document the results. In fact, it would make better content if she failed spectacularly.

She kind of didn't want to fail, though.

One of Joy's shortcomings—at least, she thought of it as a shortcoming—was that she needed people to like her. Why else would she have the career she had? And some nagging, needy part of her wanted Nix to like and approve of her.

If she tried organic gardening and did a good job—if she managed to produce a passable head of lettuce, maybe—then she might earn his grudging approval.

The fact that she wanted his approval was only a byproduct of her flawed upbringing, she assured herself.

It had nothing to do with Nix himself, or the way his T-shirt had stretched across his back, making her want to run her hands over those shoulders.

It had nothing to do with that at all.

AT OTTER BLUFF the next day, Nix began working on the bathroom flooring.

Evan had selected a ceramic tile in the color of beach sand, and

Nix was laying them out on the floor, trying to establish the arrangement of the tiles before he did anything permanent.

Tile was tricky. You had to make sure everything was aligned properly, which included cutting pieces to fit the oddly shaped spots around the toilet and tub. Then there was the whole question of grout—both the application of it and the sealing of it.

He'd done some of that before, in the bathroom of the tiny house. But this bathroom was four times the size of his own, so it was a longer, more complicated process.

While he laid out pieces of tile, using spacers between each to ensure uniformity, he had time to let his mind wander.

Predictably, it wandered to Joy Maxwell.

She'd apologized for disparaging his house in that first video, so that was something. Even if she'd only said it to smooth things over with him, it had been nice to hear.

He suspected she hadn't just said it to appease him, though. Her more recent blog posts and videos had changed in tone to emphasize her own quirks and weaknesses rather than those of his house. Would she have made that change if she weren't truly sorry for offending him?

Part of him said she was none of his business. What she felt or believed or didn't feel had nothing to do with him. As long as she paid her rent on time and kept the place in good condition, none of the rest of it mattered.

But the house mattered to him, and he didn't like the idea of it being used as a stunt—as though Joy Maxwell were competing on *Survivor: Tiny House Edition.*

She'd apologized, and she'd changed the tone of her videos and her blog, and that counted for something. But she'd probably done it to ease her way with him and not because she really had changed her mind.

Well, maybe he'd do what he could to help her change it.

The idea came on slowly, sneaking up on him while he wasn't looking. What if he helped her see the magic of living a simple life close to nature? Because to him, it really was magic. Living in the tiny house, waking up to the hills and the grass and the wandering deer, tending his garden, taking long walks by the creek—those things all created a hum of contentment inside him that nothing else could match.

Maybe Joy Maxwell had to be taught how to feel the hum.

Nix had enough to do without dealing with her as well. He had his job at the market, he had his work at Otter Bluff, he had his tiny house business to plan and work on and coax into being.

He didn't have time for Joy Maxwell.

And yet. Would it kill him to extend a hand of friendship to her to help her understand what she'd been missing all that time she'd lived in L.A.?

It was a humanitarian good deed, that's all. It had nothing to do with the way she looked.

That's what he told himself, anyway.

CHAPTER 9

By the end of Joy's first month in the tiny house, she couldn't wait to see Amber.

Joy's friend was scheduled to arrive in Cambria on Friday evening and stay until Sunday afternoon.

Joy had suggested that Amber book one of the hotels on Moonstone Beach. If she stayed in the tiny house with Joy, she'd have to sleep on the pull-out sofa, and everybody knew those things were barely disguised torture devices.

But Amber insisted she wouldn't hear of it.

"I want to experience tiny house living!" Amber said on the phone. "It's half the point of me coming there! Please, can I stay with you? I don't mind the sofa bed."

"Of course you can."

Secretly, Joy had hoped Amber might get a hotel room with two beds so Joy could escape the tiny house for a weekend. It would be a novelty to sleep in a bedroom with ceilings high enough for her to stand up. But Amber's enthusiasm was such that Joy couldn't disappoint her.

"I can't wait," Amber said. "I'm excited to see the house."

"Well ... we'll see if you still feel that way once you get here."

AMBER ARRIVED at the tiny house at sunset on Friday, just as Joy was writing a blog post about her adventures trying to cook meals using miniature appliances. She used a selection of photos she'd taken of the kitchen, the countertop staged with partially chopped carrots and onions, the undersized oven laden with a casserole dish full of Joy's homemade macaroni and cheese.

The photos would go on both the blog and Instagram, and the whole thing would be supplemented with a YouTube video offering a detailed kitchen tour along with amusing anecdotes about Joy's struggles.

She was just wrapping up the blog when she heard Amber's car tires crunching on the dirt road that led to the house.

Joy ran out onto the porch to meet her, then rushed down the steps and over to Amber's car as she parked.

"Oh, my God, you're here!" Joy threw her arms around her friend as soon as she got out of the car. "I've missed you so much."

"I've missed you, too. God, it was a long drive up here." Amber hugged Joy tightly, then held her at arm's length to get a look at her. "Jeez, you look good. And would you get a load of that sunset?" Amber turned to bask in the beauty of orange and pink hues peeking out from behind the hills. Higher above them, the sky darkened to a deep blue.

"You get to look at this every day? I swear, if I lived here, I'd never leave."

Joy's first reaction to that was surprise. Surely Amber was just saying that to be nice. This place was in the middle of nowhere, so basic she might as well have been living in a cave. It wasn't until Amber mentioned the sunset that Joy really noticed it. The hills and trees were in silhouette, and the sky nearest the horizon was the shade of a ripe peach. From where they stood, there was no visible civilization. They might have been the first people to inhabit the earth.

"Well, come on in. Let me show you the place," Joy said.

"I can't wait. I want to see everything."

Everything didn't amount to much, so it didn't take long for Joy to give Amber the complete tour of the tiny house.

She started in the kitchen, since that was the subject of her latest blog post, moved on to the bathroom and living area, then progressed to the sleeping loft.

"This is super cozy." Amber stretched out on Joy's bed. "And oh, wow, there's a skylight. You get to fall asleep looking at the stars through the trees."

Amber made that sound so nice. Joy hadn't really noticed the stars —she'd been too preoccupied with the worry that she might bump her head if she sat up. She wouldn't have—the ceiling was too high for that, even if it wasn't high enough for standing—but it felt that way.

"Why don't you sleep up here?" Joy asked impulsively. "I'll take the pullout."

"Oh, I can't do that. I don't want to put you out of your bed."

"It's fine. Really. You're my guest, I want you to be comfortable."

Amber seemed so in love with the sleeping loft and the skylight that Joy wanted her friend to have it. Besides, if the sofa bed was painfully uncomfortable, it would give her something else to blog about.

"Are you sure?"

Amber looked so happy, Joy knew it was the right move.

"Absolutely."

"Oh, wow." Amber wiggled on the bed, unable to control her enthusiasm. "Meanwhile, what's for dinner? I'm starving."

"How do you feel about homemade mac and cheese?"

They ate at a little dining table that collapsed flat against the wall when not in use. They sat on low stools that nested together in a narrow kitchen cabinet when they weren't needed.

Amber ate the mac and cheese while Joy had a salad she'd bought at the grocery store where Nix worked. Thankfully, she hadn't run into him while she'd shopped.

"This is really good." Amber held up a forkful of pasta. "Why aren't you having any? You went to all that effort to make it, and you're eating a salad?"

"I made it for Instagram," Joy said. "I couldn't blog about the perils of working in a tiny kitchen without showing what I was cooking. It looked good on the screen."

"I'll bet it looked good. It *is* good. So have some."

"The pound," Joy said.

She'd long since lost the one extra pound she'd complained about that day at the gym. But now, the phrase *the pound* had become shorthand for Joy's concerns about her weight, her body, and her general fitness for posing scantily clad on camera.

"If you're worried about the pound, this has got to be a great place for trail running. Or hiking."

"There's a gym on Main Street," Joy said. "I joined last week. It's small, but they've got a good spin class."

Amber lifted her wineglass—they were sharing a bottle of Chardonnay—and gave Joy a look of harsh judgment.

"What?" Joy asked.

"I just don't think you're enjoying what this place has to offer." Amber took a sip of wine, then put her glass down and picked up her fork. "In L.A., you had to go to the gym because exercising outside in your neighborhood wasn't much of an option with the heat and the traffic and everything. But here? God. You can go right out your front door and hike in one of the most beautiful settings I've ever seen. Have you even been to the beach?"

"Of course I have. I got some good selfies on the Moonstone Beach boardwalk."

"Selfies."

"Yes. Speaking of which, while you're here, it would be a huge help if you could take some photos of me out there on the rocks at sunset, that kind of thing."

When Joy had been at the height of her popularity, she'd had an assistant to help with camera work. But cost-cutting measures had left her to do everything by herself.

"Sure."

Amber seemed to be agreeing, but Joy knew from her tone that she was still judging the crap out of her.

"Okay, what?"

"Joy. When I asked if you'd been to the beach, I meant, have you just gone to enjoy it? Have you just … I don't know … relaxed and watched the waves and felt the way a person is supposed to feel when they're chilling out in a beautiful place?"

"I'm not here for fun. I'm here for work."

"Well, that doesn't mean you can't do both, does it?"

~

BY THE TIME Nix was laying the bathroom tile for real instead of as a trial run, he'd come up with a few ideas for how to bring Joy Maxwell around to the pleasures of tiny house living in general, and tiny house living in Cambria in particular.

He still wasn't sure why he cared, but he did. It wasn't entirely altruistic, either. He wanted her to know she'd been wrong. He wanted her to admit it—not just to him, but to all of her viewers and readers.

First, though, he needed a way in.

When he'd been out there tending his garden, he'd mentioned that he had some books on organic gardening she could borrow. That was a good start.

He gathered the books and took them out there on his day off from the market, after the bathroom tiles were placed but before he put in the grout.

He needed to think of something other than flooring.

Nix made it to the property around eleven a.m. The day was bright and cool, and a light breeze whispered through the trees. The grass was tall and emerald green, and a chorus of birds greeted his arrival.

When he got there, he was surprised to find an unfamiliar car parked next to Joy's SUV.

Boyfriend? Friend? A relative, maybe?

Nix was intrigued to know what kinds of people Joy Maxwell hung out with.

He climbed up onto the porch and knocked on the door, calling to her. "Hey, Joy? It's Nix."

The woman who opened the door was not Joy.

She was a little shorter than Joy and darker, with brunette hair and deep brown eyes. Her face was put together as though the parts hadn't all come from the same kit—nose a little too long, mouth a little too wide—but the overall effect was appealing when she smiled, which she was doing now.

"Well, hello. You must be the landlord."

"I must be."

She turned and called into the house, "Joy, your hunky landlord is here."

Hunky. Interesting. He certainly would not have described himself that way, but it was intriguing that she had. Maybe the two of them had been talking about him. Maybe Joy had described him that way.

"Nix." He offered his hand, and she took it.

"Amber."

"And you're Joy's, what? Sister?"

"Friend. I'm also an admirer of your work. You built this place yourself?"

"I did."

"It's amazing. Seriously. I could live here forever if it weren't for my Starbucks habit."

Amber was bubbly with enthusiasm and happiness, and Nix found himself smiling. Hard to help it with all those positive vibes rushing around him.

"Thank you. I appreciate it. I don't think Joy feels the same way."

She reached out and put a hand on his arm. "Don't take that personally. It's just Joy. She's used to a certain kind of lifestyle, you know?"

"I gathered." He rubbed the stubble on his chin and wondered what *it's just Joy* meant in a deeper sense.

Amber's hand was still on his arm when Joy emerged from somewhere deep in the house—probably the shower, given her wet hair.

"Hey." Nix waved his fingers at her with his free hand.

"Hello." Joy looked at the hand on Nix's arm, then at her friend. Amber caught the look and snatched her hand back.

Again, *interesting.*

"Ah ... I brought you these books." Nix held up the organic gardening references he'd brought. "Just in case you want to give it a try."

"Oh. Thank you." Joy took the books from him then stood awkwardly in the doorway as though she were unsure what the conventions of social behavior demanded of her.

Amber had no such uncertainty.

"Do you have a minute? Come in! I was just about to make tea. Would you like some? I'd love to hear more about the house from the perspective of the guy who built it. Can you stay a little? Please?"

He could see the alarm in Joy's eyes, but what could he do?

"Sure. Thanks. I'd love to."

CHAPTER 10

Amber continued to gush about the house while she heated a kettle on the two-burner stove.

"I love the shelf over here with the dolphins. Did you make that?"

"I did." He was sitting at the little folded-out dining table, watching Amber work.

"So you're a woodcarver, too?"

He shrugged. "Not really. It's just something I did because I had the idea. I thought the dolphins might come out looking like weasels, given that it was my first time doing that kind of thing. But it went okay."

"I love the built-in cabinetry, the storage. But the skylight in the loft is my favorite. I went to sleep last night looking at the stars."

"Joy gave you the loft?"

"She did! She says it makes her feel claustrophobic, but I love it."

The glow he felt from Amber's praise faded as he registered the dig from Joy. Nix should have been used to Joy's criticism by now, but somehow, he wasn't.

"I like the small space for sleeping," Nix said mildly. "It feels safe. Like I'm going into my cave to hibernate."

"Exactly!" Amber said.

All this time, Joy didn't say much of anything. He got the sense that she didn't want him here, though to his mind, he was being perfectly pleasant.

"So, how was the pullout?" he asked Joy.

"Not nearly as bad as I thought it would be. The memory foam mattress was actually pretty comfortable."

Not as bad as I thought it would be was probably the best compliment he was likely to get out of her.

JOY COULDN'T HAVE a private word with Amber inside the house because it was too small. So she grabbed Amber's hand and pulled her toward the front door.

"Let me show you the organic garden," she said to her friend. When Nix started to get up, she said, "Sit down. Stay. Relax. Watch the kettle for us. We'll be right back." And she practically dragged Amber outside.

"What are you doing?" Amber said once they were out of Nix's earshot. "Can't I see the organic garden later?"

"You're going to see it now."

Joy marched up the trail toward the raised planting beds, and Amber followed.

When they were out there, far enough away from the house that they wouldn't be overheard, Joy turned on Amber.

"What are you doing?"

Amber blinked at her. "What are you talking about?"

"All of that, back there." Joy gestured toward the house with one arm. "The flirting."

"I wasn't flirting."

"Yes, you were."

Amber waggled her head in a *maybe not, maybe so* gesture. "Well … I might have been. A little."

Joy pointed a finger at her friend in triumph. "Aha!"

"So what if I was? He's pretty scrumptious."

Hearing Amber describe Nix as scrumptious only inflamed Joy's ire. "He is not scrumptious! He's my landlord."

"Can't he be both?"

Okay, he *was* both, but somehow Joy couldn't admit that part to her friend. Instead, she took a different approach.

"You cannot make a move on my landlord, Amber. What if … what if you go out with him, and things end badly, and then he kicks me out of the house, and I have nowhere to go? I'll be living in a box on the side of the road just because you thought he was scrumptious!"

Amber side-eyed Joy. "You've lost your mind."

"No! I haven't! I just don't want to lose my living arrangements!"

Amber ticked off points on her fingers. "One, just because I was flirting doesn't mean he and I are going to embark on a torrid affair. Even though that sounds really good to me."

"Amber!"

"Two," she continued, "even if we did embark on said torrid affair, that doesn't mean it would end badly. Three, if it did end badly, that doesn't mean he would kick you out. He seems like a reasonable guy. I'm sure he could keep his feelings about me separate from his business arrangement with you. Even though I'm a hard woman to get over. So I'm told."

Joy shoved her fists onto her hips and glared at Amber. "Nice speech. Are you finished?"

"Yes. Yes, I am."

"Fine. Just … don't flirt with my landlord. Please?" She softened her voice into a gentle plea.

A smile spread on Amber's face. "You're into him. That's why you don't want me to flirt with him. You're jealous. You want him for yourself."

Joy was shocked by the accusation—mostly because it was true. Amber had picked up on it so quickly and unerringly that Joy felt exposed, as though all of her secrets, all of her inner thoughts, were on full display under a spotlight.

"I do not want him for myself."

"Bullshit," Amber said. But she didn't seem angry—in fact, she seemed delighted. "Now that we've got that settled, let's go back in."

"Wait." Joy stopped.

"What?"

"You've got that look."

Amber was all innocence, eyebrows raised in question. "What look? Me?"

"That look that says you're up to something. Like you've got some kind of whacky plan you'd see in a 1950s sitcom."

"Not at all," Amber said. "Come on. We're being rude."

Joy followed her back to the house feeling a sense of impending doom that had everything to do with her scrumptious landlord.

Nix knew there was some kind of undercurrent between Joy and Amber, but he didn't know the source. Clearly, it had something to do with him, but what?

Joy didn't seem to like him very much—maybe she was angry that Amber had invited him in and was being nice to him.

Yeah, it was probably that. The best thing to do was to excuse himself, offer his help with the gardening should Joy decide to try it, and leave.

Only, he didn't really want to leave. He liked Amber, and he was flattered by how much she loved the tiny house. Her perk and enthusiasm were infectious. And he could admit that maybe some part of him—a part that he wasn't particularly proud of—liked making Joy uncomfortable.

That part wanted to stay as long as he could manage, just to spite her.

When the women came back to the house, he assumed they'd had some kind of come-to-Jesus talk out there at the planting beds. Probably Joy telling Amber that Nix was leaving, so she'd better stop being hospitable.

That explained the defiant look in Amber's eyes when she poured

Nix a cup of tea, put it in front of him with a bowl of sugar and a carton of milk, and said, "So, Nix. Joy says she hasn't gotten around the area that much since she's been here. How about showing us around? If you've got time, that is."

Nix's eyebrows shot up in surprise. Either Amber was doing this to piss off Joy, or she was flirting with him. Maybe both.

Either way, he couldn't help wanting to see where it might go.

"I've got time." He took a sip of his tea. "I'd love to play tour guide."

Joy's mouth fell open, then she snapped it closed. "I … excuse me for a minute. I left something upstairs."

She climbed into the loft, probably to experience her rage in privacy.

~

JOY SAT ON THE BED—SHE'D have paced, but there wasn't room—and silently fumed at Amber.

They'd been friends long enough that Joy knew exactly what Amber was up to. She thought Joy had a thing for Nix, and she was planning to force the two of them together.

Damn it.

For one thing, Joy most certainly did not have a thing for Nix. Unless *a thing* meant irritation and annoyance. For another, if she *did* have a thing, it was her own business, and it should be up to her whether to pursue it. The hypothetical thing was Joy's, not Amber's. So why was Amber intent on interfering?

Now that Amber had done what she'd done, Joy had no way out of this three-person outing—unless she fell out of the loft and broke a leg. For a moment, she actually considered it.

"Joy, what are you doing up there?" Amber called to her. "Come on down. Nix has some great ideas for where we can go today."

I've got an idea for where both of you can go.

"Just a minute," she said instead, trying to make her voice sound chirpy. "I'll be right down."

CHAPTER 11

The first item on the agenda was lunch. Nix had arrived at the tiny house late in the morning, so it was nearly noon by the time they got into Joy's car and headed out to see the local sights.

He could have taken them anywhere: Linn's, with its famous olallieberry pie; Robin's, with its charming atmosphere in the heart of downtown; or the Moonstone Beach Bar and Grill, with its spectacular view of the ocean.

But the idea was to impress them with what the local area had to offer, so he opted for something different.

"Just head north on Highway 1," he told Joy as she maneuvered her car down Santa Rosa Creek Road toward town.

"And then what?" she asked.

"Then, just keep going."

"Are you going to tell me where we're headed?" She sounded no less irritable than she had back at the house.

"Not yet. You'll see."

"Great."

She didn't sound like it was great. She sounded like she thought he was a pain in the ass.

They moved north through Cambria, past San Simeon, and

beyond. To their right, grazing cattle dotted the rolling green hills. To the left, the vast blue ocean stretched out to the horizon, puffy white clouds hovering above.

"This is gorgeous," Amber gushed. "Oh, my God. Look at those cows. It's like they were placed there just to look good."

"You can see Hearst Castle up on the hill. Have either of you ever been?" Nix asked.

Neither of them had.

"Well, we can put that on the list sometime," he said.

"There's a list?" Joy asked.

"There could be, if you really want to see the area."

"I love that there's a list. Can we get through it before I go home, do you think?" Amber asked.

"Probably not," Joy said. "I'm sure Nix is busy."

~

JOY DIDN'T WANT to be the person she was currently exhibiting to both Amber and Nix.

She was fully aware that she was being snippy and disagreeable. But how could she be otherwise? She'd planned to have a low-key weekend, just herself and her best friend, and now here she was spending the day with her annoying landlord, watching him and Amber get along famously.

Joy wasn't sure what part of that bothered her most—his intrusion into her plans, or the fact that he seemed to like Amber better than he liked her.

She'd thought Amber was scheming to bring Nix and Joy together, but maybe she wasn't. Maybe she wanted him for herself.

After all, she'd called him *scrumptious.*

Joy didn't want Nix, of course. But that didn't mean she wanted Amber to get involved with him.

They rose into the hills of Big Sur, and just when Joy thought Nix intended for them to drive forever, he directed her to turn left into a hotel parking lot.

Not just a hotel, she saw as she found a parking spot and maneuvered the SUV into it. This was some sort of complex, with a hotel, a restaurant, a gift shop, an outdoor snack bar, and a gas station.

"Is the restaurant good?" Amber asked.

"I prefer the snack bar, actually," Nix said. "Good burgers."

Joy didn't eat burgers, and she was worried about the pound, and this place didn't look like somewhere you could get a decent salad or even a grilled chicken breast.

"I'm game," Amber said. "I like a good burger."

"But first," Nix said, "let me show you why it was worth the drive." They got out of the car, and he led the women across the parking lot, past the snack bar, toward a lawn area, and over to a railing that overlooked the single most awe-inspiring view Joy had ever seen.

"Oh ... God," Amber said.

They were standing above a four hundred-foot drop to a rocky black-sand beach. Atop the bluff where they stood, towering pines and cypresses shaded them, and below, cliff faces studded with greenery plummeted to the crashing waves. The water near the shore was a deep blue fading into turquoise, then foaming into white peaks.

Joy had always taken pride in the Los Angeles–area beaches, as though she'd had anything to do with them other than visiting in a well-chosen bikini. But this was so much grander. So much ... more.

In Southern California, the shoreline tended toward broad, flat stretches of sand reaching out to an ocean empty of anything to distinguish it. To the east were roads and traffic and buildings, and to the west was one endless expanse of water.

Here, the drama of nature reigned. The view was rugged and somehow desolate, awe-inspiring and humbling. Joy felt small and insignificant in comparison, but that was comforting, in its way. If she didn't matter, then neither did her mistakes. Neither did her shortcomings.

"What do you think?" Nix asked from where he stood beside her.

"I'll admit this was worth the drive." Joy's voice was thick with suppressed emotion.

"There you go." He sounded pleased. "Now, who wants to get a burger?"

~

As Nix watched Joy eat, he thought that it must be hell being a woman.

She'd ordered a veggie burger with double the lettuce and tomato, and upon receiving it, she'd discarded the bun. Now she was eating the plain veggie patty and the pile of lettuce and tomato with a knife and fork.

"So, you're a vegetarian, then?" Nix asked. "And, what, gluten-free?"

"No," Joy said.

"No to which part?"

"Both."

"She's worried about the pound," Amber added before taking a big bite of her own cheeseburger, which she'd ordered with a side of fries.

"The pound?" Nix asked.

"Amber ..." Joy meant it as a plea.

Amber proceeded anyway. "When Joy eats real food—like the kind of things the rest of us eat—she gains a pound, then goes through hell trying to take it off. She and that same pound are in a battle to the death."

Joy kept her eyes on her food instead of on him. Was she blushing? It seemed as though Amber had embarrassed her, and Nix felt bad about that. He hadn't intended it.

"Well ... for what it's worth, you look great," he said, trying to make amends.

"If I look great, it's because I stay on top of the pound," she said. "Now, can we talk about something else, please?"

~

The truth was, Joy would have died for one of those cheeseburgers.

They looked delicious—so juicy and thick, and the smell of the fries wafted to her and made her almost weak with hunger.

But the pound didn't care what Joy wanted. It didn't care if she was hungry. The pound taunted her, harassed her, stalked her like some vicious wild animal that would pounce at the slightest provocation.

So she told herself she liked the veggie patty and the lettuce and tomato. She told herself it was fine.

It wasn't fine, though, and that was pissing her off. If they'd gone to the restaurant instead of the snack bar, at least she'd be eating a real salad right now.

But the view—that made it all worth it. After lunch, Joy snapped some photos and had Amber take some of her as she posed against the wooden railing, the breathtaking view at her back.

"Do you always do that?" Nix wanted to know as Amber handed Joy's phone back to her after the photo shoot.

"Do what?"

"Take photos instead of living in the moment."

"I'm living in the moment," Joy protested.

"Yes, she always does that," Amber said.

And that made Joy feel like she had to defend herself—again. "The photos are for my blog and for Instagram. It's how I make my living. I've explained that."

"Right. I get it." He looked out over the view, his shoulder brushing hers as he stood beside her. "But sometimes you've got to just forget all that and …you know. Be."

AMBER CONTINUED to exclaim over the natural beauty as the three of them walked a path through the trees and down toward the end of the property. Joy hung back as Nix and Amber walked up ahead, chatting about the various points of interest.

Joy had started out angry and irritated about Amber's flirtation with Nix, but now she just felt resigned.

Joy's Instagram got dozens of comments every day telling her how beautiful she was, but Amber was the one who could effortlessly draw a man into her orbit. Why? What did she have that Joy didn't have?

And why do I care? It's not as though I'm interested in Nix.

The idea of herself and Nix as a couple was ludicrous. What would Joy do with a crunchy, Birkenstock-wearing, kale-eating, organic-farming man like him?

Even as she had the thought, she knew there were a lot of things she could do with him—most of them distinctly R-rated.

Stop it, she told herself. *Just stop.*

Actually, this could be good. If Amber and Nix got together, it would make Amber happy, and Joy wanted her friend to be happy. Also, it might make Nix more agreeable, and that would benefit Joy as she continued to live in his house.

Up ahead on the trail, Nix and Amber talked out of Joy's earshot. While she didn't know what they were saying, she got the gist of Amber's end of it. Joy's friend was laughing, tossing her hair, and doing that flirty thing Joy had seen her do so many times before. And he seemed to be responding to her. Why else would both of them have forgotten Joy was here?

Ah, well, none of that mattered. She focused on her blog, her Instagram, and her eventual book. This place was full of picturesque scenery that would serve her purposes perfectly. She pulled out her phone and got to work taking pictures.

~

ON THE WAY back to Cambria, Nix had Joy pull off into a parking lot overlooking the ocean.

"Okay, what now?" Joy's question could have been laden with snark, but she kept her tone neutral, even curious. Their first destination had been much better than she'd anticipated, so maybe this one would be, too.

"Elephant seals," he said.

"Elephant seals?" Amber piped in from the back seat.

"Yeah. This is their mating ground. There's an observation area, and ... well, you'll see."

Catching the aroma wafting up from the beach, Joy wasn't optimistic. But when she got to the railing and looked over onto the beach, she couldn't help but feel charmed.

Lying on the beach, so densely packed they might have been a living, breathing carpet, were hundreds—maybe thousands—of fat, lumbering, roaring elephant seals, their bodies long and thick and their bulbous, elongated noses making it obvious how they'd gotten their name.

Elephant seals dragged themselves into the surf and out again. Others fought, bellowing and nosing one another. Some lay in the sun, using their front flippers to throw wet sand onto their bodies.

"Oh my God," Joy said in awe. "There are so many of them!"

"Before they built this observation area, people used to just park on the side of the highway and go down onto the beach to see them. Which was super dangerous, not only for the elephant seals but for the tourists. This is better. You get a good view without disturbing them," Nix told her.

"How do they know to come here?" Amber asked.

"I'm not sure," Nix said. "But they do."

Joy was so absorbed watching the animals that it took her a while to notice that Nix and Amber were standing so close to one another that their shoulders pressed together.

She found herself looking at that spot—that point of connection between them—vicariously feeling the warmth of him, the tingle of electricity Amber was probably feeling.

She told herself she'd be happy for Amber if she and Nix ended up together. She told herself it was fine.

~

AFTER THAT, Joy made an excuse for why she had to end the outing and get back to the tiny house. Work, she said. She tried to upload her blog posts on a regular schedule, and she had one due today.

"Oh." Amber's shoulders fell with disappointment.

"But if you two want to keep going, you can drop me off at the house. I don't mind." The last part was a lie, but she knew she *shouldn't* mind, and she was trying to be gracious.

"That's okay." Nix stretched his long legs out in the passenger side of Joy's SUV, as much as he could in a confined space. "I have something to get back to, anyway. I have to grout a bathroom floor." He told them about Otter Bluff and his project to renovate the place for Evan. "I'm not on any kind of deadline, exactly, but I don't want to drag it out too long, either."

"But can we do this again?" Amber asked. "I'm leaving Sunday, but I don't have to go until afternoon. Maybe you can show us more of the area?"

Say no, Joy urged him mentally. *Please say no.*

"Sure," he said. "Give me a call. Joy has my number."

The way he'd phrased it—*Joy has my number*—indicated he was asking Amber to call him, not Joy.

Well, fine.

CHAPTER 12

When she and Amber were back at the tiny house and Nix had left them, Joy was subdued as she got herself set up in front of her laptop on the tiny dining table.

"Are you okay?" Amber asked.

"Of course. I just need to get this blog post written and posted so I don't throw off my schedule."

"You seemed … annoyed. All day. Or most of it, anyway. Is everything all right?"

"Yes, Amber."

Amber narrowed her eyes at Joy. "Okay, the way you said that —*yes, Amber*—tells me you're full of shit. Everything is not okay. So spill it, or our next twenty-four hours together is going to be damned awkward. It's not like there's anywhere we can go to get space from each other."

Joy sighed, closed her laptop, and turned in her chair to face Amber.

"It's just weird that you were flirting with Nix, that's all."

Amber blinked a few times. "I wasn't flirting."

"Oh, my God. Yes, you were. Which is fine. I mean, why shouldn't you? But you definitely were."

Amber put her fists on her hips and glared at her best friend. "I was just happy. I was having fun. Not that you'd recognize something like that, even if it smacked you on the ass and called you Sally."

Joy's mouth fell open. "What are you talking about?"

Amber perched on the edge of the sofa and faced Joy. "Look. This could be a new start for you. A change of pace, which you really, really need. But it's not going to do you any good if you keep trying to live like you were in L.A. I mean, it wasn't working for you there, why should it work for you here?"

Joy closed the laptop and went to the sofa to sit beside Amber. "What do you mean it wasn't working? I was doing fine in L.A. Other than the money issue."

"No, you weren't." Amber softened her tone and laid a hand on Joy's jean-clad knee. "Joy, I've known you for a long time. And you know I love you. That's why I've got to be honest with you."

"Okay."

"The whole materialistic, selfie-taking hot-girl thing you've got going on? It's not doing you any favors."

Joy felt a hot ball of dread forming in her stomach. Amber had always been supportive, had always played the cheerleader for Joy. Had she disapproved of her all this time?

"I don't know what you mean." It came out barely above a whisper.

"Joy. The Prada purses and the Louboutins and all of that are fun—don't get me wrong. But they're not making you happy. You haven't been happy for a long time."

Joy didn't answer. She just looked at the floor, feeling the hot sting of indignation and shame. Indignation, because none of this seemed fair. Shame, because it did seem true.

"You've never said any of this before."

"I've wanted to." Amber's voice was gentle. "But then, when you decided to come here? I thought I might not have to. I thought the change of scenery might help. But then, seeing you picking at that veggie patty and lettuce? You're starving yourself over a pound, and for what? Joy, you don't really think that your weight matters that much, do you? Do you really think your body in a swimsuit is all you have to offer?"

Tears burned in Joy's eyes, and she blinked to hold them back. "It doesn't matter what I think. My followers—"

"To hell with your followers." Amber turned on the sofa to face Joy more fully and gave her an encouraging smile. "They don't know you like I do. They don't know how you used to laugh and have fun, how you used to be warm and kind and funny before you got into the whole Internet thing. But I do. I know you. And I know that the pound only has as much power as you choose to give it."

The speech was devastating, and Joy tried not to show that it had hit its mark. She nodded and squeezed Amber's hand. "I know. I get that. I'll think about what you said."

"Good." Amber offered another upbeat smile, then went outside to sit on the porch and enjoy the outdoors.

When she was gone, Joy went back to the table, opened her laptop again, and stared at the screen. She couldn't seem to focus on anything. Whenever she tried, Amber's voice came back to her.

They don't know how you used to laugh and have fun, how you used to be warm and kind and funny before you got into the whole Internet thing.

Used to.

Had she really changed that much? Was Amber really still friends with her only because of the memory of who Joy used to be?

And who would she be now if she just let herself do what she wanted, let herself be who she wanted? Who would she be without the adoration of thousands of anonymous people online?

A cheeseburger wasn't just a cheeseburger, and the pound—and its friends—would mean ridicule and judgment and scorn. As much as she wanted to let go, as much as she wanted to embrace fun and food and, God, even love, all of those things took courage.

More courage than Joy had.

She wanted to be brave, she just didn't know how.

When Amber had walked with Nix on the trail and Joy had fallen behind, Nix had expected an enjoyable bout of flirting. He wasn't interested in Amber, really—and even if he had been, she was going home in a day or two—but who didn't like flirting? Who didn't enjoy a little harmless banter with an attractive woman?

But that wasn't what happened. Instead, Amber took that time to talk to him about Joy.

She'd started with an explanation of Joy's finer qualities—loyalty, kindness, and intelligence among them—and then she'd apologize for her friend's attitude that day.

"She's not usually so negative," Amber had told him. "But she's going through some stuff right now, so."

Nix didn't know what it was that Joy might be going through, and he was certain it was none of his business. But he was also certain that he wanted to find out.

Nix drove back to Otter Bluff from his place on Santa Rosa Creek Road thinking about it.

If Joy had been a bit standoffish with him, it might be because he'd been a dick to her before. He was making a sincere effort to be pleasant and hospitable now, but he'd definitely been prickly with her after he'd seen that first video. So maybe she was just feeling residual annoyance from that.

He brought it up with Evan on the phone that afternoon when Nix called to update him on the renovation plan.

"I probably irritated the shit out of her by tagging along with her and her friend like that," he said. "But, hell, I was just trying to be nice." He was sitting on the patio in an Adirondack chair, sipping from a bottle of beer and looking at the sunlight on the ocean as he talked.

"So you just showed up and invited yourself on an outing?"

"No. No, no. I showed up to lend Joy some books on organic gardening that, let's face it, she doesn't want and she'll probably never take off the shelf. And then her friend asked me to show them around."

"*Hmm*. The friend asked you," Evan said.

"Right. I mean, I knew Joy didn't want me to go, but I did it anyway, because when an attractive woman asks you to spend the day with her and her attractive friend, what kind of asshole says no?"

"Not you," Evan said mildly.

"Damn right."

"Well . . . what are the chances Joy is jealous?" Evan asked.

"Jealous? About what? Why?"

"I don't know. I mean, maybe she's got the hots for you. Her friend was the one to invite you along, and maybe the friend was being a little overly friendly. . . ."

"Joy Maxwell does not have the hots for me. In fact, it's my considered opinion that she can't stand me."

"Well . . ."

"What?" Nix demanded.

"It's just, women don't always mean what you think they mean."

"Truer words were never spoken," Nix said.

"I'm just saying, maybe Joy's attitude was a female competition thing."

"You think so?"

"Who the hell knows?" Evan said.

Certainly not Nix.

"Of course," Evan went on, "it's also possible that she's repulsed by you and cringed at the very idea of spending time with you."

"Yeah . . . you know, I've thought of that, but thanks for bringing it up."

Nix ended the call even less certain about the motives of women than he'd been before. Maybe Joy liked him and was jealous about the attention Amber had given him. Maybe she couldn't stand him. Or maybe she had family problems, or a hangnail, or one of those irritating tension headaches you couldn't get rid of.

The mysteries of women eluded him. More often than not, the women themselves did, too.

CHAPTER 13

Joy and Amber ate dinner that night at a fish and chips place in Morro Bay. Amber had a pile of hot, steaming fish and french fries in front of her, while Joy was picking at a salad with fat-free dressing.

Looking at Amber's food and then at her own almost had Joy in tears.

The pound was back despite all of Joy's work to keep it away, despite all of the fat-free salads and all of the spin classes and workouts. Not only that, she'd looked in the mirror this morning and had seen signs of fine lines fanning out from the corners of her eyes, and more beginning to form around her mouth.

She was in her thirties now, and she wouldn't be able to keep the signs of aging at bay forever. She could hide the pound with careful clothing choices. She could hide the lines with good makeup. But that was now. What about later, when she couldn't hide them anymore? Who would she be then? What would she do when her followers deserted her—as they were already starting to do—and her career plummeted into obscurity?

"Are you sure you don't want some of this?" Amber gestured toward her plate.

"No, thank you. This salad is fine." Joy tried to smile, but it came out wobbly.

"If you're worried about the pound coming back—"

"It's back!" Joy let her fork drop onto her plate. "It's back already, and I can't make it go away, Amber! No matter how many salads I eat or spin classes I take, I just can't make it go away!"

Amber's expression softened, and she tilted her head slightly as she regarded her friend. "Well ... I don't want this to sound harsh, because I don't mean it that way. But ... you're not twenty-two anymore. At some point, the pound is going to stay."

"I know I'm not twenty-two anymore! Look at this!" Joy pointed to the corner of one eye.

Amber leaned in closer. "What am I looking at?"

"Wrinkles! That's what you're looking at! Should I get Botox, maybe? Is it time for that?"

Amber peered at the spot Joy had indicated, then leaned back in her chair and arranged her features in a patient expression that Joy thought would serve her well when she had kids one day.

"You don't need Botox."

"Well, I need something."

"No argument there."

Was that some kind of dig? Joy thought it probably was, but Amber was too kind for it to be a dig. So what was it?

"What do you mean by that?" Joy tried to keep the defensiveness out of her voice, to present it as a neutral question.

"I mean, you definitely need something, and it's not Botox, and it's not another damned salad." Amber gestured toward Joy's plate. "What you need is ... is to stop worrying about how you look and start thinking about how you *feel*. Start enjoying things, for God's sake. Joy, when did you stop living just for the sake of having fun and experiencing things? When did it all get to be about how things look on Instagram?"

Part of Joy wanted to get up, turn around, and walk away so she wouldn't have to have this conversation. But another part of her knew —really knew—that it was a conversation she needed to have. So she stayed where she was, took a deep breath, let it out, and willed herself to respond honestly and not defensively.

"I'm worried about it because that's how I make my living, Amber."

"I get that. I honestly do. But that's not going to last forever, is it? I mean, aging happens to all of us, and there's nothing you can do to stop it. There aren't a whole lot of successful influencers out there in their forties and fifties, so you were going to have to come up with another plan eventually."

"But—"

"It's not making you happy, Joy, and it hasn't for a long time. I can see that. If you're going to need a change of plan at some point, why not now? Why not make a new life for yourself that feels better than the one you had?"

It was a fair point, but it seemed to Joy that Amber was missing a key detail.

"That's why I'm here, isn't it? In Cambria? I'm trying something new. Testing out a new life."

Amber folded her arms on the table and leaned toward Joy. "Yes. But the change of scenery isn't going to work unless you actually let it change *you*."

JOY WAS SUBDUED on the drive home from Morro Bay. Amber kept glancing at her furtively from the passenger seat.

"You're mad, aren't you?" Amber said.

"No."

"You are. You're mad. And you should really just say so, so we can—"

"I'm really not." Joy kept her voice soft and her eyes on the road. "I'm just …thinking. It's clear you've had that on your mind for a while, and now that you've said it, I just … I need to think about it."

"Well … that's good." Amber nodded. "I'm glad. And Joy? I really hope you took it in the spirit I meant it. I just care about you, and I want you to be happy."

"I know. I do."

"Are you going to see Nix again?" Amber asked after a while.

"Nix? Why?"

Amber shrugged. "Because if you do decide to let yourself have a little fun, that doesn't seem like a bad place to start."

NIX HAD LEFT it open about whether he would get together with Joy and Amber on Sunday morning, before Amber had to leave for L.A. But he wasn't sure why he'd done that. Mostly to be nice, he guessed. The fact was, Joy obviously didn't want that, which gave the whole thing a level of tension that he'd just as soon avoid.

There was some kind of weird dynamic going on. Amber had started out flirting with him, but then she'd shifted over to trying to sell him on all of Joy's various attributes.

And regardless of what he'd been talking to Amber about, the more he spoke to her—the more he hung out with her—the more irritated Joy seemed to get.

A female competition thing, probably, and he didn't need it.

Besides, he was busy. He had a job. He had the Otter Bluff project.

The last thing he wanted was to lose valuable time getting mired in a woman situation he didn't understand.

So he got up on Sunday morning, showered, made his first cup of coffee, then texted Joy, asking her to please tell Amber he couldn't make it.

Sorry, something came up. You should still take her to see Hearst Castle, though. It's amazing.

He sent the text, not expecting to get any response. The answer came within minutes, though.

Thanks for letting me know. I'll tell her.

Then, after a pause:

Thank you for yesterday. Amber and I both had a good time.

That came as a surprise. The last thing he'd thought was that Joy had experienced anything resembling fun.

No problem, he wrote back. *Let me know if you want to do it again sometime. Just the two of us.*

He sent it before he gave himself a chance to think about it. Yes, he'd begged off today because of the screaming tension he'd had to deal with the day before. But the tension had to do with the Joy-Amber dynamic. If it was just Joy, it might be fine.

That's what he told himself.

He also told himself that he hadn't just asked her out on a date. Of course not. He was just being hospitable. He was just being a good neighbor.

So why was he nervous about how she would respond?

~

JOY LOOKED at the text message Nix had sent for much longer than it took to read it.

Was he asking her out? It really looked like he was asking her out.

"What's that?" Amber bustled around in the tiny kitchen, making a pot of coffee.

"Oh ... it's nothing. It's just ... Nix can't make it today. But he thinks we should go to Hearst Castle anyway."

"Oh." Amber frowned, a bag of ground coffee in one hand and the coffee pot in the other. "That's too bad. I had a scheme planned."

"You had a scheme?" Joy's eyebrows rose.

"Yeah. I was going to wait until we had the whole outing planned, then I was gonna back out at the last second, when he was already here and the tickets were already bought and everything."

Joy regarded her friend. "Why in the world were you going to do that?"

"So the two of you would have to go together, obviously. It's called a setup, in case you're unfamiliar with the concept."

"Seriously?"

"Sure. Why not?" Amber set up the coffeemaker, measuring coffee into the filter. "We talked about you maybe going out with him. You know, as part of the whole Joy-gets-her-groove-on project."

"I'm not sure that's an actual thing," Joy said.

"Well, it should be."

"And anyway," Joy went on, "you flirted with him a lot yesterday. I thought maybe you and he—"

"I wasn't flirting. I mean, yes, it started out that way. But once I caught on that you like him, I stopped. After that, I was telling him about you."

"You were?"

"Yes." Amber poured the water into the reservoir and turned on the machine. "I told him how awesome and fun you are, and what a great person you are. Though, it really would have helped my case if you'd been in a better mood yesterday."

"I was in a bad mood because I had to eat a veggie patty and lettuce!" Joy protested.

"Lesson learned," Amber said. "Next time, prepare by eating a cheeseburger. You'll be in a better mood, and you can work off the calories later in the date." She waggled her eyebrows suggestively.

Joy considered objecting, but what was the point? The scenario Amber had presented to her sounded like a pretty good time.

"Actually ..." She held out her phone so Amber could see the screen. "He just asked me out. Kind of. I think."

Amber's eyes widened, and she bounced up and down on her toes a little. "He did?"

"Read it."

Amber rushed over to where Joy sat and looked at the phone.

"Oh, my God. Yes. That's definitely him asking you out."

"Are you sure? Maybe he's just being nice."

"The first part of the text—the part about doing it again—was him being nice. But the part about it being just the two of you? That's him asking you out."

It really was, wasn't it?

"He's my landlord, though," Joy said.

"He's your really hot landlord."

"Still." It could lead to potential problems, couldn't it? If she went out with Nix—on a real date—and it ended badly, she'd be stuck dealing with a landlord who hated her. That could be awkward as hell. On the other hand, how bad could it be? She was only in the tiny house temporarily, anyway. If she had to move, it would only speed up the timeline on something she was going to do anyway.

"Remember what we talked about," Amber told her. "You need more fun in your life. You need more pleasure." She waggled the eyebrows again. "Eat some real food. Go out with a hot man. Maybe sleep with him, if you feel like it. Get out and see what the world has to offer you without taking a selfie of it and putting it on Instagram. Just try it and see."

Joy had to admit the idea was appealing.

CHAPTER 14

Joy wrote about Amber's idea in her next blog post.

Physically, I'm here on the Central Coast amid the trees and the grass, with the ocean at my feet. But mentally, I'm still in L.A. wondering where the fast pace, the designer stores, and the trendy nightlife went.

My best friend, Amber, told me it's pointless to change my surroundings if I don't let my surroundings change me. So, I'm going to try an experiment. For the next two weeks, I'm going to say no to materialism and yes to hedonism.

I'm going to buy less and experience more. Walks on the beach?Picnics by the creek? Good food and good wine and long talks with good people? Yes, please. I vow to live in the moment and experience all that Cambria and tiny house living have to offer, without judgment and without worrying about how I look while I do it.

I'm not saying it'll be easy. But it should be interesting.

Joy reread what she'd written, edited a few sentences, read it again, and then hit PUBLISH.

It seemed like a simple enough plan—just have fun without milking every moment for good Instagram posts—but for some reason, it made her so nervous she thought she might be sick.

If she ate what she wanted, she was going to gain weight. If she just enjoyed her surroundings without thinking about monetary gain, her income might plummet. And if she said yes to a date with Nix? Well. She might have a great time, or she might be slammed by disappointment and heartbreak.

Well, what good experiment came without risk?

Amber was right. It was time for a change, not just of address but of attitude.

Joy took a deep breath as she sat cross-legged on her bed in the loft and set her laptop aside.

Where to start in this quest for pleasure?

A sexual adventure seemed like a big step she wasn't ready for. But ice cream was almost as tempting as sex, so she decided to start there.

~

JOY COULDN'T REMEMBER the last time she'd eaten ice cream. Well, that wasn't strictly true. She'd eaten it a couple of weeks ago, but it was that crappy low-calorie, low-fat, low-taste stuff that was supposed to be a miracle food but wasn't. Real ice cream hadn't passed her lips in so long that it might as well have happened during another life.

Surely there was a place on Main Street that sold ice cream. Cambria was a tourist town, after all.

She got into her SUV and headed down the tree-lined, winding road toward town. When she got there, she started at the east end of Main Street and headed west at a leisurely pace, keeping her eye out for her target.

She found Mojo's almost immediately. The place billed itself as a coffeehouse, but a large freestanding sign in the shape of an ice cream cone placed on the sidewalk had her looking for the nearest parking spot.

Joy had been watching her weight for so long she'd almost forgotten that buying and enjoying an ice cream cone was something a person could do. She parked and walked across the street to the shop feeling as though she were about to commit a crime.

I can do this, she thought. *I can eat some ice cream, and it doesn't mean I'll immediately gain ten pounds and be unworthy of love.*

When had she gotten to the point that she needed a pep talk just to eat? When had she decided that her entire sense of self should be wrapped up in her weight? When had she forgotten that she had other qualities besides a single-digit jeans size?

She walked into the shop, approached the ice cream freezer, and found herself overwhelmed by the choices.

Salted caramel? Cookies and cream? Double fudge?

The teenaged girl behind the counter waited patiently while Joy decided.

"Would you like to sample something?" she asked.

"Um … no, thanks. That's okay. I'll just get this one." She pointed to an ice cream with the unlikely name of Rooster Tracks. She paid, and the girl assembled the cone and handed it to Joy.

It looked huge.

At the first lick, Joy almost swooned. She closed her eyes, ran her tongue over the ice cream, and savored the flavors of vanilla and fudge. A rooster track—a mini peanut butter cup—burst open in her mouth when she bit into it, and she moaned.

"I feel like I should offer you a cigarette and promise to call you in the morning," a voice said.

Her eyes flew open to find Nix standing there, grinning at her.

Joy felt her cheeks pink up in a blush of embarrassment.

"It's just, this is really good," she said.

"I gathered. I came in for coffee, but after that, I'll have what you're having."

~

When Nix had come into the shop and had seen Joy in there, he'd been torn between friendly courtesy and turning around and leaving before she saw him. After all, she'd never answered his text, which probably meant she didn't want to go out with him. That was fine, but he could do without facing rejection on a simple trip to Mojo's.

But when he'd seen the ecstasy on her face, when he'd watched her tongue dart out and sweep over the ice cream, her eyes closed … and then the moan, it had been impossible not to imagine her exactly like that, in his bed, but without the ice cream.

And having imagined it, it had been equally impossible not to say so.

Now, having said it, he felt a little bit bad for embarrassing her. But her blush delighted him, so maybe it had been worth it.

"One of those, please," Nix said to the girl behind the counter, pointing at Joy's cone.

~

ALL JOY HAD WANTED WAS to enjoy a little harmless hedonism. How had she ended up at a table in a coffeehouse eating ice cream with the admittedly delectable Nix Landry? Life was funny that way. Open the door to a small amount of pleasure, and the universe sent you the opportunity for so much more.

The problem was, she wasn't sure she was ready for quite that much self-indulgent abandon.

As they sat beside the shop's front window, sunlight streaming in and highlighting Nix's glorious hair, Joy decided that she hadn't fully appreciated just how beautiful he was.

It wasn't just the hair. He had perfectly sculpted cheekbones, long eyelashes that lay gently on his cheeks when he closed his eyes, and flawless skin that would probably have been pale if he didn't spend so much time in the sun. And those eyes. Their color was so improbably light, with just a hint of sky blue, that she couldn't help feeling that she was being drawn in by them.

No wonder Amber had been a little bit smitten.

"Amber really likes you," Joy said, then caught a drip of melting ice cream with her tongue.

"She's nice. And she's a good friend to you." He looked at her meaningfully, and Joy wondered if he was referring to how Amber had tried to play matchmaker instead of pursuing him herself. Instead of getting into that, Joy opted for the generic answer.

"She really is."

He licked his ice cream, then focused that pale gaze on Joy. "She thinks you and I should go out, you know."

Suddenly, Joy's mouth was dry. "Um ... does she?"

"*Mmm hmm.* She asked me whether I was seeing someone, and she said you weren't, either. Then she spent a full ten minutes talking about how great you are."

Joy froze, speechless. She'd known all of that because Amber had told her. But now that it was out there—now that Nix was laying it on the table—she didn't know how to respond.

"Wow," was all she could think to say.

Nix finished his cone, wiped his mouth with a napkin from the dispenser on the table, balled up the napkin, and tossed it into a trash can ten feet from where they sat. Then he gave Joy a tentative grin that made her feel all warm and soft inside.

"Look. I know you and I got off to a bad start," he said. "But it means a lot to Amber that you and I go out. You should think about it. For her sake." Then he got up, gave her a wave, and left.

~

NIX LEFT Mojo's wondering how big an idiot he actually was.

Joy didn't like him. She was generally surly and critical, and there was a good chance that going out with her would feel like a particularly brutal visit to the dentist. And yet, he'd not only asked her out via text but had doubled down in person.

What was he thinking? Was he that shallow that he would pursue a woman just because of how she looked?

But it wasn't just about how she looked. It was more than that. Nix liked to think he had good instincts about people, and his instinct said Joy was more than she let on.

He'd seen her angrily eating a veggie patty and iceberg lettuce, and now he'd seen her blissfully devouring an ice cream cone. What did that tell him? She was a woman who'd been holding herself back, and who maybe was ready to stop doing that.

She was, maybe, ready to let herself go.

That would be a beautiful sight when it happened, and he wouldn't mind being there to see it.

He didn't know what her story was—why she'd been so repressed up to now and what had happened in her life to make her want to change. But he found that he really wanted to know.

She was tightly knotted, but it seemed possible that she'd started pulling on some threads in an effort to free herself from all of that tension.

Nix wouldn't mind pulling on a few threads himself, just to see what happened.

He drove back to Otter Bluff, let himself inside, and decided that Joy Maxwell would be a fine thing to think about while applying grout.

~

WHEN JOY GOT BACK to the tiny house, she texted Amber.

All I did was eat some ice cream, and now everything's spinning out of control.

Almost immediately, three dots bounced on her screen, indicating that Amber was formulating a response.

You're going to need to explain that.

So she did.

I went to town and got an ice cream cone, and I guess I made an obscene sound because, Amber, I haven't had ice cream in so long and it was soooo good. But I ran into Nix and he heard the sound and now he's got ideas.

Amber responded: *!!!!*

It turns out he really was asking me out before, and now he's asked again, and I really have to answer him at this point, Joy wrote.

So answer him! Amber responded. Then: *Just in case that wasn't clear enough, say yes!*

She wanted to. She really did. But then what? When everything went to hell, as it always did, she'd be stuck handing her monthly rent check to a guy who was trying not to strangle her.

Then again, she couldn't seem to forget how he'd looked sitting across from her, the sunlight on his hair, those long eyelashes resting on his skin.

She wanted to touch that skin. Maybe even lick it the way she'd licked that incredible ice cream.

I'm going to do it, Joy wrote.

She'd intended for her hedonism project to progress a bit more slowly than this. After all, it was a big jump from ice cream to getting involved with a hot organic farmer.

Still, in for a penny ...

Yay! Amber wrote. *Keep me posted, and you have to tell me everything.*

CHAPTER 15

Joy and Nix had their first date a couple of days after the ice cream incident. She'd let him choose the place, since he knew the town better than she did.

He opted to take her to The Sandpiper, a restaurant on Moonstone Beach Drive with a view of the ocean.

He picked her up at six, knocking on the door of the tiny house exactly on time.

When she opened the door, she was momentarily speechless.

Usually when she saw Nix, he was wearing torn jeans, sandals, and a T-shirt that looked like it had been through the wash so many times it might dissolve into dust at any moment. His hair was usually tied back to keep it out of his way.

Today, though, he'd made an effort.

Pressed khakis, a blue chambray shirt open at the throat and turned up at the elbows, and a pair of loafers that looked like they'd been shined recently. And the hair—loose and wavy, thick and lustrous. She wanted to bury her hands in it. Usually, he had a day or two worth of stubble when she saw him, but today he was freshly shaved. He smelled faintly of spicy aftershave.

"Wow," she blurted out before she could stop herself.

Nix's eyebrows rose and he gave her a slow grin that made her feel alarmingly hot and melty. "Wow yourself."

Joy was wearing the only dressy outfit she'd managed to wedge into the closet at the tiny house: her little black dress with an off-the-shoulder neckline and a swingy skirt. On her feet were the sole pair of designer shoes she'd kept out of storage.

"It's too dressy, right?" she said, doubting herself. "It's probably too dressy for Cambria, but most of my clothes are in storage, so—"

"It's perfect. You look great." From the way he was looking at her, Joy knew he meant it.

"Well, let me just grab my purse, and we can go."

NIX WAS FEELING pleased with himself as he drove to The Sandpiper. He'd been uncertain whether it was a good idea to ask Joy out, but now, with her sitting beside him looking the way she looked, he couldn't help but think it had been an inspired bit of brilliance.

"I read your blog post." He kept his voice casual and his eyes on the road.

"You did? Which one?"

"The one where you said you want to become a hedonist." He glanced at her, and her blush was adorable.

"Oh. That one."

He grinned. "You know, I think it's a great idea."

"You do?"

"Yeah. I really do. I mean, hedonism's bad if it gets out of hand, but a little fun? A little harmless enjoyment? I'm all for that."

She gave him a knowing, mischievous look out of the corner of her eye that required him to shift in his seat.

"I suppose you have ideas about that?"

She was flirting with him—shamelessly—and he realized how long it had been since he'd enjoyed a little suggestive banter with a woman.

"I might," he said.

"Such as?"

"Let's start with a good meal. No salads, no grilled chicken breast with steamed vegetables. A real meal. Then we'll go from there."

She didn't object, and that seemed like a good sign.

~

Oh. My. God.

Joy had almost forgotten what carbs tasted like, and now, as she savored the flavors of seafood pasta with lemon butter sauce, she nearly blacked out with bliss.

She heard a helpless whimpering sound, then realized it was coming from her.

She snapped her eyes open, embarrassed.

"I … uh … I'm sorry about that."

"Don't be. Watching you eat pasta is the most satisfying sexual experience I've had for a while."

Damn it, there she went, blushing again. She could feel the heat in her cheeks.

"It's just … carbs. It's been a long time."

He put down his own fork, folded his arms on the table, and regarded her. "Tell me something about women, would you?"

"Sure. I mean, I'm not our spokeswoman, but I'll try."

"What are you afraid will happen if you enjoy yourself a little? What's the worst-case scenario?"

The worst-case scenario is that once I start, I won't be able to stop. I'll fall into a pit of need and desire so deep I'll never be able to dig myself out of it.

And then I'll be lost forever.

That wasn't the kind of thing you say to someone on a first date, but he'd asked a real question, and she tried to give him a real answer.

"Self-control is a slippery slope," she told him. "Once you give in, it's too easy to keep giving in. I mean, it's like alcoholism, right? Nobody asks a recovering alcoholic why they can't have just one drink. But if you're dieting, everybody wants to know why you can't have just one piece of cake."

"Fair point," he said. "But what if you take self-control so far that you're not enjoying life anymore?"

What if, indeed?

Joy had been at that point for a while. Everybody thought it must be great to be a size four—as though the lack of body fat meant she didn't have any worries, any problems. But they didn't know what it took to get that way, and they didn't know what it cost her to worry over every mouthful, every pound.

When other people saw her in a bikini, they saw ... well, whatever they wanted to. Sexuality. Perfection. Some construct of female beauty.

But when Joy saw herself in that same bikini, she saw the bumps of cellulite along her outer thighs, the visible veins in her calves, the fact that her boobs weren't as high as they used to be. She saw failure and unattainable goals and the unstoppable effects of time.

After a while, she realized she was lost in her thoughts and hadn't said anything.

"I can't do it anymore," she said finally.

He cocked his head at her. "Do what?"

She gestured with a forkful of pasta. "The ... the salads and the pound and the bathroom scale! What's the point? I miss carbs." She slurped the pasta into her mouth and moaned in pleasure.

Part of her thought that if she gained five pounds—or even ten—she'd be unworthy of love. But her love life hadn't exactly been going gangbusters as it was, so what did she have to lose?

Nix might not want her anymore if he saw how monstrous her desires were, how deep that empty, gaping pit of her need. But he could help her fulfill some of those needs before that happened, couldn't he?

As she ate more pasta, drank more wine, reached for a hunk of warm bread from the basket on the table, she realized he was smiling at her.

"You're horrified," she said. Because wasn't that how everyone reacted to a woman finally feeding her hunger? Wasn't that how people reacted to a woman fulfilling her desires?

"No," he said. "No, actually. I'm charmed."

He'd say that, wouldn't he? They all claimed to find everything about you adorable—until the moment they left.

~

NIX WAS ABSOLUTELY delighted by the sight of Joy in the throes of pleasure.

Of course he enjoyed it on the level that most guys would—one that suggested nudity and orgasms at some point in their relationship—but he also enjoyed it on a more basic human level.

She was, for the moment, happy, and he'd had a role in making her that way.

It was intoxicating.

He basked in the food, the wine, the view, and the atmosphere, but all of that paled in comparison with knowing that Joy was having a good time.

"Dessert?" he said when she'd finished her pasta.

She hesitated for just a moment. Then: "Oh … God, yes."

~

BY THE TIME they left the restaurant, Joy was so full she could barely move.

Between that and the wine they'd shared, she felt more relaxed and at ease than she had in weeks—maybe months. Maybe even years.

"Come on." He took her hand. "Let's take a walk. The Moonstone Beach boardwalk is what people come to Cambria to see."

She'd seen it, of course—it had been one of the first places she'd visited when she'd come to town—but then, she'd been looking at the rocky coastline in the context of how it would show on Instagram. Now, she vowed to enjoy it for its own sake. She vowed to really see it for the first time.

The evening was mild as the sun eased toward the horizon. On the boardwalk, couples and families walked hand-in-hand, and dog walkers held leashes as their charges sniffed the plant life.

Joy saw the rough boards and wished she'd worn different shoes.

She struggled for a few yards, then Nix said, "Let's go down onto the sand, and you can take off your shoes."

"Good idea."

They walked down a staircase to the beach, and Joy slipped off her shoes and felt the cool sand seep between her toes.

It was heaven.

She held the shoes in one hand and Nix's hand in the other as their fingers intertwined. She reflected, just for a moment, on the simple joy of holding hands with a man.

"This is lovely," she said as they made their way toward the waterline.

~

YOU'RE LOVELY.

That had been the natural response to what Joy had said. But Nix sensed it wouldn't be the right thing to say. How many men had complimented her on her looks? How many people had reinforced to her that her appearance was the only thing that mattered?

He resisted the temptation to be just another one of those guys.

"It is," he said instead. "I'm glad you're enjoying it."

Nix had grown up in Cambria and had seen Moonstone Beach thousands of times. But seeing it through Joy's eyes made everything seem new.

"I'm wondering …" he said.

"Wondering what?"

"If it's okay to kiss you." He stopped and turned toward her with the ocean at his back.

She grinned, and the salt-scented breeze ruffled her hair. "Let's try it and find out."

~

THERE WERE SO many things Joy could be worried about right now.

What if things between them went wrong? What if he made her life as his tenant miserable in some fit of spite? What if things got awkward and she kept running into him around town? What if he turned out to be so much less—so much more disappointing—than she expected? Or what if she liked him—really liked him—and he broke her heart?

Instead of thinking about any of that, she reminded herself to stay in the moment, feel the feelings, and enjoy what there was to enjoy.

He touched his lips to hers gently at first, tentatively, and then both of them sank deeper into the kiss, relaxing and opening to each other.

Had Joy thought the pasta was bliss?

This was so much better. So much *more.*

She put her hands on his shoulders, lifting up on her tiptoes to reach him better, and her entire body filled with liquid warmth as his mouth explored hers.

She realized she was making that same sound she'd made when she'd tasted the pasta.

"Wow," she said when they parted.

Nix grinned. "A two-wow night. I must be doing okay."

CHAPTER 16

How was your date? Amber texted the next morning.

Joy was lying in bed in the loft, looking at the early morning sky through the skylight.

Oh, my God. You should have tasted the pasta, Joy responded.

You ate pasta?!!

I did. I finished the whole plate, and then we had dessert. I'm going to hell.

A moment later, Amber responded: *Why would you think you're going to hell for eating pasta? It's a meal, not murder.*

It was a fair question. Why did Joy equate food with sin? Why did anyone?

What about Nix? Amber asked. *Did you like him? Did you have fun? Are you going to see him again?*

That was a harder question than just asking about pasta. Yes, she liked him. Yes, she'd had fun. As for whether she'd see him again? Men were strange, fickle creatures. Joy's accuracy in predicting whether a first date would lead to a second one was notoriously poor. Dates she'd thought were disastrous led to ardent pleas for a follow-up, while others that she'd thoroughly enjoyed had been met with silence.

Did she want to see Nix again? Yes. But did he share those feelings? He was a man. Who knew?

She tried to distill all of that into a succinct text message.

I had a good time, and I think he did, too. We'll see.

Did anything happen? Amber asked.

On a first date? No! Joy said. *We kissed, though.*

Ooh! How was that?

How to answer? It had been lovely. Delicious. It had been hot and intriguing and had made her insides feel like warm butter.

Better than the pasta, she wrote.

~

NOW THAT THE grout in the bathroom at Otter Bluff had been applied, it was time to seal it.

The job required zero brain power, so Nix spent the time while he worked thinking about Joy.

She hadn't been what he'd expected.

After the ice cream incident, he'd had some hope that she might let herself enjoy the evening, but there was no way to be sure. He figured there was at least some chance she'd go back to the self-denial of dry salad, which wouldn't bode well for him.

Her blog post—the one about hedonism—had provided more hope.

The Joy he'd spent the evening with the night before had been an entirely different person than the uptight, snobbish woman he'd met when she'd first come to Cambria. He'd wondered if she was hiding under there someplace, and it turned out, she was.

Just add carbs.

If she was this much happier when she allowed herself a little pleasure, why would she ever go back to self-denial?

It was a balancing act, obviously. You couldn't get so involved in indulging yourself that you became self-destructive. But a little enjoyment here and there made all the difference, as he'd seen last night.

He wanted to see more of what happened when Joy was happy and having fun.

~

WHEN NIX FINISHED SEALING the grout, he showered, dressed, and went to the market to work the afternoon shift.

Louise poked her head into the break room while he was tying on his apron.

"So? How'd it go?" She smiled expectantly.

"How did what go? Driving to work? Fine, thanks. I got here safely."

She wadded up a hand towel she'd been holding and threw it at him. "Your date, doofus. How was it?"

"It was … interesting," he said.

"Uh oh. That bad?"

"No. It was interesting good."

"Oh." She perked up. "So when are you going to see her again?"

"I haven't asked yet."

Louise's eyes widened in alarm. "Tell me you at least called her or texted her. It's after two!"

"Is there some sort of deadline that I missed?" he asked.

"Not yet, but it's coming up."

"I wish there was some kind of instruction book for these things," he said.

"You don't need an instruction book. You've got me." She came closer to him and planted her feet, her fists on her hips. "Where's your phone?"

He dug it out of his pocket and handed it to her with some reluctance.

"Okay, let's see …" Louise pulled up the texting app and found Joy's name. Nix felt fortunate that he hadn't texted anything personal to Joy—at least, not yet.

"What are you doing?" Nix asked, nervous tension in his voice. "Show me before you send anything."

"Relax. I know what I'm doing." Her thumbs moved over the screen as she typed.

"Seriously, Louise. Don't send anything too—"

"Here." She turned the phone toward him to show him the screen.

I had a really good time last night.

Well, that seemed harmless enough.

"Okay," he said. "Send it."

"Not yet. I've got to add some more stuff."

"Louise—"

She typed, a look of smug satisfaction on her face, and showed him what she'd written.

I had a really good time last night. I can't stop thinking about you.

Nix's first reaction was to object that she'd gone too far. Then again, it was true, wasn't it? He really hadn't stopped thinking about Joy since he'd left her. Though, the text suggested something sexual, something prurient, and that wasn't exactly true. Yes, he did find her attractive, and yes, the kiss had been phenomenal—the best he'd had in a very long time—but …

"Hello? Anyone in there?" Louise said, interrupting Nix's thoughts.

"I just don't want to be too pushy," Nix said. "Or too … I don't know … *suggestive.* I don't want to make her uncomfortable, or …"

"Have you been thinking about her?" Louise pressed.

"Well, yes, but—"

"Fine." She pressed her finger to the screen, and he heard the tinny whoosh of a text being sent merrily to its destination.

"Wait! We were still talking about it!" Nix said.

She handed his phone back to him, smirking. "Too much talk. Not enough action."

~

JOY HAD BEEN GOING through her day trying not to think about Nix.

The date had been fine—better than fine—but she wasn't about to get into that girly thing where she obsessed over whether he'd call, and when, and what he was going to say when he did, and what she was going to say in response, and all of the immature longing and insecurity that involved.

She'd done that enough times in the past to know it was counterproductive. It was also annoying as hell. So, she simply wouldn't do it this time. Instead, she vowed to regard the date as a pleasant one-time occurrence that might or might not lead to an encore.

Either way, it was fine.

Having given herself that rousing pep talk, she was dismayed to find that her heart rate sped and she felt a peculiar tingle when his text came in.

He couldn't stop thinking about her? Oh, God. That was just the kind of talk that, coming from a man who looked the way he did, was likely to get her into trouble.

She was standing in the produce section at the Cookie Crock—Cambria's rival market to the one where Nix worked—one hand on her cart and the other on her phone as she reread his text.

Actually, she was probably making this thing more complicated than it needed to be.

There was no reason she shouldn't be able to take things as they came, enjoying time with him without expectations and without her usual neuroses.

But that was a scenario for an ideal world, not the one in which Joy actually lived. In fact, she'd had too much real-life experience to assume this would be anything but disastrous.

Joy's dating experience usually followed a pattern: A man would see her on Instagram or on YouTube and assume she was an easy lay because she'd posed in a swimsuit. He would take her out, make a move that was too much too soon, then treat her like shit when she said no. Or, alternatively, she might be attracted and lonely, and she might say yes. In that event, he would treat her like an object or, worse, an achievement he could show off to his friends. The moment she revealed herself emotionally in an honest and human way—the moment she admitted to frailties or insecurities—he would stop answering her texts and her calls.

Just because Nix seemed different didn't mean he was.

Just because she'd had a nice time, too—just because she'd *liked* him—didn't mean things with him would end any differently than they usually did.

So, where did that leave her?

She decided her best approach was to be open to more but not to reveal her own feelings, her own needs.

I had a good time, too, she texted him.

And that was enough for now. He didn't need to know that she hadn't stopped thinking about him, either.

Can we do it again sometime? he wrote.

We'll see, Joy responded.

Don't shut him down, but don't let him get too cocky, she thought. Even if what she'd really wanted to say was, *How about right now?*

CHAPTER 17

The *we'll see* meant Nix had to wait, and while he waited, he read Joy's blog.

She posted almost every day, sometimes just a few sentences, and sometimes a long rumination on whatever was on her mind.

It occurred to him that his dating life would have been so much easier if every woman he'd gotten involved with had posted her thoughts and feelings as clearly and frequently as Joy did.

My past has made me believe that my only value is in how I look, she wrote, *and that I owe it to people to be pretty. As though it's my job. There has to be more than that.*

Nix read the words at the kitchen table at Otter Bluff, a mug of coffee at his side. He'd just woken up, and he was wearing a pair of pajama pants and a T-shirt, his hair mussed.

Was that how Joy felt?

It was a significant revelation, and Nix found himself admiring her for having had it and also for being brave enough to go public with it. He wanted to know more—like what, exactly, had happened in her past to make her feel that way.

Not that anything had to happen, other than Joy being female in the world. Nix didn't consider himself to be the most aware guy out there—he tried, but he was sure he was lacking in thousands of ways he didn't understand—but even he could see that. Anybody who consumed American media for an hour could get a hell of a lesson in female beauty standards.

BEING BOMBARDED with that day after day, as a little girl and then later as a woman, had to screw with your head.

He thought of Joy eating her veggie patty and iceberg lettuce, angry and probably hungry, and it tugged at him.

Of course there was more to her than her appearance, and he wanted to find out exactly what. He wanted to learn her, read her like a textbook and absorb all of the complex and profound lessons she contained.

Part of it was curiosity. He'd always been curious about people, had always wanted to know what made them who they were. But part of it was just … Joy.

Unbidden, the image of her came to him—her eyes closed, her tongue running along a scoop of ice cream—and that alone was enough to make the blood rush straight to his nether regions.

It wasn't about how beautiful she'd been at that moment—at least, not entirely. It was about the pure magic and wonder of watching someone experience a moment of bliss.

God, he wanted to see her again.

She had layers, and the more of them he uncovered, the more he wanted to delve into her.

And *that* thought wasn't doing anything to relieve his current physical tension.

Ah, well. Nothing he couldn't take care of himself temporarily, until he'd earned the real thing.

~

JOY KNEW the current direction her blog had taken was likely to ruin her career.

Nobody wanted revelations from her. They wanted what she'd always provided: pretty pictures of an aspirational lifestyle.

Blog views were down, Instagram hits were down, and income was down along with them. But this wasn't just about money. This was about so much more. It was about figuring out where she was going from here with her life and who she was going to be when she got there.

She didn't need money right away, anyway. Her condo had sold quickly, and that had given her enough cash that she could live in the tiny house—or somewhere else, when her lease was up—for a while without having to worry about it.

Joy would have to come up with a career plan eventually, but how could she know what she wanted to do when she didn't know who she was?

She thought about all of that as she took a morning walk on Nix's property. One thing she'd promised herself was that she wouldn't take pictures—at least, none that she would post on social media. Any images she captured would be just for her. She wanted to experience the walk without the static of worrying how it would look to others. She wanted to bask.

She just wanted to *be*.

A path from the tiny house led to a creek running through the property, and she let herself enjoy the burble of water over rocks, the cool breeze whispering through the trees, the chitter of birds and the rustle of a squirrel dashing through the grass.

Nature actually wasn't half bad.

Surely there was nature in Los Angeles, even amid the bustle of a large city. Why hadn't she noticed it? There were the beaches, sure, and that was good. That was fine. But this was different. This was quiet and peaceful and untouched.

She could see why Nix loved it here.

At the thought of Nix, she remembered the kiss they had shared and how it had made her feel. Not that she needed any kind of trigger to remember it—she seemed to be remembering it a lot, at odd moments, sometimes for no reason.

He was interesting and nice and fun, and so attractive. But he was drawn to her for her looks, of course. All of the men in her life were. She was so tired of working to be pretty, working to be thin and perfect. Would he still be interested in her if she wasn't those things? If she just let all of that go?

Probably not, a voice in her head answered her. The voice was Joy but also not Joy. It was the voice of her own self-doubt, and it sounded remarkably like her mother.

If she decided to see him again, she would have to do it with the full knowledge that he was probably like all of the others—he'd probably run when the conquest was complete or when she dropped the hot-girl facade.

Because that's all it was—a facade. She'd thought it was her, but it wasn't. And now that she knew that, there was a big, empty space where her true self should have been.

She needed to fill that space, and she had to be careful, selective, about what she filled it with.

Joy sat down on a large, flat rock on the bank of the creek and pulled her knees up to her chin, wrapping her arms around her legs.

Funny, when she and Amber had come up with the tiny house plan, Joy had thought of it as a gimmick. If she could just play-act at having made a major life transition, with all of the bumps and setbacks that suggested, then she could regain her fan base.

Now that she was here, though, she wasn't play-acting. The life transition actually seemed to be happening.

Where was she supposed to go from here, though? Now that she'd realized the old Joy had to be torn down, burned, and done away with, how did she go about building a new and better one?

I don't even know what I like.

And that was true, wasn't it? Joy had been modeling a vision of what she thought other people liked, not what she did. And now, she didn't even know herself.

That seemed like the first step. She needed to find out what she liked, what she enjoyed, what filled her up and gave her pleasure, without regard to what the world might think of it.

I need to brainstorm. I need a list.

Buoyed by the thought, she got up, brushed some stray dirt off her jeans, then went back to the tiny house to start drawing up a set of plans for the new and improved Joy Maxwell.

"A LIST?" Amber asked when Joy called her later that day.

"Yeah. Of things I want to try that I might enjoy."

"Like a bucket list?" Amber asked.

"No, no. A bucket list is stuff you really want to do and that you're afraid you might not get to before you die. This is different. This is … an experiment."

"An experiment."

"Yeah. It's stuff I don't know if I'll like, but I might. I want to find out what I enjoy."

Amber sighed. "Oh, Joy. How can you not even know what you like? I blame your mother for all of this. If she'd only—"

"Less pity, more ideas," Joy said, interrupting her.

"It's not pity, it's sympathy."

"Well, less of that, too. I mean, I appreciate it. I do. But this isn't a sympathize-with-Joy talk. It's a brainstorming talk."

"You want to brainstorm about what kinds of things you might like if you only gave them a chance."

"Right."

"*Hmm*. This could be fun."

"There you go." Joy sat on the porch at the tiny house with her phone on speaker and a notepad and pen in her hands. "First category: food."

"I hope there's also going to be a sex category."

Oh, there will be.

"Let's start small," Joy said, her pen poised. "Now, I've never tried boba tea. What else have you got?"

CHAPTER 18

Nix was in his car, ready to head back to Otter Bluff after work, when he saw the list.

He had his e-mail set to alert him whenever Joy posted to her blog, and he told himself it would keep until he got home. But he couldn't resist. He clicked on the link, thinking he'd just take a peek to see what the topic was before heading back to Otter Bluff.

Once he saw what she'd written, though, he was riveted and didn't move until he'd read the last word.

It was a treasure trove of information, from a dating perspective.

She had so many categories: food, adventure, travel (a subset of adventure), entertainment, and—sweet Jesus—sex.

His immediate impulse was to offer to cross off the entire sex category in one day, but then he decided subtlety and nuance were his friends.

I can help you with number eight, he texted her.

In number eight, she'd stated that she'd never eaten fresh homemade pasta. In an unlikely but fortunate coincidence, he'd gotten a pasta maker for Christmas the year before. He still hadn't taken it out of the box.

Number eight? she wrote back.

Fresh pasta. Come to Otter Bluff for dinner tomorrow and we'll tick off that box for you.

For a minute or two, nothing happened, and he worried he might get another *we'll see.* Then, her response came.

What time?

NIX HAD the following day off, and he spent the morning painting the master bathroom in a pale taupe that Evan had chosen. When he was done, he cleaned up the paint mess, showered in the bathroom he hadn't worked on yet, got dressed, and applied himself to the question of how to make fresh pasta.

"I've never made fresh pasta before," he told Louise on the phone. She was at the market, but he'd caught her on a break.

"Well … I've never done macramé, so there's that."

"No. It's about Joy. I invited her for dinner and said I'd make fresh pasta, only I don't know how."

"Why did you say you'd do it, then?" Her voice held the frustration of a woman who did not now, nor would she ever, understand men.

"It was on her list." He explained about the list, and about how he'd used it to persuade her to go out with him again. Or, in this case, stay in.

"Oh. And you're hoping to tick off the pasta box and then move on to some things lower on the list," Louise said.

Nix felt a rush of annoyance that he was so transparent.

"I kinda doubt we're going to get to anything else if the pasta sucks."

"Fair point. But why are you calling me?"

"Don't you know how to make pasta?"

"Why would I know that?"

"You're Italian."

Louise made a scoffing noise. "That just means I know how to *eat* it."

"Oh." He tried not to sound disappointed. "Well … I'll try

YouTube."

"Not so fast, Noodle Boy. My mom makes great pasta. I'll give you her number."

Nix had met Louise's mother a few times—in Cambria, it was hard not to run into people—but he wasn't sure he knew her well enough to impose on her.

"Are you sure she won't mind?"

"Are you kidding? She'll love it. I'll call ahead and tell her she's going to hear form you."

~

NIX WAITED until he'd gotten a text from Louise saying her mother was on board. Then he called the number he'd been given.

"Mrs. Lombardi? This is Nix Landry. Louise said—"

He barely got a word in after that.

Mrs. Lombardi talked about Louise, cooking, Cambria, dating, the necessity for "a nice boy" like him to find someone, and how he really needed to put on a few pounds. Then she insisted that he needed to come to her place for a practice run—something he wasn't sure he'd have time for, given the fact that he still needed to plan the menu, buy ingredients, and make Otter Bluff suitable for female company.

Mrs. Lombardi didn't wait for him to say whether he actually planned to come—she simply assumed he would. She gave him her address and said she'd be waiting.

"And bring your own machine," she told him. "It won't help if you learn on mine and then don't know how to use the one you've got."

She hung up before he could protest.

~

FORTUNATELY, Nix had brought the pasta machine to Otter Bluff with him along with his other belongings when he'd moved out of the tiny house. It was in a box in the garage, and he didn't know which one.

He had so few belongings that it didn't take long to find it at the bottom of a carton marked MISCELLANEOUS.

He'd intended to donate it to a local thrift store for the sake of minimalism, but now he was thankful he hadn't.

When he arrived at Mrs. Lombardi's house, she opened the door, grabbed his arm, and pulled him inside as though she thought he might flee if she wasn't fast enough to catch him.

"Pasta is the perfect food for love!" she declared.

He considered that, his eyebrows raised. "Is it? I'd have thought seafood, what with the oysters and all."

She waved off the comment. "Pasta is sensual. You twirl the fork, you accept the food into your mouth. Then you gently suck the stray noddles in through your lips, feeling the textures on your tongue...."

Thinking of Joy doing all those things, Nix started to feel a little warm. He cleared his throat. "I can see your point."

~

OVER THE NEXT hour or so, she showed him how to make the dough directly on the granite countertop, making a well in the center of the flour and cracking an egg into it; how to set up his pasta machine; how to roll out sheets of pasta; and how to cut those sheets into fettuccini noodles.

"This is important." She held the newly cut noodles draped over her hand. "You have to hang it to dry, or it'll stick together." She hung the noodles over a gizmo apparently created for that purpose.

"I don't have one of those." He pointed at the gizmo.

"You can borrow mine. Now, let's see you do it."

~

BY THE TIME Nix got back to Otter Bluff, he'd been given thorough lessons not only for making the pasta, but also for making a simple sauce with fresh tomatoes, basil, and olive oil. He'd considered trying a more complex sauce, but Mrs. Lombardi had wisely counseled him against it, saying he'd have enough to deal with as it was.

He already knew how to make an excellent salad from organic vegetables, and that would round out the meal nicely.

He went to the market, gathered the things he needed—including a good bottle of wine—and paid. Louise was behind the register.

"So? Did Mom take care of you?"

"She did. I'm pretty sure I'm expected to be married by next Christmas."

"And you'll be expected to bring the wife to Mom's place for Christmas dinner," she added.

"Tell her thanks from me, would you? I mean, I already did, but …"

"You got it. Good luck!"

JOY PONDERED how to dress for a night eating pasta at Nix's place.

Pre-Cambria, she'd have worn something upscale with a designer label—something that looked casual but that said she'd paid hundreds of dollars to put together the look.

But this called for something different.

She browsed through her meager wardrobe and selected a pair of jeans that made her ass look great and a soft cable-knit sweater that was just low-cut enough to be sexy but not low-cut enough to be slutty.

She'd rescued a pair of soft leather boots from her storage unit, and those completed the casual-but-attractive look she was going for.

She brushed out her hair, letting it fall loosely around her shoulders, and took care with her makeup, shooting for a level of glamor she thought of as casual plus; the idea was to look at first glance like she was wearing nothing on her face, but to appear just a little more vibrant, just a little more *there*.

Once she was satisfied, she used her Google Maps app to navigate her way to Otter Bluff.

She was nervous, she could admit that. As she drove, she picked apart the reasons for her anxiety.

One: He'd read her blog, so she couldn't present the usual persona she used with men. Nix knew more about the real her than was standard in these situations.

Two: She was going there to eat pasta, something she'd never done in front of a man until she'd met Nix. What if the sight of her feeding her hunger repulsed him? What if she moaned again and it made her seem out of control, like some ravenous beast who couldn't rein in her impulses?

Three: What if the pasta led to sex? Usually, she'd have been encouraged by that thought, but in her experience, sex led to goodbye, and she really liked Nix. If the goodbye was going to come, she'd rather it be later instead of sooner.

And four: Liking Nix made her feel vulnerable, and she hated vulnerability.

Well, she couldn't do anything about items one, two, and four, but three? That she could control. She promised herself there would be no sex tonight.

Though the right pasta dish might feel just as good.

~

By the time Nix opened the door for Joy, he figured he was as ready as he was going to be.

He felt a certain amount of anxiety, but he felt good and hopeful, too. Introducing someone to homemade pasta was God's work, so he had that going for him.

Looking at her as she stood on the doorstep at Otter Bluff, it occurred to Nix that she'd already changed since she'd gotten to Cambria. She was less polished but more relaxed. Less upscale, more natural. He liked the change, and he couldn't help smiling like an idiot.

"So ... can I come in?"

Nix had been so wrapped up in taking her in that he'd neglected to invite her into the house.

"Oh. Right. Of course." He stood back to let her pass.

First, there was the small talk about Otter Bluff.

"Oh, my God." Joy stared out the bank of windows in the front room that looked out onto a close-up and unobstructed ocean view. "You really live here now?"

"For another few months." He'd already explained about the house and Evan and his agreement to renovate the place while he lived there, so he updated her on his progress. "I finished the master bathroom," he told her. "Want to see?"

He led her into the bathroom and stood back, feeling proud of what he'd accomplished.

"This is really nice," she said, and it seemed like she meant it.

He pulled out his phone and brought up a photo of what the bathroom had looked like before, in all of its chipped-tile, powder-blue-bathtub glory.

Her mouth fell open as she looked at the before shot. "Now I'm even more impressed."

Nix reflected briefly on the manly pride that came from being complimented by a woman on home improvement tasks.

"Well … should we get to the pasta?" he said.

~

NIX LED Joy into the kitchen, where he'd laid out the ingredients and equipment for the pasta.

"Did you renovate the kitchen, too?" she asked. "It's really nice."

"Nah. I wish I could take credit, but the kitchen was the one room the previous owner had redone before she sold the place." He leaned his hip against the counter, one hand tucked into his pocket. "I … ah … wondered whether I should have everything ready before you got here, but then I thought it might be fun to wait so we could do it together. I hope that's okay." He looked uncertain, and Joy thought it was cute that he was nervous, too.

"It's great," she said. "I don't really cook, though."

"That's okay, I know what I'm doing," he assured her. "I got lessons from my friend's Italian mom."

CHAPTER 19

They worked together, side by side, to make the dough and roll it out with Nix's pasta machine. They hung the noodles on the rack Mrs. Lombardi had loaned him, and then Joy chopped tomatoes on a cutting board at the kitchen island while Nix put a big pot of water on the stove.

Joy had worried about the possible sexual repercussions of the date, but this was just ... fun.

Working together, making a mess with flour, talking about this and that ... it was different than any date Joy could remember. Usually, the entire date was focused on the guy trying to impress Joy so he could get her into bed. But this was companionable. Low-key. She found herself relaxing, her self-consciousness fading as she became absorbed in the tasks and smells and textures of cooking.

By the time they sat down to dinner, she was hungry and happy. Nix poured her a glass of pinot noir, and they settled in at a small table he'd set up on the back patio, the waves crashing into the bluffs below them.

"This is amazing," she said, indicating the ocean, the horizon, and their front-row seats.

"Usually it's too windy out here in the afternoons and evenings for this kind of thing, but today we got lucky." He shrugged.

She took a sip of the wine. "Okay. Time to check off that list." She twirled some pasta onto her fork, put it into her mouth, and drew one stray noodle in slowly between her lips, her eyes closed.

Then she moaned, "Oh, God."

~

NIX WAS MESMERIZED, and a blood engorgement problem was causing him to shift a little in his seat. It was just like Mrs. Lombardi had said. Sensual. The perfect food for love.

His mouth was dry and his mind was blank, and when she recovered enough to tell him the food was delicious, he couldn't respond at first.

"Nix? Are you okay?" She looked at him with her fork in her hand, her eyebrows raised.

He cleared his throat. "Uh … fine. Yes. I'm fine."

He'd suspected it at Mojo's, and now he knew it for sure: watching Joy eat was, in itself, a satisfying sexual experience.

He was nothing if not ambitious, though. He was certain he could improve on it, if given a chance.

He was hoping he'd get the chance sooner rather than later.

~

WHEN DINNER WAS OVER, they carried their plates back into the house and put them in the sink. Joy made moves to start cleaning up, but Nix stopped her.

"I'll do that later. You're my guest. You don't have to clean up."

Instead, she poured herself another glass of wine, refilled Nix's glass, and sat on the sofa in the living room, patting the seat beside her in invitation.

"So, that's one item ticked off your list," he said.

"Yes. And it was so much fun! I can't wait to hit some more things on the checklist."

"Speaking of which." He put his knee up on the sofa so he could face her more fully. "I saw another one we could maybe take care of now, if you want."

"Which is?"

Joy was fully prepared for this to be a come-on, an invitation into his bedroom that would change the whole dynamic of the date. But what he suggested was different than what she'd thought.

"You wrote that you've never kissed a guy without worrying about whether it was going to turn into sex," he said.

She blinked a few times. "Yeah. I did write that."

"So, let's cross that one off. If you want to."

She stared at him, then her lips curved into a slow smile. "I'm not sure that's possible."

"What? The kissing?"

"No. The part where I'm not worried about whether it will lead to sex."

"Oh, well, that's not an issue."

"It's not?"

"Nope." He held his hand over his heart. "I, Phoenix Landry, give you my solemn vow that I will not make any moves on you tonight beyond kissing, no matter what, even if you beg me. No touching below the neck."

"But above the neck is okay?" Joy asked.

"Well, I was hoping to run my hands through your hair. It's really nice hair."

She giggled. "Even if I beg you," she repeated.

"Right. Even if you get on your knees and ..." He seemed to rethink where he was going with that. "Even if you say please."

God, he was adorable. And it really would be nice to kiss him without worries, without expectations, without anything but the pleasure of kissing for its own sake.

"All right," she said.

"All right?"

"Let's do it." Now she was the one rethinking her language. "The kissing, I mean."

NIX WONDERED if his proposal had sounded to Joy like a gimmick or an angle. It wasn't. Yes, he wanted to get her into bed. Eventually. But right now, he really did want her to be able to fulfill her list item. He really did want her to be able to enjoy a kiss for kissing's sake, without expectation and without anxiety.

It was a thing men didn't have to deal with—the constant weighing of risk vs. reward that came with a kiss. For him, a kiss was always just a kiss when he wanted it to be. But he could see that for Joy, and probably for all women, it was likely fraught not only with expectation but also with potential danger.

He had an opportunity to give her what she wanted in exactly the way she wanted it, and he wasn't about to squander it.

He leaned forward, looked to her in case she'd changed her mind, and, when she gave him a slight, barely perceptible nod, he gently touched his lips to hers.

They'd kissed before, but this was different. This was the fulfillment of a specific thing she'd wanted but had never had. He deepened the kiss, leaning in and slightly parting his lips.

Joy tasted lightly of pinot noir, and she smelled like shampoo and some faint floral perfume. He tilted his head and gently touched his tongue to hers.

If he'd thought the moan was erotic when it was inspired by ice cream or pasta, it was so much more so when elicited by his own touch. It was a subtle sound—a kind of hum from deep in her throat—and it made him feel a rush of desire so strong he nearly swooned—if men could be said to swoon.

He remembered his promise to her—no sex, even if she begged him—and also remembered what he'd said about his hands and her hair.

That, at least, he could do.

He brought his hands up to her face, pressed them to her cheeks, then ran them into her hair, feeling its silky thickness through his fingers.

Usually at this point he'd be pondering how he could transition this whole thing into the bedroom. But not this time. This time, he was fully present in the moment, the way he'd always urged Joy to be.

He had to admit, there was something to be said for this kissing-only concept.

A FEW MOMENTS into the kiss—after Nix slid his hands into her hair and after she let out that explicitly sexual sound of bliss—Joy started rethinking the limits they'd set on this particular activity.

"Um … I …" She was having a hard time gathering her thoughts because he was running his lips along her jawline. Her head was thrown back, her eyes closed as she felt the sensation of his kisses like a current of electricity through her body.

"*Mmm?*" He murmured his encouragement without removing his mouth from her skin.

"I think … maybe it wouldn't be so bad if we … you know. Moved things …" She gasped. "Below the neck."

"Nope." He continued what he was doing.

Had he really said no? She wondered if she'd heard him wrong from within her fog of pleasure.

"Really? Because—"

"I made a promise." He moved his mouth back to hers and devoured her, caressing her with his tongue and drawing her lower lip in between his teeth for a gentle nip.

"Yes, but …" She lost the thread of the conversation again, then forced herself back on track. "If I say … that you don't really have to … you know … keep it …"

"A promise is a promise."

His lips and his tongue and his hands in her hair were everything —the whole world.

"Oh." The word sounded breathy and sad.

~

NIX HAD FACED challenges in his life. Getting through AP Calculus in high school, for one. And then there was the time he'd taken a law office job he wasn't qualified for.

But none of the previous challenges he'd faced and then either met or failed to meet had been quite like this one.

A beautiful, warm woman was inviting herself into his bed, and he had to say no.

God knew he didn't want to, but he'd made a promise, and this was a test. If he failed to keep this promise, he might not get a chance to show her he could keep the next one. Worse than that, if he didn't do what he'd said he would, she wouldn't get to tick the box next to the kissing item on her list. And that meant she would never be able to simply enjoy being with a man without all of the baggage that came with it.

He'd set out to give her that, and he wasn't going to turn back now.

~

NIX WAS KEEPING his nothing-below-the-neck promise. But Joy wasn't sticking to the limits they'd set.

She laid her palms against his chest, then began running them downward. But before she could get very far, he caught her hands in his and stopped her.

"Nope," he said again. He brought her hands to his mouth and kissed them, then let go and sat back with a satisfied smile on his face.

"Really?" she said.

"Really."

Joy wasn't sure whether to feel rejected or pleased.

"How did you enjoy it?" he asked. "A kiss without the possibility of sex?"

She was silent for a moment, still coming back into herself after what felt like an out-of-body experience.

"It was lovely." She could feel herself smiling like a lovesick fool.

"Good. I'm glad."

"I … uh … I guess I'd better go," she said. "Before we …"

"Yeah. Probably best."

"I had a great time, Nix. Thank you." She pressed a kiss to his lips that was much more chaste than the last one.

"I did, too. I'd walk you to the door, but I have a situation." He glanced down toward his lap.

"Oh." She giggled a little, then gathered up her purse and her jacket and headed for the door, giving him a little three-fingered wave as she went.

~

NIX WAS ENCHANTED by Joy's giggle. He'd heard it a couple of times tonight, and it delighted him. When he'd met her, he wouldn't have thought her capable of such a simple, innocent expression of pleasure.

He wanted to make her do it again and again. And if she happened to be naked when it happened, well, so much the better.

He got up with some discomfort and went to take care of his situation.

CHAPTER 20

Joy's original intention had been to delay having sex with Nix in order to protect her heart. Who'd have thought that simply kissing him would put her heart in more danger than if she'd just gone all the way?

The kiss had been amazing. Miraculous. The fact that they'd agreed it wouldn't lead to anything else had allowed her to be fully present for it, enjoying it for its own sake instead of seeing it as a bridge to something else.

Okay, yes, she'd tried to take it further, and Nix had surely wanted that, too. But he'd kept his promise to her.

Even though he'd had to deny himself something he wanted, he'd kept his promise.

How many men in her life had ever done that?

She thought about that the morning after the date as she took a run up Santa Rosa Creek Road. The weather was mild, and she enjoyed the feeling of the cool ocean air on her skin, her muscles warm and loose, the trees above her offering a canopy of shade.

Usually, on the morning after she'd eaten something calorie-laden like the pasta, she'd be running to atone for her indulgence. But today, she reminded herself to run just for the sake of it. Just for the pure thrill of enjoying her own vibrant strength.

She ran up the road for two and a half miles according to her pedometer, then turned around for a total of five. When she got back to the tiny house, a sheen of sweat on her skin, she looked at the outdoor tub with her hands on her hips, considering.

When she'd first seen the thing, she'd thought there was no way she would ever take a bath outdoors—it had seemed so … rural. But now the sight of the tub situated just off the porch was more enticing than she'd have expected.

Why not?

No one ever came out here except Nix, and he only showed up in the afternoons, usually, to tend his garden. The odds of him visiting at exactly the wrong time were slim.

She'd decided to enjoy whatever the tiny house experience had to offer, and this was one of those things. Bathing in the shade of a sycamore tree with the breeze murmuring through the leaves and the birds singing their unknowable songs?

Again, why not?

She went to the tub, plugged the drain, and started the tap. When the tub was full, the water just the right temperature, she went into the house, got a towel, and brought it outside.

Joy hesitated, then stripped off her running clothes and stepped into the tub. She let out a sigh of contentment as she lowered herself into the hot water.

~

NIX COULD ADMIT, if pressed, that he'd manufactured a reason to go to the tiny house. He didn't need to weed his planting beds—he'd done it just the day before—but if he went out there and did it again, he might get to see Joy, which seemed to him like a very good thing.

The day was so nice that he decided to park his car just inside the gate to the property and walk the rest of the way.

He wasn't trying to be especially quiet, but he wasn't making noise, either; just the crunch of his shoes on the dirt road.

She didn't hear him, probably because she was wearing earbuds, listening to something—music? A podcast?—as she soaked in the tub he'd installed.

Her head was back against the edge of the tub, her eyes closed, her face smooth and relaxed.

Her shoulders, bare and pale and perfect, peeked out above the rim of the tub.

He froze, not knowing what to do.

If she saw him, she'd be self-conscious and it would ruin what was obviously a good time. If she didn't see him, well, that was kind of creepy. He didn't want to be that guy who stood there watching a naked woman without her knowledge.

So, two choices: call out to her so she'd know he was there, or turn around and go home.

God, she was beautiful. Not just physically, either—he found unbearable beauty in the way she was unfolding, opening herself to new experiences and new pleasures. He felt privileged to be a part of it.

Still, he couldn't stand here and watch her without her knowing. He turned and started back toward his car.

He'd barely gotten three steps away before he heard her squealing, the bath water splashing.

"Oh my God. Nix! How long have you been there?!"

He winced and turned around slowly to find her still in the tub, but sitting upright now and clutching a towel to her body.

"Sorry. Sorry." He held his hands up in helpless surrender and closed his eyes. "I wasn't watching you. I promise. I was only there for a second."

"Well, what were you doing if you weren't watching me?"

The sight of her had made his excuse for being here fly right out of his head, and he scrambled to get it back. "I … uh … I came out here to do some gardening, that's all. Then I saw you, and I didn't want to interrupt … you seemed like you were having a really nice time … so I was just going to leave. But then you saw me, and … and here we are."

It was a fairly thorough summary, given how flustered he was.

"Oh, God. I knew this whole outdoor bathtub thing was a mistake," she said.

"No! No, it isn't. I'll just go so you can continue"—he made a vague gesture with his hands—"doing what you were doing. Just pretend I was never here."

"You don't have to do that. You came all the way out here. Ugh. Just … turn around while I get out."

The thought of her getting out of the tub on his account, before she was ready, disturbing her peaceful reverie, filled him with regret. But he turned his back to her as she instructed.

He heard the splashing as she got out of the water.

"Okay, I'm just going to go inside now. Don't turn around until you hear the door close."

"Got it."

He heard her steps on the porch, then the opening of the door. Then, with not a small amount of sorrow, he heard the door close.

He sighed, turned back around, and headed toward the garden.

~

JOY HAD A COUPLE OF CHOICES: she could believe that Nix had been standing there spying on her, or she could believe he'd innocently stumbled onto her lying in the bathtub and had been leaving to preserve her privacy when she'd seen him.

She chose to believe the latter—that he'd been a victim of circumstance. After all, what would she have done in the same situation? If she'd seen Nix naked in the tub, lying with his face to the sun, his eyes closed …

Oh, God. That wasn't useful. That kind of thinking was going to get her into trouble.

She dried off, dressed, and wondered what to do next. Should she go out to the garden and talk to him? What if he'd come wanting to be alone with his plants?

Don't be stupid, she told herself. *The plants are an excuse. He came here to see me.*

That thought made a little trill of excitement bubble up in her chest. That was the truth, wasn't it? He came here for her, and the gardening was a convenient ruse.

She blow-dried her hair, put on just a hint of makeup, and gave herself a pep talk before going out there to see him.

It's just friendly. It's just a friendly visit. And there's not going to be any kissing today. Even though he just saw me naked.

NIX WAS out at his garden, looking for nonexistent weeds, when Joy came walking up the path to meet him.

"Hey." He gave her a weak wave. "I'm sorry about earlier. I really didn't mean—"

"Right. I know." She dismissed his apology with a wave of her arm. "I get it."

"Okay." He nodded, his hands stuffed into the pockets of his jeans. He raked a hand through his hair—it was loose today—and grinned sheepishly. "I do kind of have a confession, though."

"You do?"

"Yeah. I didn't really have to weed the garden." He indicated the weedless expanse of his planting beds. "I just wanted to see you. Though, I didn't expect to see quite so much of you."

She laughed and blushed, and the sight of it warmed him and made him feel happy and full.

"I ... ah ... noticed you've got some stuff sprouting," he said. "I didn't know you planted anything."

Joy's eyes widened, and she went to the raised bed Nix had designated as hers. She peered down at the tiny green shoots stretching up from the soil and squealed in delight.

"Oh my God! Yes! I planted some carrots and cucumbers, but I didn't think it would work! Look at them!" She jumped up and down a few times in excitement, clapping her hands like a child at Christmas.

If he hadn't already fallen in love with her, that would have been the moment. Seeing her bubble over with excitement over her sprouting seeds would have sent him over the edge into a zone of no return. He'd already been more than halfway there, anyway.

"You did it," he said, feeling more simple happiness than he had in months, maybe years.

"I did." She came to him and threw her arms around him.

~

JOY HADN'T MEANT to kiss him. She really hadn't. But she was so excited about her delicate, sprouting plants, and he looked so good with the sunlight on his hair, those pale eyes smiling at her.

She couldn't seem to help herself.

And anyway, this wasn't something unprecedented between them, was it?

She linked her arms around his neck and pressed her lips to his, and as they sank into the kiss, her entire body sighed with relief, as though it had been holding the tension of years of unrealized hopes and suppressed fears, and it had finally put down that baggage and felt the freedom of release.

They broke the kiss, and she rested her forehead lightly against his.

"I guess I got a little excited," she said. "About the plants, I mean."

"I guess you did." His breath was warm on her, and his fragrance smelled like home.

"Oh boy," she said. Nothing else, just that.

He sighed. "Yeah."

~

HE KNEW what the *oh boy* meant, because he felt it himself. It meant they both were getting deep into this thing, and if it didn't work out, somebody was going to get hurt.

Likely, both of them.

But why shouldn't it work? Sure, all of Nix's romantic relationships had eventually failed. But it only took one. Why shouldn't it be this one?

If Joy had been just any woman he was dating, he'd have tried to transition the kiss into something more. He'd have invited himself into the house, and from there, he'd have tried to persuade her to take him into her bed.

But Joy wasn't just any woman. He couldn't have said why, exactly. Why this time was different, why this woman was more. But he knew it was true, and that would just have to do.

So instead, he cleared his throat and gathered his faculties.

"Have I told you anything about fertilizing the soil yet? I … ah … we should do that."

CHAPTER 21

"So you've kissed a few times. Now what?"

Joy was on the phone with Amber that evening, after she'd cooked dinner in her little kitchen and tidied up the tiny house. She gave Amber's question full consideration before answering.

"I don't know. We keep dating, I guess. And we keep hitting things on my list. It's been really fun so far."

"I saw the pictures of your little sprouts on Instagram," Amber said. "You said you were going to do the organic gardening thing, but I didn't really believe it. But there it was, happening!"

"I got so excited I accidentally kissed Nix." Joy was up in the loft sitting on her bed, and she could admit she was starting to see the coziness of the space that Amber had recognized when she'd visited.

"You accidentally kissed him."

"Well ... yes."

"Like, you were just celebrating and your lips smacked into his."

"Something like that." Joy grinned like an idiot remembering it.

"You want my two cents?" Amber asked.

"Always."

"This guy is good for you. I really think he is. I mean, the whole tone of our phone conversations and your blog posts has changed. You've changed. For the better, Joy."

Her first impulse was to deny it, but why? It was true.

"You think so?" she said.

"I do."

"You know what else?" Joy shifted her position on the bed, settling in and getting comfortable with the early evening glow from the skylight shining down on her. "My blog views are up. Everything kind of plummeted when I started this thing, but now? It's starting to gain traction, Amber. Just like we hoped it would."

"That's wonderful, Joy." From the warmth in Amber's voice, Joy knew she meant it. "But remember, you're doing this for you, not just for views."

"I know." For the first time, she actually did know.

They chatted about other things for a while— Amber's job and her family, mostly—then Joy said, "You really think Nix is good for me?"

"*Yes.*" Amber put heavy emphasis on the word. "He's different than anyone else you've dated, and that's a good thing, Joy. That's a very good thing."

~

NIX, Louise, and Leon were playing darts at Ted's, a dive bar off Main Street, a couple of nights after Nix had seen Joy in the bathtub. Nix had just beaten Louise, and now he and Leon were competing in a best two out of three match.

The bar was dark and smelled like old sweat and spilled Budweiser. The floor was sticky under Nix's feet, and the sound system was running through a playlist of 1980s greatest hits.

"You walked in on her in the tub and you didn't make a move?" Leon asked, shaking his head. "Man, that's a wasted opportunity."

"No, it wasn't." Nix lined up and took his three shots for a total of thirty-two points. "It was respectful, asswipe."

"It was," Louise agreed from where she sat on a barstool far enough back that she was unlikely to get pegged by an errant dart.

"Whether that's a good thing or not depends on whether she's looking for a nice guy or for someone who's going to use her hard and then throw her away like yesterday's newspaper."

Nix and Leon both stopped what they were doing and looked at her.

"Hey, I'm not gonna lie. Those are some of my fondest memories," she said.

"Well, that's not what I've got in mind," Nix said.

"That's sweet, dude. Really. I'm kind of choking up a little," Leon deadpanned.

"Asshole," Nix observed mildly.

Leon took his shots and got a paltry eighteen points. Apparently deciding to ignore the crappiness of his score, he did a little victory dance, waving his arms in the air and swinging his hips.

"So, what's your next move?" Louise asked Nix. She wasn't talking about darts.

He shrugged as though he hadn't thought about it much, but in fact, he had. "The list is my best bet."

"The things-she-wants-to-do list?" Louise asked.

"That's the one." He took a swig from the bottle of beer he'd been nursing. "Gives me an excuse for asking her out. Tuesday is skydiving day, that kind of thing."

"Holy shit. She wants to skydive?" Leon said.

"That's just an example," Nix said. "No, she doesn't actually want to skydive."

"That's a relief," Louise said. "No woman's worth risking your life for."

Privately, Nix thought she might be wrong about that. And the fact that he was thinking that way was at least as scary as actual skydiving would have been.

"Shove over," Nix told Leon. "It's my turn."

~

THEY DATED STEADILY over the next month. Sometimes they did things on Joy's list—she'd never been kayaking, so they did that—and other times, they just ate a meal together or took a walk or saw some local attraction.

Occasionally, they hung out at his place or hers, but that made it too hard not to sleep together, and Joy wasn't ready for that. So they usually spent time in public places that didn't pose much of a danger.

The dates often ended with kissing, and the kissing made Joy want to do more. Which made her ask herself why she kept saying no.

"You're scared, obviously," Amber told her on the phone one night.

Joy's first impulse was to deny it, but she kept her mouth closed because she didn't want to lie.

"Nix isn't scary," she said instead. "He's sweet and kind and generous. He's—"

"He's scary as shit, and you know it," Amber said, interrupting her. "Not because you think he'll hurt you. But because you think you'll screw things up and hurt yourself."

Joy was lying on her bed looking up through the skylight at the stars. "You know what's annoying?"

"What?"

"You always being right."

"Also, you don't trust him," Amber put in.

"Well ... we're still getting to know each other, but I'm pretty sure he's not a closet serial killer."

"Very funny. But you know what I mean. You don't trust him to stick. Because no one ever has."

Joy was quiet as Amber's words sank in. Joy's father hadn't stuck—he'd left when she was five years old. And none of her boyfriends had stuck. Some left after they got what they wanted—usually sex—and others left as soon as Joy revealed some crack in her pretty Instagram girl persona.

When she found out that her father had died, Joy had taken it hard, even though she hadn't seen him in decades. Because there had always been the hope that maybe, someday, she would. All it had taken was two weeks of Joy being off—two weeks of her bad mood, her dark thoughts, her grief—and Trevor had fled like he was being chased by gunmen.

Nobody stuck.

"Joy?" Amber spoke up after Joy had been silent for a while. "Are you still there? I didn't mean to hurt your feelings. All I meant was—"

"It's okay." Joy dismissed Amber's apology. "No, you're right."

And there was another factor, as well. Joy had already been in Cambria for two and a half months, and her original intention had been to stay for six. What good would it do for her to fall in love with Nix if she was leaving in a few months? And what if Nix was dating her knowing he had a built-in out once her lease was up?

"It's possible I have a trust problem," she said after a while.

"You think?" Amber's voice was heavy with sarcasm.

"So, what am I supposed to do about it?"

"You know," Amber said, "you could just … embrace the risk."

"Embrace the risk," Joy repeated.

"Yeah. You know what they say. No risk, no reward."

CHAPTER 22

They went out to dinner one night in mid-June, sharing a basket of fried clams in Morro Bay as the sun set over the water.

He and Joy had been dating long enough that Nix had finished renovating the second bathroom, and he still hadn't progressed to second base.

He suspected he might have been friend-zoned—if being friend-zoned included kissing.

Nothing to do but ask her.

"So, I was wondering ..." He picked up a fried clam, popped it into his mouth, and chewed. They were sitting on a patio facing the water, a light ocean breeze ruffling their hair.

"You were wondering what?" Joy asked.

"I was wondering if ... maybe you've decided that you just want to be friends with me. Which is okay, but I'd like to know if that's the case. Because I have feelings that are decidedly beyond friendly, and if I need to scale back my expectations—"

"What?" Joy blinked at him in surprise, a clam frozen between her fingers in the space between the basket and her mouth. "No. That's not ... no. I don't want to be friends."

"You don't?"

"Well ... no. I'd have thought all of the kissing would have made that clear."

He gave her a shy half grin that melted something deep inside her chest. "That's good to know."

"Why did you think that? If you think I'm not interested in you, then—"

"It's just..." He shrugged and avoided her gaze. "We've been seeing each other awhile now, and ... I mean, first base is great ..."

"But you're swinging for the home run," she finished for him.

His eyes widened as he rushed to correct any misunderstandings. "When you're ready. Of course. I'm not looking to rush things, it's just ... I'd like to know if things are going that way eventually."

"Right. Of course." Joy put down her clam and turned in her seat to face him more fully. "That's fair."

"So, what are your thoughts?"

Joy's thoughts were swinging wildly from *oh God, yes* to panic to *how soon can we get to your place* to stark fear that once he had what he wanted, he wouldn't want her.

He'd been patient, and she'd been holding him off, and at some point things either had to move forward or they had to end.

She could see that.

"Okay." She picked up her napkin and wiped her fingers carefully. "Let's go back to your place."

He stared at her as though he wasn't quite certain she'd said what he thought she'd said. "Really?"

"Sure. I'd say the tiny house, but Otter Bluff has that nice ocean view."

"It ... it does."

"We can sit out on the deck afterward and enjoy the ocean."

"Afterward."

"Yep." She grinned at him, and her excitement began to outweigh her doubts.

His eyebrows shot up, and he hunted in his wallet for some cash for the tip. "Let's go."

ON THE DRIVE from Morro Bay to Cambria, Joy kept thinking about the pound.

Except it wasn't just a pound anymore, was it? It had, just as she'd predicted, invited its friends. Now it was five pounds—enough that she was contemplating moving up to the next pants size.

What if she took her clothes off and Nix was disappointed by her body?

He'd seen her bikini shots on Instagram—he'd told her that. But that was before the five pounds. The last time she'd gained five pounds, she'd been targeted by hate and ridicule on social media, and that had been bad enough. Facing judgment and scorn in Nix's bedroom would be so much worse.

Of course he was too nice to say anything. He would never judge her—at least not out loud. But what if he privately thought she was so much less attractive than he'd expected her to be? What if everything about her was a letdown?

"Is everything okay?" he asked as he drove. He shot a concerned look at her. "You've gotten really quiet."

"I'm fine."

"Are you sure? If you've changed your mind—"

"I haven't." That much was true. She really did want him, really did want to feel his body against hers, touch his skin, breathe in every inch of him.

She just hoped he wouldn't change his mind about her when the time came.

THEY HELD hands as they went up the front walk, and then, on the front porch, he turned to her and they wrapped themselves up in each other's arms, falling into a deep and satisfying kiss.

He still had one arm wrapped tightly around her as he fished around in his pocket for his keys and opened the front door.

He pulled her inside, and then she was grabbing at his T-shirt, pulling it off over his head.

He had a beautiful body—lean and strong—and she had a flash of worry about her own as he pulled off her shirt just as she had his. She was thankful she'd worn a pretty bra.

"Come on. Let's go in the bedroom." She took him by the hand and led him down the hallway.

When they got in there, she was thankful that the room was dark. He reached out to turn on a light, but she caught his hand before he could. She kissed the hand, then led him away from the light switch, hoping the move was more subtle than it felt.

"I want to see you," he said, but he left the light off as they made their way to the bed with only the light from a full moon casting a silvery glow on the room.

She lay down on the bed and he reached for her belt buckle. "I think about this all the time," he said, his voice rough.

She did, too. She let him undress her, then took him into her arms.

AFTERWARD, Joy had expected them to enjoy closeness and warmth and happy relaxation.

Instead, they got awkwardness, insecurity, and regret.

"If there was something I should have done, or something I did that I shouldn't have done ..." Nix lay on his back, looking at the ceiling with Joy beside him. They weren't touching.

"No. It wasn't your fault." Joy, like Nix, stared at the ceiling as though the answers to the universe might be up there in the paint. "You did everything you could."

It had gone well at first. There had been more kissing, and a lot of touching, and some truly amazing things he'd done with his tongue. And then ... nothing. Joy had thought she might get to the finish line, but she'd stalled when she was just inches away.

"Do you normally ..." He left the rest of the sentence unfinished, but it was clear what he was asking.

She quickly did the math: truth vs. lie, fact vs. face-saving fiction.

"Ah … well, no. Not when I'm … you know. With someone." She opted for truth because he was special, and he deserved it.

"What about alone?"

She felt her face redden. "Yes. It usually goes okay when I'm alone."

"Oh."

Joy heard a universe of meaning in the *oh.*

Oh, so it's just me, then. Oh, I'm inept as a lover. Oh, then it's entirely my fault.

And, *Oh, if no one else has achieved it, either, then maybe it's you.*

Joy had really thought it might happen this time. She was so attracted to Nix, and everything he'd done to her had felt so good. Her hopes had been so high.

Maybe that was the problem. Maybe the weight of her expectation had crushed her potential orgasm like a paper cup under someone's shoe.

"Maybe if we try again." He raked his hand through his hair. "If you could give me a little more … you know. Instruction."

"Maybe."

But the moment was gone—she knew that. Now that they'd tried and failed to ring her bell, he felt awkward, and she felt awkward, and another go at it—at least, right now—wasn't going to help anything.

Joy had long since learned that faking it smoothed things over considerably. But she hadn't wanted to fake it with Nix. She'd wanted whatever happened between them to be real.

She rolled onto her side to look at him. "I still had a really great time."

"Yeah." He looked at the ceiling instead of at her.

~

"So … it happened. We finally … you know."

Joy and Amber were having lunch at a café in Santa Barbara, which they'd determined was an equitable halfway point between Los Angeles and Cambria. Joy was picking at a salad—which she'd ordered because she actually wanted a salad—and Amber was working her way through a BLT with fries.

When Amber heard the news, her eyes widened and she dropped the fry she was holding onto her plate. "Oh, my God. You did? How was it? Was it awesome?"

Joy's miserable face answered for her.

"Oh, no." Amber's expression fell. "What happened?"

"The usual." Joy looked at her plate, her hands in her lap. "You know I never …I've told you how I …"

"Uh oh."

"Yeah. The grand finale didn't happen. And he tried so hard, Amber. He really did. I give him an A for effort. It's just …"

"He got an A, but you didn't get an O," Amber offered.

"Exactly. Which would have been fine. It's fine! I still had a good time. It still felt great, and it was so nice to be close to him, but afterward …"

"He had an ego problem."

"Yes."

"Which ruined everything."

"Yeah. It kind of did."

Amber considered that. "Well, what have you done in the past when guys had ego problems … after?"

"They didn't." Joy scrunched up her face in an expression of regret. "I kind of … you know. Faked it."

"You faked it."

"Yes! So that this kind of thing wouldn't happen!"

"But you didn't fake it with Nix."

"No." Joy couldn't really explain why she hadn't. It was just a feeling, really. A feeling that he deserved her honesty, her authenticity. And there was also the feeling that she wanted more this time. She didn't want to fake ecstasy anymore. She wanted the real thing.

"Look." Amber wiped her fingers on her napkin and focused on Joy. "I think it's good that you didn't fake it. I mean, yes, it hurt his confidence, maybe. But now he's got no other recourse but to up his game."

Joy could see Amber's point. But what if, instead of upping his game, Nix decided to forfeit? Or, what if he wasn't the problem at all? What if Joy was the one who needed to improve her play?

She'd been holding back her real thoughts, so now she just let them spill out.

"It's the five pounds," Joy said. "I know it is."

"Wait ... what?" Amber looked as though the confusion caused by that sentence was causing her physical pain.

"I was so worried about whether he'd like my body now that I've gained five pounds that I just ... couldn't."

Amber's mouth fell open, and she gave Joy a withering look. "Did *he* get to the finish line?"

"Yes. Of course he did."

"Then he liked your body just fine. The penis doesn't lie."

Amber delivered that last line just as the waitress arrived at their table.

"Uh ... I hate to interrupt, but would you two like dessert?"

Nix tried to tell himself everything was fine.

Of course it was.

He and Joy had shared a lovely time together, even if it hadn't gone exactly the way he'd planned. She'd seemed to have fun even without the fireworks he'd expected to give her. And anyway, any disappointment she might have felt wasn't his fault. After all, she'd told him it had always been that way between her and her partners.

He would just try again. He'd ask her for feedback, and he would act on it. He'd be patient and persistent, and it would happen.

That was what the rational part of his brain told him. But the irrational part—the part that whispered to him at his most vulnerable moments—had another take on things.

What if she lied about the other guys? What if I really am the problem? What if my technique sucks? What then?

Nobody had complained about his technique before, but that didn't mean anything. It was possible they were just being kind.

He thought about all of that as he stood in the flooring aisle at The Home Depot, looking at samples of hardwood for Otter Bluff.

He tried to weigh the merits of dark vs. light colors in terms of what would hide scratches and dirt the best, but his mind kept going back to Joy.

He wanted another chance, but what if she didn't give him one? What if she'd written him off as bad in bed, and he never got to show her that he could do better? That he could learn?

"Anything I can help you with?"

Nix looked up to see a guy in an orange apron looking at him expectantly.

"Yeah. What do women want? Sexually, I mean?"

The guy regarded him with skepticism. "Dude, I don't know what you're planning to do with that flooring, but I guarantee it wasn't made for that."

CHAPTER 23

Joy's organic vegetables continued to grow, and she wrote about it on her blog and posted photos to Instagram. She gained another pound and tried not to worry about it. The audience for her blog grew, and her ad revenue grew along with it—though not to anywhere near what she'd earned at her peak.

She and Nix took another go at it—a few times—with similar results. He tried valiantly and tirelessly to push her over the edge, and she tried valiantly and tirelessly to get there. No luck so far, but she loved being with him, and they both tried to tell themselves it was enough.

"You know, I don't really think it's me," he said one night when they were lying naked in each other's arms after another effort. "I mean, the things I'm doing have always worked for me before."

"I've been telling you that." Her head lay on his chest, and she could hear the steady thump of his heart. "I've been telling you it's not you."

"Yeah, but … you *would* say that, wouldn't you?"

"I guess I would," she conceded. "But it's really true."

They were both quiet for a while, then he spoke softly into the darkness. "I've got a theory."

"*Mm*. Do you?"

"Yeah. It's got something to do with the fact that you never want me to keep the lights on. And the fact that you never really let me look at you."

From the tone of his voice, she could tell he was nervous about saying it, not knowing how she'd react.

When she didn't say anything, he pressed on. "Joy? Why don't you think I'll like your body? You're beautiful."

Her eyes welled up with tears, and she didn't answer him.

"I mean, you have all those photos out there on Instagram, with the bikinis and the lingerie. So you don't mind people seeing you. But with me ..." He didn't finish the thought.

She pulled away from him. She couldn't help it. The move was automatic, involuntary.

"Joy ..."

"I just need ..." She got up and padded to the bathroom in the darkness, and she stayed in there long enough to make it clear that he shouldn't bring up the topic again.

~

JOY HADN'T VISITED her mother since she'd moved to Cambria, but now she had no choice—it was her mother's birthday, and Delores didn't have any other family.

Nix offered to go with her, but Joy made excuses.

"Really, that's sweet, but you don't have to. This is just a thing I have to get done. Like dropping off my dry cleaning." Once it was out of her mouth, she realized it sounded cold and uncaring. But it was an accurate reflection of how Joy felt about visiting her mom—if going to the dry cleaners involved a large dollop of regret and self-loathing.

She bought a gift—Delores's favorite perfume—wrapped it, picked up a cake from a bakery near her mother's place, and knocked on the door at just after one p.m. on the day Delores turned 56.

"Oh. Joy. I didn't know you were coming." Delores stood on the doorstep in an expensive pastel pants ensemble.

"Of course I came. It's your birthday." She tried to keep her tone upbeat.

"Well, come on in." Delores stepped aside to allow Joy to enter.

They chatted a little about Delores's day—she didn't have anything planned until evening, when she'd be having a birthday dinner with a couple of women from her book club—Joy's life in the tiny house, and the news that one of Joy's cousins had gotten engaged. Then Delores opened her gift and made the appropriate noises about how much she loved it.

The whole thing was tense and awkward but mostly fine until Joy was standing at the kitchen counter cutting the cake. Delores, scrutinizing her, said, "Have you gained weight?"

Joy's knife froze in mid-cut.

"Um ... a little. Why?"

Delores's face arranged itself into an expression of dismay. "Oh, Joy. Don't start letting yourself go. You're not as young as you used to be, and if you want to find a relationship ..."

Tension and anxiety coursed through Joy, and she advised herself to do what she always did—smile, say nothing, and get out as quickly as possible. But somehow, her mouth didn't do what her brain was telling it to.

She put down the knife and turned toward her mother.

"It's six pounds, Mom. I'm hardly letting myself go."

"Six! Oh, honey. They say if you gain five pounds or more, it's so much harder to take it back off. You never should have let it get this far. Now, my friend Sheila has a detox smoothie recipe that I—"

"I don't need a detox smoothie!" Joy stood with her eyes clamped shut, fists clenched at her sides.

"Well, you don't need to raise your voice with me, either."

Standing in her mother's kitchen, Joy had a sudden burst of clarity about why she didn't like her body, why she didn't trust a man to accept her the way she was, why she'd thought the only thing she had to offer was her physical attractiveness.

"Mom, has it ever occurred to you that your focus on my weight and how I look might have done some damage?"

Delores looked stunned, blinking like a newly hatched bird. "Damage? Look at you. You're beautiful. That doesn't come without work, without sacrifice. Once you lose that six pounds—"

"I don't want to lose the six pounds." Only once it was out of her mouth did Joy realize it was true. She didn't want to do this anymore —the dieting, the weighing, the worrying. She couldn't.

"What do you mean you don't want to? Look at me, I'm still a size six at my age. Do you think that wasn't hard? Do you think I got here by … by eating cake?" She gestured toward the cake Joy had brought.

Oh, God, here we go again.

It was the same thing, over and over. Except that now, Joy had decided she wasn't going to take it anymore.

"I guess not." She grabbed a chunk of the cake with her bare hand and threw it into the sink. "I should have known cake is off the menu for you, huh?" Another fistful—*plop*—into the sink.

"Joy, what in the world are you—"

"And God forbid I should eat anything like this." *Plop,* another chunk. Tears had begun streaming down Joy's cheeks, and her hand was a mitt of frosting and crumbs. "God forbid I should enjoy anything." *Plop.* "Because you would never approve of that, would you?" She was using both hands now, shoveling up birthday cake and dumping it into the sink. "And you will never, ever approve of me unless I'm tiny and thin and beautiful." She picked up the empty cake board and threw that into the trash, both of her hands covered in frosting. "But you know what? I'm sick of it. I'm sick to death of it. And I'm done." She pointedly licked a bit of frosting off of one finger. "*Mmm.* Delicious. Too bad you're not having any."

She wiped her hands on a dish towel, grabbed her purse, and stormed out the door.

JOY WAS CRYING, and her hands were still slick with the remnants of birthday cake and frosting, when she pulled up outside Amber's apartment building forty minutes later, having made her way through L.A.'s afternoon traffic.

She rang the bell and no one answered, so she dug her cell phone out of her purse, trying not to get frosting on everything inside.

"Joy? Hey, there. I thought you'd be at your mom's house right now."

Something about Amber's voice—about the way she sounded warm and welcoming and glad to hear from her—made Joy cry even harder.

"Oh, no. What's going on? What happened?" Amber asked in alarm.

"My mother. That's what happened."

"Oh, God. Where are you? I'll be right there."

~

ONCE AMBER HAD ARRIVED and let Joy into her apartment, Joy washed the remains of the cake off her hands, wiped the smeared mascara off her face, and sat down at the kitchen table with a cup of herbal tea Amber had insisted she accept for its soothing properties.

"Okay, let's have it." Amber put her hand on Joy's arm for support. "What did she do?"

Joy went through it—the comments about her weight and her failure to find a lasting relationship, Joy's response, and the messy, disastrous fate of the cake.

"Oh, shit. You really did that?" Amber clapped a hand over her mouth in shock. "You beat up your mother's birthday cake?"

Now that Amber had put it that way, Joy could see the humor in it, and she smirked. "You should have seen it. It was like some kind of bakery-themed crime scene."

Amber laughed, a helpless kind of laughter that bubbled up from inside her and could not be stopped until it had run its course. "I'm sorry. I'm sorry." She wiped the tears of mirth from her eyes. "I know it's not funny. It's just …"

"It's kind of funny," Joy admitted.

"It is! I can just see her face." Amber arranged her features into a spot-on parody of Delores's shocked scowl, which made Joy dissolve into laughter.

"I just ... It's like I had an out of body experience," Joy said. "Like I was watching someone else destroy the cake. It was like this horrifying train wreck that I couldn't stop, and maybe didn't even want to."

Amber caught her breath and wiped her eyes with a napkin. "Oh my God. I wish I'd been there. I really do."

"I kind of wish I hadn't."

Joy grew somber as she thought of the implications of what had happened. Her relationship with her mother had never been the best, but now it might be irreparable. Was it worth saving just because Delores was her mother? Was it possible to create a new and better relationship with her?

"Joy, I'm damned proud of you." Amber put her hand on Joy's arm again and gave it a gentle squeeze. "You've put up with her bullshit long enough."

"I don't know if she can change, Amber. I don't know if either of us can."

"Listen to me." Amber waited until Joy looked at her, really looked at her, then went on. "She might not change. But you can choose not to let the things she says affect you."

"But they do affect me. They do."

"That's why you're not really letting Nix in."

Joy knew it would come back to Nix. Because, of course, Amber was right. The things Delores had said to Joy all of her life, the things she'd valued about her, made it impossible for Joy to trust a man—or to trust herself to be enough for one.

"You have to talk to him about it," Amber said.

Joy let out a weary sigh. "Oh ... God. Do I have to?"

"I really think you do. And the fact that you don't want to pretty much proves the point, doesn't it?"

CHAPTER 24

Joy avoided Nix for a few days after that. Not because she wanted to stay at a distance from him, but because she didn't. She knew Amber was right and she had to talk to him about her insecurities. But first, she had to gear up for it.

"Are we okay?" Nix asked over the phone when she'd put him off for the second time. "Are you … Is this … Please tell me you're not breaking up with me and you're too scared to say it out loud."

"No! It's not that. I swear. It's just … I have some things I'm working out. And I'm going to tell you about them, but I'm not ready yet."

"Okay. But, while you're working things out, I have something for you to think about."

"What's that?"

"I love you."

NIX HADN'T EXPECTED to tell Joy he loved her. He'd felt it for a while now, but he hadn't planned to blurt it out like that.

He tried not to make too much of the fact that she hadn't said it back.

Thank you, that's what she'd said. As though he'd given her a gift.

Well, it was a gift, wasn't it? He was giving her the gift of his love, freely and without expectation, and if he was one goddamned lucky bastard, she might choose to give him hers in return.

She had to choose it, though. He didn't want her to say it just because he had. He didn't want her to respond out of obligation.

He ran all of it over in his mind as he and Leon tore the flooring out of the living room at Otter Bluff.

The old floor was a tired and worn carpet with stains in some places and flattened by wear in others. They'd already moved the furniture into the spare bedroom, and they were halfway through pulling the carpet up, rolling it as they went so it could be deposited into Leon's pickup truck.

"You okay?" Leon asked when they'd been working for a while in silence.

"Sure. I've just got some stuff on my mind."

Leon didn't ask what was on Nix's mind—probably because he didn't care. But that didn't stop Nix from blurting it out anyway, much as he'd blurted out his declaration of love for Joy.

"What does it mean if you tell a woman you love her and she doesn't say it back?"

Leon paused with a piece of old carpeting rolled up under his arm. "Ah, geez. Do I look like I know? I haven't had a date since that chick at the wine bar. I'm not exactly an expert."

"Maybe if you stopped calling them *chicks* . . ." Nix suggested.

"Yeah, yeah." Leon said it amiably enough, even if he was showing Nix his middle finger while he said it. "The point is, I don't know shit."

"Noted."

"Though, if I'm guessing," he went on, "I'd say it means she doesn't love you, dude. It might be time to move on."

Nix's reaction was to disregard the advice, not only because it was coming from Leon, but also because moving on wasn't an option. He'd meant what he said—he loved Joy. And that meant he was in it, no matter what. If at some point she declared that she didn't want him, well, that would be one thing. But she hadn't done that. She just hadn't said she did.

Which meant there was hope.

~

JOY WORKED up her nerve and called Nix. He'd be working on Otter Bluff in the morning, he told her, and then he was doing an afternoon shift at the market.

She showed up at Otter Bluff at just after nine a.m. with lattes and scones from a local coffeehouse. The message, she supposed, was *I didn't say I loved you, so here's some compensatory coffee.* As a gesture, it was inadequate, but it was all she could come up with on the fly.

She hadn't told him she was coming, so she knocked on the door with some hesitation.

He answered it in full construction-guy mode: faded jeans, work boots, a plain white T-shirt sprinkled with dust, his hair tied back to keep it out of his way.

"Hey." He looked happy to see her, and she felt some of her anxiety lift from her shoulders.

"I brought coffee." She held up the drink carrier in one hand. "And scones." She held up the bag in the other.

"Wow. That's great. Thank you. Come on in."

~

NIX'S first thought when he saw her was that she'd brought the coffee and scones as a way of softening the blow so she could tell him in a friendly way that she didn't want to see him anymore.

But as she walked in the door, she came up to him, leaned in, let her chest press against his, and kissed him, her hands occupied with the things she'd brought.

The kiss didn't say she was just being friendly before cutting him off at the knees. The kiss said she missed him and was glad to see him and maybe even was thinking about the whole *I love you* thing.

"Try not to … you know … look at anything." He followed her into the living room, where the carpet was gone and only the subflooring remained. "I'm in the middle of redoing the floor. I mean, obviously."

She put the coffee and scones on the kitchen island and they talked about flooring for a while—what he was going to install, why he'd chosen it, and what would come next when he was done with that.

They took their food and drinks out onto the patio, because right now, that was the only place where there was somewhere to sit.

"So, this is a pleasant surprise," he said when they were settled into their Adirondack chairs. "I wasn't sure when I was going to hear from you again. You know … after what I said."

"I liked what you said."

"Did you?" He couldn't help grinning.

"I did. I mean, it did freak me out a little bit. But I liked it."

Not dumping him, then. Things were looking up.

~

JOY WASN'T sure how to launch into the things she needed to say. She supposed she could take the direct approach, but then he wouldn't have the necessary context. Instead, she started with the background.

"I went to visit my mom a couple of days ago. It was her birthday."

"Right. How was that?"

"It was awful." She told him about the fight and about the cake. "I was trying to connect with her, you know? Just … connect. And all she could talk about was my weight gain and the fact that I would never find someone to love me if I didn't lose it."

He started to say something, and she put up a hand to stop him. "I just need to get through this," she said.

He nodded. "Okay."

"I used to act when I was a kid, did you know that? Did I ever mention it?"

"No. But I think I read something about that when I was Googling you for the rental application."

"Yeah, well. I did. And I did pageants before that."

"Pageants."

"Beauty pageants. Miss Teen This and Little Miss That. With the hair and the makeup and the dresses. And the swimsuits. I started my first diet when I was eight years old."

He looked like he wanted to say something again, but he didn't. He just reached out and took her hand.

"So, that's the context, Nix. Intellectually, I know the six pounds I've put on since I came here isn't important. I know it doesn't matter. I mean, it's only six pounds, right? But ..."

"But the messages you've gotten since childhood are that it does matter."

"The messages I've gotten are that my weight—my body, my looks—are *all* that matter. Every pageant, every audition, somebody had something to say about my weight. And now I'm getting older! Keeping the weight off isn't as easy anymore, and ... and I don't even want to do it! But if my looks are all that anyone likes about me, then what happens when I get wrinkles or I gain another five pounds or ... I know there's more about me that's worthy of love, Nix. I do know that. But knowing it and feeling it are two different things."

HE COULD SEE the issues now—could see it all laid out before him like a puzzle that needed to be solved.

Joy was in transition to a place where she wanted to think about more than just the way she looked. But she wasn't sure where that transition would leave her and how the people in her life would feel about her once it was complete.

So, when he said he loved her, did he love the old Joy or the one she was becoming? And if he'd meant the old one, where would that leave her as she continued to change?

"When I saw your pictures on Instagram, I thought you were incredibly hot."

"Nix, that's not—"

He put up a hand to stop her. "I thought you were incredibly hot, but I didn't really fall for you until I started getting to know you. Honestly? It was when you started to change. Seeing you go from the person you were when you showed up to the person you are now? And knowing it's all still in progress? It's been a beautiful thing, Joy, and I can't wait to find out where you end up."

He meant every word of it.

His worry was that, when she finished transforming, she wouldn't have a place for him in her new life.

"What if you don't want me anymore once I'm done doing whatever it is I'm doing?" she said.

"What if you don't want me?" he countered.

She gave him a wistful smile, then looked out toward the water. "The unanswered questions are ... unsettling."

He shrugged. "All of the most important things are."

CHAPTER 25

Now that they'd had the conversation Joy needed them to have, they resumed seeing each other. And they resumed Nix's efforts to fully satisfy her in bed.

"I've got an idea," he said one night. They were at the tiny house because Otter Bluff was still too torn up from the renovations.

"What might that be?"

They lay upstairs in the sleeping loft, partially undressed on the bed, where they'd been making out like teenagers.

Nix reached into his jeans pocket and pulled out a dark blue bandana.

"What's that for?" Joy asked.

"It's a blindfold."

She was mildly horrified. "You want to blindfold me?"

"It's for me."

She sat up on the bed and looked at him. "Is this the first step in some bondage fantasy I don't know about? Because—"

"It's an experiment. You worry about what I think when I see you. So, what if I can't see you?"

"I thought you wanted to see me."

"I do. And we'll get there, I hope. But for now, why not try it and find out what happens?"

JOY AGREED TO THE EXPERIMENT, and Nix went to work using only his other senses. Which, he reflected, was not much of a hardship.

He did all of the things he knew she liked, and he talked to her—when his mouth wasn't otherwise occupied—about how good she felt, how delicious she tasted, how much he loved her scent.

He couldn't see the look on her face, but he could hear the noises she was making, and he could feel the tension in her body. He knew the experiment would be a success when she grabbed handfuls of his hair and cried out in what sounded like pain, but which clearly wasn't.

JOY FELT like her body had been torn apart and then put back together in an arrangement that was infinitely preferable to the original.

She and Nix lay together afterward, both of them warm and naked and covered in a light sheen of sweat, the blindfold long since discarded.

"That was a really good idea." Joy had her body wrapped around his, her face pressed to his warm neck.

"Maybe my best idea ever."

"Someone's feeling pleased with himself."

"And rightly so." He pressed a kiss to the top of her head.

Joy had experienced perfectly pleasurable orgasms, though never with a partner until now. But if the others had been like small earthquakes, this one had the power to level a metropolis.

No wonder people made such a big deal about sex. She'd never really understood it before.

It was on the tip of her tongue to say she loved him. But she didn't want him to think it was the post-coital glow talking. When she said it, she wanted him to know it had come from her heart, not from other body parts.

"Thank you," she said instead. "That was amazing. It was … I've never …"

"You're welcome." He snuggled her a little closer.

The sleeping loft really was cozy, as though they were safe and comfortable in a burrow with a view of the stars. She was surprised she hadn't recognized what a lovely place it was until now.

He didn't usually spend the entire night with her, but this time, he did. Joy slept better than she had in weeks.

~

"So, how are things going with you and Nix?" Amber had planned to come to the tiny house for a visit, but her work schedule got in the way, and she'd called to say she couldn't make it. Their conversation had evolved from the logistics of her canceled visit to a discussion of Joy's love life.

"Great. Really great," Joy said. "Incredibly awesome, in fact. Earth-shaking."

Amber was silent for a moment as she decoded what Joy was trying to say.

"Really?" she said.

"Really."

"Oh, my God. He's achieved what no man has achieved before him. He must be insufferable right now."

Joy giggled. "He's fairly proud of himself, but I'll give it to him. He earned it."

"You sound so … so happy," Amber said.

"I'm more relaxed than I've ever been, I'll tell you that."

"That's so great. Too bad you can't put it in your blog."

Well, she could, she supposed—she wouldn't be the first person to overshare on the Internet—but she wouldn't. What had happened between herself and Nix was precious and private, and she would hold it close to her heart. It wasn't for public consumption.

She didn't need to, anyway. Her blog had picked up enough readers—along with reader engagement—that she was beginning to think the book idea might actually happen.

"The blog—that's another thing that's going well." Joy told Amber about her steady increase in revenue and how happy she was with the number of positive reader comments. "I'm about ready to start writing a book proposal."

"You know, Nix isn't the only one who's feeling proud of himself. I'm pretty proud of me, too," Amber said. "This whole tiny house thing was my idea, remember."

"I do remember."

When Joy had come here, she'd expected to fake the part about her personal transformation. She hadn't expected it to actually happen. There was an authenticity to the blog that hadn't been present in any of her work before.

"Oh, and I almost forgot!" she said. "Have you seen the photos of my organic vegetables? They look just like the books say they're supposed to! I can't believe it!"

"You used to scoff at organic gardening. You used to make fun of it."

"Well, it's actually kind of fun."

A lot of things were fun that she hadn't expected to enjoy. The only problem was that her time in the tiny house was nearing its end, and she didn't know what she was going to do when that happened.

"You know, my lease is up in a couple of months," she told Amber.

"I know."

"That's … jeez. I don't know what comes next."

"Have you talked to Nix about it?"

"Not yet."

Obviously, he knew when her lease was up—he'd written it. But he hadn't approached her about extending it or about living with him when he moved back into the tiny house.

Well, she'd embraced the uncertainty when she'd come here. What was a little more?

BY EARLY SEPTEMBER, Nix was almost done renovating Otter Bluff. He'd updated both bathrooms, redone the flooring throughout the house, painted, had people in to cover up the popcorn ceilings, hired a crew to shore up the retaining wall along the bluff, and set up a new closet organization system for the master bedroom.

He could keep going forever, he supposed, as long as Evan kept fronting the money. But really, it was almost time to go home. Which meant it was almost time for Joy to leave the tiny house.

Except that more and more, he didn't want her to leave the tiny house. He wanted to live there with her.

He hoped to propose that to her, but what he didn't want was for it to seem like a practical matter. *Hey, the lease is almost up, so you might as well shack up with me.*

No.

If they were going to do this, he wanted it to be because they loved each other and thought they might make a life together. He wanted it to be a choice made freely and enthusiastically, and not as a solution to a housing problem.

But if he brought it up now, that's exactly what it would look like. It would look like he didn't want to show his girlfriend the door because of what it might do to his sex life.

And, hell, it was partly that, wasn't it? He didn't want his sex life to evaporate just when things were getting good.

The first thing, he figured, was to decide where he stood on the whole thing. Did he want to live with Joy? Or did he just think he wanted it because it was convenient?

Taking some time to think about all of that was a good idea, but he didn't have much time to spare. There was less than a month on the lease. He could let Joy stay in the house on a month-to-month basis, but then where would he go? Evan needed to start renting Otter Bluff so he could bring in the income he'd envisioned when he bought the house in the first place.

"Nix? You okay?" Louise was looking at him strangely, and he realized he'd been holding the same can of organic beans for God knew how long.

He looked at her as they stood in the canned goods aisle at the market and willed himself to focus on the present.

"Yeah. Yes. Of course. I'm fine."

"You gonna put that can on the shelf, or are you forming a close personal relationship with it?"

"Ah … the shelf." He placed the can with its brethren and sighed.

Normally, having your slow work noticed by your boss was a bad thing, but Louise wasn't just Nix's boss, she was his friend. Besides, the place was practically deserted, as it often was near closing time on a Wednesday night.

"Seriously. Are you okay?" Louise regarded him, her eyes narrowed, her hands on her hips, poised to spot any happy lie he might offer her.

"Yes. I'm fine. I'm just … thinking."

"About Joy." It wasn't a question.

"Well, yes. And about my life. And about the fact that I have to move out of Otter Bluff, and in theory she's supposed to go back to L.A. so I can have my house back, but …"

"Is that what you want? For her to leave so you can get your house back?"

"No!" He threw his arms up, a can of beans in each hand. "No. I want … Jesus, I think I want to marry her."

"You sound like you just decided that, right this moment in the bean section."

"I did. I did just decide it right now in the bean section. God. I think I'm gonna be sick."

"Aw, Nix." She put her hand on his shoulder in a sisterly fashion. "I think it's awesome that you want to marry Joy. But …"

"But what, Louise? Tell me. Talk me down."

"I don't want to talk you down, necessarily. I just want to point out that from everything you said, her life is in flux."

"It is."

"Well, a person shouldn't make any huge decisions while they're in flux. That's all."

Damn it, she was right. So, what was the winning move, then? Wait for her to finish whatever changes she was making in her life so he could propose once she was no longer ... *fluxing*?

What if all of the changes she was making included a change in relationships? A change in who she wanted to be involved with?

He tried to shake that off. "I'd better just ... you know. Shelve these beans."

CHAPTER 26

At the height of her career as an influencer, Joy had published a book—mostly glossy photos with a few paragraphs of text for each one. Lifestyle stuff. Clothes, makeup, accessories, wellness—that kind of thing.

She'd gone through a literary agent, and even though it had been a few years ago, she and the agent were still in touch.

That meant she had someone in the business who was willing to look at her book proposal. It also meant Joy had done one of these before and had some idea how to put it together.

Over the course of a week, she sat at the little dining table in the tiny house and wrote a synopsis, an outline, and a cover letter that included information about her marketing plan, her platform, the blog, and the blog's ever-increasing audience.

By the time it was done, she was confident that there really was a book here, and it would sell pretty well if only she could get a publication deal.

This book would have more text than her previous one, but it would have a lot of photos, too. The emphasis this time would be on transformation—on reinvention. She hardly felt like the same person she'd been when she moved to the tiny house more than five months ago.

She sent all of her materials to the agent, then told herself not to think about it anymore until she heard back.

These things took time—she knew that. And there were no guarantees. Plus, the ad revenue from her blog was rising enough that if she continued living a more low-key lifestyle—wherever she ended up once she left Nix's house—she could cover her bills with a little bit to spare.

That phrase—*once I leave Nix's house*—replayed in Joy's mind at the most inconvenient times. Like when she was trying to sleep. When she should have been enjoying a satisfying REM cycle, she was looking up at the stars through the skylight and wondering where she would go from here.

Where *they* would go from here.

She pondered the question one evening after midnight as she lay in bed and watched rain patter down onto the skylight.

She and Nix were getting serious—both of them could see that. But he still spent most of his nights at Otter Bluff and she spent most of hers here. Which meant, what? That they'd both decided to take things slow, she supposed.

Which was still a good idea. She didn't want to jump into something just to get hurt.

So why was she so lonely whenever she had to sleep without him? How had she gotten so accustomed, so quickly, to the feel of him beside her?

She picked up her phone and texted him, hoping she wouldn't wake him up.

What are you doing?

He answered a moment later.

In bed with a book. You?

Can't sleep.

It's probably because you miss me, he wrote.

She responded with an emoticon that she thought communicated lighthearted, teasing judgment.

Then: *I do miss you,* she admitted.

Want me to come over? he asked.

She did. Oh, God, she did. But she had to be smart. She was holding back for a reason. This thing was almost over, wasn't it? He'd move back into his house and she'd go … where? Back to L.A.? She didn't know. What she did know was that he would, very soon, have an opportunity to cut things off with her, and she had to be ready for the possibility that he might take it.

If she kept herself at a distance, if she kept things light between them, maybe she wouldn't be hurt as badly if it happened.

Not tonight, she wrote. *It's late.*

This whole thing with Nix had been a mistake, probably. She wasn't the same person she used to be. She wasn't that pretty, glossed-up girl who could make men want her. Now, she was just herself—and she wasn't even sure yet who that was.

How could she expect Nix to want someone who didn't even really exist yet? Who was still in the process of becoming?

I meant that thing I said, he wrote.

She knew the thing he meant—the *I love you* thing. She hadn't said it back yet, even though she was more and more certain it was true. How could she say it when she still wasn't sure who she was or what she wanted?

I know you did, she wrote. *It means a lot to me.*

It wasn't the answer he wanted, but it was the only one she could give him right now.

~

It means a lot to me, Nix read, and sighed.

It means a lot to me wasn't *I love you, too.* Did that mean she didn't, or was she just too scared to say so?

Why were women so hard to figure out? Why couldn't Joy just say what she wanted so Nix could begin in earnest the business of giving it to her?

Maybe what she wanted was a life without him in it.

If that were the case, though, surely she wouldn't have texted to say she missed him.

At the beginning of the texting, Joy had been the one who couldn't sleep. Now, as the night wore on, it turned out that Nix couldn't, either.

At least they agreed on that.

~

"So, I've been looking at ads for apartments," Amber said on the phone a couple of days later. "I know you said you wanted to spend less than you did for the condo, so you might have to change neighborhoods. Something a little farther out from downtown. If you're open to sharing with a roommate, that'll help. You can stay here until you find a place. The guest bed's pretty comfortable."

Joy was being assaulted with so much information at once that it took her a moment to gather herself to respond.

"You've been looking for apartments for me?"

"Just the ads. I've got a list of good ones you can look at when you're down here."

"Oh. Wow. Amber … you didn't have to do that."

"I know, but I wanted to do it. I can't wait for you to move back down here. It's been pretty dull without you. I've been counting down the weeks until you come back."

"Oh."

Amber had grown skilled at reading the context of Joy's voice, and she did that now with flawless accuracy. "Unless you and Nix are getting to be so serious you might not come back."

Joy was silent.

"Oh, holy shit. You are. Aren't you?"

"I don't know," Joy said miserably. "I don't know! He said he loved me, Amber. But he didn't say he wanted me to stay. What does that mean? I don't know what any of it means!"

"He said he loves you?"

"Yes. A while ago."

"And what did you say?"

"I said ... I said thank you."

"*Thank you?* Oh, jeez. Why didn't you just kick the guy in the face? That would have been kinder."

"Amber ..."

"Joy, I mean ... he hasn't asked you to stay because he thinks you don't love him. He thinks you're going to bail as soon as the lease is up."

"Why does he think that?!" Joy's voice was becoming a little hysterical.

"He thinks that because you said thank you!"

Amber was right, of course. If Joy loved Nix, she had to tell him before it was too late. She just wanted to be sure. And she wanted him to be sure, too.

THE FOLLOWING WEEK, two things happened that shook Joy's confidence.

One was that she couldn't get into her jeans. And the other was that people on the Internet were starting to attack her for her weight gain.

The attackers were in the minority, thankfully—most people who responded to her blog were positive and encouraging—but there were enough of them that she felt it like a gut-punch.

You used to be hot. What happened?

Keep going this way and you're going to be unfuckable.

Response to that last one: *I'd still fuck her.*

As though that was supposed to be encouraging.

Is that a muffin top under your shirt? (Vomiting emoji.)

Oh, God, Joy told herself. *Just ignore it. Ignore it.*

It wasn't as though Joy had never had haters before. In the past, people had scrutinized her body, accused her of Photoshopping her images to create impossible perfection, criticized her clothing, her settings, her captions, her blog posts. So, this was nothing new.

When her career had started—back when she'd been acting in commercials and bit parts, and even before then, with the pageants—she'd thought positive comments on her body were affirming, reassuring. Now, she wondered why she'd ever invited that scrutiny.

Why had she even thought that being *fuckable* was a good thing? When had she decided that was a worthy goal to pursue? Was it when she was sixteen? Fifteen? Younger?

She thought about all of that as she shopped for a new, bigger pair of jeans.

Her old jeans—the go-to pair that she turned to as a default—were a designer brand that went for three hundred dollars. (She'd gotten them free in exchange for a product endorsement.) Now, she thought about the waste and excess of three hundred dollar jeans. What was the point of it?

Instead of driving down to Santa Barbara to visit a designer boutique, she went to the Target in San Luis Obispo.

She found a thirty dollar pair (if she wanted, she could buy ten for the price of the ones she no longer fit into) and tried them on in the fitting room.

The lighting in the dressing room made her ass look twice its actual size.

At least, she hoped it was just the light.

But that was ridiculous. She'd just gone from a size four to a six. Surely that was nothing to worry about.

Except that the size six she was trying on was still too snug for comfort. Was it possible she'd gone up two sizes? She hadn't stepped on the scale for a while—avoiding it was part of her new effort toward emotional wellness—so maybe.

Shit.

She got dressed, went back out into the store, and found a size eight in the style she'd already tried on. Back in the dressing room, she slipped them on, and they were perfect.

Size eight.

So, yeah, she'd gone up two sizes since she'd come to Cambria. She guessed it was possible her old jeans had stretched, and the whole question of what size she was supposed to be had been distorted.

Size eight was good. It was fine. Women all over America would love to be a size eight. So why did Joy feel so … so broken? So devastated?

She wiped away a few tears, took a deep breath, and got dressed in her own clothes again—a T-shirt and a pair of stretchy leggings that were more forgiving than her jeans had been. Then she bought two pairs of the jeans, feeling like she was failing as a human being.

Were carbs really worth all of this self-doubt and angst?

For one thing, yes, they were. Carbs were heaven. Joy couldn't believe she'd lived without them for so long. And for another thing, being a size four hadn't made her happy. It hadn't done a thing to relieve her self-doubt. The self-doubt was its own entity, a wild beast waiting to attack her regardless of how she looked or what she weighed. It had always been there. Being thin hadn't tamed it, so what was the point?

And she felt better physically since she'd started to eat more. At first she'd thought it was just the sugar high, but it wasn't. She felt stronger, more awake. More energetic.

Her daily run was easier and felt better.

Surely that was some kind of sign.

Her body was in flux, and her life was in flux.

She didn't know where she was going from here, but she did know that she couldn't go back to the way she'd been.

There was only one direction: forward.

CHAPTER 27

Nix knew all of the reasons he shouldn't ask Joy to marry him. He'd gone over them in his head a thousand times. And he was right—he shouldn't ask her. Not now, at least. Not while it looked like a convenient means of solving a housing issue.

And yet, he couldn't seem to stop wanting to do it.

God help him, he was going to propose.

One day at the market, he asked Louise to help him pick out the ring.

"I need a woman's opinion. Or, wait. Should I let her pick it out? Should I propose without a ring and then go with her to choose one? Or, no. Whenever you see people propose online or in the movies or whatever, they already have a ring. So, that's probably what I should do."

Louise stood with her hands on her hips, staring at Nix. "You've lost your goddamned mind."

That was entirely possible. He didn't deny it.

"But will you help me?" he said.

"Will I help you make a colossal error in judgment? Is that what you're asking?"

"Why? Why is it a colossal error in judgment?"

Nix was removing some old peaches from a bin in the produce section and replacing them with fresh ones while Louise watched him.

"Because she still hasn't said she loves you, Nix. Which means she's not sure where this thing with you is going. Which means you have no idea what her answer will be. And you should never, never propose unless you know the other person is going to say yes."

Those were all rational points, but Nix wasn't using his rational brain here. He was using his heart, his instincts, his needy, yearning soul.

His shoulders fell. "So, you're saying you won't help me?"

Louise regarded him sternly for a moment, then threw her hands into the air. "Oh, hell. Sure, I'll help you. It's your funeral."

THEY WENT to a jewelry store on Main Street, and when Nix didn't find anything there, they drove down to San Luis Obispo.

In the third shop they visited, Nix zeroed in on a ring with an emerald-cut diamond in the center and smaller pear-shaped diamonds on either side. The effect was delicate, elegant, and, in his opinion, lovely.

"What do you think?" He held the ring in his hand, staring at it, while the clerk looked on with unconcealed glee.

"It's pretty," Louise said. "Very pretty."

"But do you think Joy will like it?"

"How could she not?" the clerk, a well-groomed woman in her fifties, said. "It's stunning."

"She'll like it," Louise said.

"If she doesn't, we can exchange it, right?" he asked the clerk.

"Of course. Though, I can't imagine that happening."

"If she says no, he can get a refund, can't he?" Louise asked.

"Why do you think she'll say no?" Nix turned to her, offended.

"I don't think that, necessarily. But she might, Nix."

"Yes. You'll be able to get a refund if that happens," the woman confirmed.

Nix stared at the ring, seeing not just a ring but his own future—a wedding, children, fighting and making up and celebrating anniversaries, birthdays, traveling together, growing old in each other's arms.

He hadn't even known he wanted such a thing, but now, with Joy, he wanted it more than he wanted to take his next breath.

"But ... she loves expensive designer things. Is she going to be upset that it's not from Tiffany? Because—"

"If she is, then you're better off without her," Louise said.

"That was the old Joy," he said, more to himself than to either of the women. "The old Joy was about the designer stuff, but the new one—she's more down to earth. She's ... Do I buy a ring for the old Joy or the new one? Oh, God. I think I'm going to pass out."

The clerk came around to Nix's side of the counter and brought over a chair. "Here you go, honey. Believe me, you're not the first."

Nix sank into the chair gratefully.

"Nix." Louise laid a hand on his shoulder. "You buy the ring for whichever version of her that you love. If it's the wrong one, then ... well, it's better to know that now, isn't it?"

He had to admit, she had a point.

~

He was feeling a little shaky, so Louise drove them home.

She'd given up trying to talk him out of proposing—especially now that he had the ring—so instead, she focused on the question of how he would do it.

"So, what's the plan? Quiet dinner at an intimate restaurant? Hot air balloon? Flash mob?"

"Probably no on the flash mob."

"Right. Simple is better," she said.

"That's what I was thinking. Simple. Maybe we'll go for a walk someplace pretty. San Simeon Point, maybe, or Moonstone Beach. We're holding hands, we're both feeling good, and then ..."

"Then you drop to one knee and bring out the velvet box," she finished for him.

"Something like that."

Nix felt nauseated, and he was certain his face was an alarming shade of green. And yet he knew—absolutely knew—that Joy was the woman he wanted to be with for the rest of his life.

How could something that felt so right also make him feel like he had a bad case of the flu?

"You doing okay over there, slugger?" Louise shot him a look from the driver's seat.

"Yeah. Yes. Absolutely."

"Are you two going to live in the tiny house? It's one thing when there's just one of you, but now …"

"I'll live anywhere if it's with her. I'll live in a penthouse apartment or a Motel 6 or a cardboard box." As he said it, he knew it was true. She would be his home, and he would be hers, wherever that was.

"Oh, shit. You've got it bad," Louise said.

THE DAY NIX and Louise shopped for a ring, one week after Joy sent her book proposal to her agent, she got an e-mail saying that Gina loved it.

Tiny houses are huge right now. Well, you know what I mean. So is simplifying, what with the whole Marie Kondo thing. This could be great! Call me.

Joy, giddy with happiness, wrote back to her, and they set up an appointment to talk on the phone.

Once that was arranged, the first person she wanted to tell about it was Nix.

I have good news, she texted him.

So do I, I think. We should get together and talk about it.

I'm in. Where? When?!

You want to go hiking tomorrow? Maybe San Simeon Point?

Okay. But can you come over now? Or tonight?

A long pause followed before he got back to her.

Sorry, I've got work, and then some other things.

Why didn't he want to see her tonight? She got the distinct feeling he was putting her off and that it had something to do with his good news. What if he'd gotten a job offer somewhere out of town? What if he'd met someone? *Shit. Shit.*

Joy told herself not to assume anything. She'd find out tomorrow.

~

NIX HOPED his efforts to hold Joy off hadn't seemed too weird or awkward. The fact was, he was sure that if he saw her today, he'd pop the question before he was ready. Premature proposal—every guy's worst fear.

If that did happen, it would be okay, he supposed. But he really had the whole San Simeon Point thing in mind—the way she would look standing out there on the bluff above the water, the wind in her hair. The way they would both feel out there in nature, the trees swishing in the breeze above them and the sounds of the surf in their ears.

He could wait.

That didn't mean he wasn't going to drive himself crazy while he did it.

I'm asking her tomorrow, he texted to Louise.

GOOD LUCK!!!!

I'm going to go insane thinking about it until then.

Want to go out and get drunk?

He considered that.

Why not?

~

JOY SPENT the rest of the day and that evening working on her book. She had so many ideas—she'd considered telling the story chronologically, but instead, she decided to group the blog posts into themes. Each chapter could address a particular thing she'd learned during her time in the tiny house, and she'd pair it with photos, mementos, inspirational quotes on the benefits of simplicity and nature.

She was still bubbling with enthusiasm for the project when she called Gina the next day.

"Do you really like it?" she asked instead of saying hello.

"Better than that, I know I can sell it. Get me the first chapters as soon as you can. Oh, and Joy?"

"Hmm?"

"I wonder ..."

"What?"

"It might be good if you could ... you know. Lose a few pounds."

Joy was struck silent in horror.

"I mean, I'm looking at the photos you sent, and you look great. You really do. But ... they might go over better if you looked the way you did back when you were hot on Instagram."

Joy felt like she'd been slapped. Yes, Joy had been thinner when Gina had sold her previous book. But what did that matter? Why was it important?

"Are you joking?"

"No. Look, Joy, I don't mean to hurt your feelings, or ... You look fantastic. But the book, the lifestyle you're promoting ... it's aspirational. The readers will want to be you. I mean, that's the whole point, isn't it? And the better you look, the better it's going to work."

Joy felt herself start to get angry, and on top of the anger was a growing hysteria. "But you're missing the whole point! It's not aspirational. It's ...it's about how I let go of all that! It's about how I learned to be me instead of some tiny, perfect Barbie doll!"

"Joy—"

"There's going to be a whole chapter on body image and how damaging it is when you're expected to be thin and diet all the time, when none of that makes you happy! Gina—"

"Joy, calm down." Gina said some happy things about how it had only been a suggestion, and how they could alter the photos to hide the extra weight, and how Joy should forget she'd said anything about it.

But long after they hung up, Joy felt a hard, hot weight on her chest that might have been disappointment and might have been shame.

Had she been kidding herself that anyone would want her if she continued to put on weight? And, more importantly, had she been lying to herself that Nix would?

CHAPTER 28

Joy began her date with Nix feeling anxious and upset. She tried to shove those feelings down and just enjoy being with him, but the feelings were stubborn and insisted on staying.

On top of that, he was acting strangely, which increased her certainty that his good news was something that would be good for him but would somehow end their relationship.

She coached herself to pretend to be happy for him when he announced his new job or his new relationship or whatever it might be. She urged herself to be positive and supportive and not to cry.

He picked her up in the early afternoon and they drove out to the parking lot at San Simeon Cove. The sky was bright and blue, a cloudless expanse of the universe stretching out above them. It was the middle of the week, so only a handful of cars were parked near the pier.

"Are you okay?" he asked as he pulled into a parking spot and turned off the ignition.

"Yes. I'm fine. What about you? You seem … quiet."

"I've just got a lot on my mind, that's all."

That made two of them.

They got out and walked to the beach, and from there, they made their way to a path that rose up from the sand to the bluffs above.

As they walked, Nix held her hand, but he still wasn't saying anything, which made Joy's sense of impending doom even more intense.

"So, what's your good news?" she asked when she couldn't keep the question in any longer.

"I'll tell you in a bit. What's yours?"

"Well … my agent said she loved my book proposal." She kept her eyes on the ground in front of her.

"She did? That's great! That's really great, Joy. I'm so happy for you." He sounded so sincere, so genuinely pleased for her, that she couldn't bring herself to tell him the rest—that Gina had wanted her to change her body to bring the project to fruition. She wasn't going to do it, and if that meant scrapping the project, then so be it.

"Yeah. Thanks. So … we'll see what happens."

"I read all of your blog posts, and I'm not surprised she liked it. I mean, it's a great story. Everybody's into tiny houses right now—they're a trend, right?—and simplifying. And you've already got a platform, so …"

"That's what she said."

He stopped walking and turned to face her. "So why do you sound like your dog just died, Joy?"

Her eyes filled with tears and she blinked them away. Then she laughed and shook her head. "It's just … some of the comments I'm getting about my photos …"

"What have they been saying?"

She shook her head. "It doesn't matter. People are just assholes, that's all."

~

NIX HADN'T LOOKED at the comments on Joy's blog posts or on Instagram—he'd only looked at the photos and blog posts themselves—but he resolved to do it once he got home. Whatever people were saying about Joy had really upset her, and he wanted to know what it was so he could tell her it was bullshit.

Which it almost surely was.

"You know people are just jerks for their own reasons, right?" he said. "It's not about you. It's about their own petty insecurities."

"I know."

"But what the agent said—that's good news, right?" Better to focus on what was going right rather than whatever was going wrong.

"Sure."

"So what's got you so upset?"

She didn't answer.

So far, this outing was going to shit before it had really started, and he wasn't sure why. The ring box was in his jacket pocket, and he felt it there as though its presence was a black hole sucking everything in the vicinity into it. He couldn't think of anything else. What would she think of it? Would she wear it? How would he give it to her? What would she say?

They walked a little farther, and she stopped, pulled her hand out of his, and turned to him.

"Look, Nix. Whatever your news is, it's probably better to just come out with it. If you're planning to break up with me—"

"What?" He took a step back from her as though he'd been pushed. "What are you talking about?"

"I'm talking about whatever it is you brought me here to tell me. What is it, Nix? A new job someplace far away? Or … are you seeing someone else? Just say it. Please."

"That's what you think?" He stared at her, dazed.

"I don't know what to think!"

"But … I told you I had *good* news. None of those things would be good news."

"They would be to you."

Oh, shit. He'd bungled this whole thing. He'd brought her here to propose, and all this time she'd been bracing herself to get dumped.

"No. That's not … no." He squeezed his eyes shut and shook his head.

"Then what? And don't tell me we'll talk about it later. I don't want to talk about it later."

He had two choices: he could propose right now, here on the trail, or he could put her off until another time, when his plans weren't turning to ash in a massive dumpster fire. Plan A or Plan B. Go for the gold or call a time out.

He opted for Plan A.

"Well, this isn't how I planned to do this, but …" Shaking, he pulled the ring box out of his jacket pocket and lowered himself to one knee in the dirt. "I …God, I had a whole speech planned, but I'm so nervous I forgot it."

She stared at him, wide-eyed.

"I love you, Joy. And even though you haven't said it yet, I think you love me. I want to spend the rest of my life with you. You just … you make me happy." He opened the lid of the ring box and held it out to her. "Will you marry me?"

JOY'S BRAIN simply shut down for a moment. She was so shocked by what Nix had said that she couldn't form a response, couldn't think, and could barely remember who she was or what she was doing here. She stood with both hands clapped over her mouth, trying to remember to breathe.

"Joy?" he prompted her. "If you don't like the ring, we can exchange it, pick out something you like better."

Still, nothing.

"Um … could you say something, please? Joy?"

"You … you want to marry me?"

"Yes. That's the general idea." He tried to offer her a winning smile, but it trembled a little on his face.

Once her brain started to work again, its initial response was panic. He wanted to *marry* her? Why? Because the lease was almost up and he wanted his house back? Because it was easier than evicting her? Because he thought he was in love with some Instagram image, some woman who no longer existed? Who possibly never had?

"I ... ah ... I think you should get up."

~

IT WASN'T until she told him to get up off the ground that he realized this thing might not go the way he wanted it to.

Yes, the date had started out with some awkwardness, but he'd been certain the proposal would change all that. He'd been certain she would say yes.

Instead, she'd said, *I think you should get up.*

Still shaking, he did.

He looked down at the ring in the box. In every mental run-through he'd done of this moment, she'd taken it by now. Why hadn't she taken it?

"So, you're saying no, then?"

~

HE LOOKED SO sad standing there with his ring box in his hand.

Joy didn't know what to say to him. She only knew that the conflicting messages bombarding her were making her feel more panic than elation.

She loved him, but she was afraid of how badly he could hurt her if he chose to. She trusted that he was telling her the truth about his feelings, but she didn't trust that his feelings wouldn't change. She wanted him, but she didn't know if he would keep wanting her in the long run, when neither of them really knew for sure who she was becoming.

"I'm saying ... that I don't know what to say."

He snapped the box closed and shoved it back into his pocket. "Well, that's just great."

"If this is about the lease ..." she began.

"Joy? I don't give a fuck about the fucking lease."

His anger broke the dam that had been holding back her shame. Her cheeks burned and she couldn't meet his gaze. "Nix—"

"Do you really think I proposed to you because … because your *lease* is almost up? That's the most ridiculous, insulting—"

"I think … I think we're in a period of change, where something has to happen, and maybe you didn't know what's next for us, so you … you did this."

He laughed bitterly and threw his head back to stare at the trees above them. "You don't have a very high opinion of me, then."

"I—"

"Louise warned me. She pointed out that you've never said you love me. And if you've never said it, then maybe you don't."

The tears that had been filling her eyes began to fall. "Please, that's not—"

"I think we should go back." He turned and headed back up the trail without waiting for her.

CHAPTER 29

"You warned me. Oh, shit. You warned me and I didn't listen." Nix let his head fall against the back of Louise's sofa and groaned. "Why didn't I listen? What the hell is wrong with me?"

"You're in love." Louise sat beside him and patted his hand in a soothing, sisterly fashion.

"Also, you're a man, which means you're starting out behind the curve when it comes to making sensible decisions with women," said Clara, Louise's wife, who was in the kitchen making Nix a soothing cup of herbal tea.

"It's all ruined now, isn't it? Things were going fine, and I fucked it up."

"Not necessarily," Louise said.

He lifted his head to look at her. "Which part?"

She considered that. "Either one. It's not necessarily fucked up, and if it is, then it wasn't necessarily fine in the first place."

Which was it? Were things hopeless and he just hadn't been able to see it? Or could he salvage things between himself and Joy?

"Well … what do I do now? Now that I've asked her and she said no … Do I just walk away?"

Clara set the mug of tea on the side table next to Nix. "Do you want to walk away?"

Nix squeezed his eyes shut and pressed the heels of his hands to his eyelids. "No. No. I just … I just want Joy."

"Then you two have to have a talk," Louise said. "A real talk about whether she's just not ready yet, or …"

"Or if she'll never be ready. Not with me."

"Well … yeah."

He'd said he didn't want to walk away, but the idea was tempting. Not because he didn't love Joy—of course he did. And not because he was angry with her for saying no. He was tempted to change his name and move to another country because of the humiliation. He'd been on his knee, for Christ's sake. He'd been kneeling in the dirt with the damned ring in his hand, and she'd looked at him with horror instead of love.

Well, she'd never said she loved him, had she? He was sure she did, though—he was certain of it. But maybe he'd just been deluding himself.

"So, how did you leave it?" Clara asked, bringing him out of his reverie.

He groaned again and ran both hands through his hair. "We stalked back to the car without saying anything, and I drove her home and got the hell out of there. I might have actually burned rubber."

Louise winced. "Well, that wasn't very mature."

"Mature? Really? Screw mature. She hurt me."

"And you wanted to hurt her back, so you acted like an ass," Louise said. "Would you have preferred that she just said yes even though she wasn't sure? If she's going to dump you, better it should happen now instead of later, after the deposits have been paid. Or, God forbid, even later than that, when you have to figure out who gets custody of the kids."

She was right. He knew she was right. But that didn't make it hurt any less.

"Shit. I mean, you're right, but … shit."

"So, what are you going to do?" Clara asked softly.

"I don't know. I just . . . I don't know."

~

In the wake of the failed proposal, Joy didn't know what to do any more than Nix did.

At least, she had a friend on the way to help.

Joy had called Amber and said it was an emergency. Joy had wanted to go down to L.A. to talk it out with her friend, but Amber's apartment was being treated for mold, so Amber decided to come north instead.

Secretly, Joy thought Amber had made that part up to keep Joy in Cambria, where she and Nix might manage to see each other and patch things up.

She also suspected that Amber thought Joy would run away from her problems at the first opportunity. Which, to be fair, she might have.

Amber got to Cambria that evening after a four-hour drive. She'd brought a bottle of wine and a pizza, and the two of them sat on the sofa in the tiny house eating and drinking while Joy poured out the details of what had happened.

"I just . . . froze. I froze like some girl in a horror movie who sees the killer standing there with a chainsaw and just lets him come and get her instead of running away."

"I've gotta tell you. It doesn't bode well for you and Nix that you're comparing him to a chainsaw murderer." Amber quirked one eyebrow upward and took a drink of her wine.

"I didn't mean it that way." Joy frowned. "Or maybe I did. Because he's killing me, Amber. He really is killing me with his . . . his eyes and his hair and his . . ." She gestured vaguely with one hand. "His niceness! How am I supposed to resist all of that? How am I supposed to say no?"

"Here's an idea." Amber pointed one finger at her friend. "Maybe don't say no if you don't want to."

Amber knew everything about Joy. She knew Joy better than

anyone else in the world. And yet Joy still couldn't tell her about the conflicting feelings that had caused her to flee from Nix. She couldn't tell her, because none of it made sense when spoken out loud. How could she explain that she was afraid of being too happy, because that would make the fall, when it came, so much more disastrous? How could she explain that if her mother, her agent, and the public at large couldn't accept the new, less perfect Joy, surely Nix couldn't be expected to accept her, either.

How could she explain that, having rejected the idea of her value lying in her beauty, she now had no idea where her value actually did lie? And if she didn't know, how could anyone else?

"I'm in flux," she said, because that, at least, was both clear and true. "When I did all of this—when I came to Cambria—I expected to pretend to change. But instead, I'm actually changing. My priorities are changing, and I … I don't know where I'm going to land when all of this changing is done. How can I make a major life decision when I don't even know what I want?"

Amber looked at her for a while, then nodded slowly, her wine-glass in her hand. "That part, I agree with. It makes sense. So, you need to tell him that. Just the way you told me."

"I'll sound crazy. I'll sound like some kind of …"

"You don't sound crazy to me. You sound like you need some time. If he can't or won't give you that, then that tells you something important about him, doesn't it?"

Joy supposed it did. But knowing that important thing wouldn't make it any less painful if it turned out to be true.

NIX WAS HURT, and that might have accounted for why he was acting like a dick.

He called Joy a couple of days after the failed proposal to talk about the lease. Which was the most dickish, least Nixish thing he could have done.

"I've finished the renovations on Otter Bluff, so I wondered if you can vacate the tiny house by the first."

He was standing at the kitchen island at Otter Bluff holding onto his phone so tightly that his knuckles were white.

"I … you want to know when I can vacate." Joy sounded vaguely stunned.

"Well, yes. I have to let Evan know when he can start renting Otter Bluff. Which really should be as soon as possible, because he's losing income on it every day he has to wait. So …"

"Right. Of course." Her tone had gone from hurt to cold. "You don't have to wait until the first. I can be out in a couple of days."

Nix squeezed his eyes closed. "Joy, you don't have to—"

"No, no, of course. I don't want Evan to lose income."

"Look. I didn't mean—"

"And you don't have to worry," she went on. "I'll leave it in pristine condition."

"I'm sure you will. That's not—"

She hung up on him while he was still talking.

~

JOY HAD INTENDED to have the talk with Nix that Amber had suggested. She really had. But it seemed now that the whole thing was moot.

When Nix had asked her to vacate the tiny house, he'd made his position clear.

Packing her things didn't take long. The bulk of her time in the moving-out process involved cleaning the place from top to bottom as a matter of pride. She didn't want him thinking she didn't respect his house, and she didn't want him to see any trace of her here once she was gone.

If he wanted her out, then she'd erase her presence so thoroughly it'd be as though she'd never been here.

With rubber gloves on her hands, she scrubbed the shower stall, the toilet, and the bathroom floor. She scoured the kitchen sink and polished the wood floors throughout the house. She vacuumed the upholstered furniture, cleaned the windows, and put fresh sheets on the bed. She even cleaned inside the oven, though she'd only used it sparingly.

Then she put her things in her car and took one last look around before heading out of town.

She was standing on the porch looking at Nix's gorgeous plot of land when her cell phone rang.

The screen said it was Gina.

Joy was tempted not to answer the call in case it was another critique of her body weight.

But avoiding whatever Gina had to say didn't seem like a good option, so she picked up the call.

"Hi, Gina. How are you today?" She tried to keep her voice bright.

"I'm very well, Joy. And you're going to be, too, when you hear what I've been up to."

It turned out, Gina had an offer for Joy's book from a prominent publisher, with an advance that was modest by the standards of the publishing world but that was still more than Joy had anticipated.

"Oh. Gina, that's ... that's really great. But I'm not going to lose weight, so if that's a deal-breaker—"

"Joy, that was just a suggestion. And I still think it's a good idea. But nothing like that even came up with the acquiring editor, so that's fine. It's your call."

All of this was good news—the best news—and yet Joy still felt the sting of judgment at Gina's words.

They talked a little while about the details of the contract, and by the time they hung up, Joy knew she should feel good about herself. She'd set out to turn this tiny-house adventure into a book deal, and she'd done it.

She'd achieved her goal. So why did she feel so *lost*?

With the tiny house cleaned out and Joy ready to go, she wondered what to do with Nix's key. If they'd been on good terms, she'd have taken it to him—or she wouldn't have to because they'd be living together—but they weren't. Instead, she drove to Otter Bluff and put the key in the mailbox before getting onto Highway 1 and heading south toward Los Angeles.

CHAPTER 30

Nix had thought he'd have time to figure out what to do about Joy. He'd thought he could arrange his thoughts and then talk to her, smooth things over before she did anything crazy like leaving town.

When he saw his key in the mailbox at Otter Bluff, he knew he'd miscalculated.

He called her, and she didn't pick up.

He texted her, and she didn't respond.

Finally, he drove out to his place, thinking maybe she'd left a note there. All he found was his tiny house, spotless and gleaming, with no trace of Joy left.

He stood in the doorway looking around, frozen, unable to move or to figure out what to do next.

Should he chase her down? Hard when he didn't even know where she'd gone. Should he just walk away? She'd turned down his proposal and she still hadn't said she loved him. Maybe it was time to accept that she didn't, and move on.

But he didn't want to move on. He didn't want to accept the defeat and rally. He didn't want any of that.

He was angry that she'd left without talking to him, but he

could see that she might be angry, too. He'd been an ass out there on the trail when she'd declined his proposal. He'd been an ass again on the phone when he'd asked when she could vacate the house.

When could she *vacate*? Thinking about it, he could hardly believe the size or scope of his idiocy. He'd been hurt, and so he'd been cold and heartless toward her.

And so, yeah, if she was mad, maybe there was a reason.

He went into the house, climbed into the loft, and stretched out on the perfectly made bed, staring up through the skylight to the bright blue beyond.

He'd let her go.

Not just that, he'd pushed her away.

All because his male ego was unable to fathom that she might not be ready for marriage.

He pulled his phone out of his pocket and called Louise.

"She's gone," he said. "She's just ..." His voice broke. "She's just fucking gone."

"Oh shit," she said. "Where are you?"

~

THE GOOD THING ABOUT REAL, true friends was that they would drop whatever they were doing and come running when your girlfriend packed up and absconded for parts unknown.

Louise was at the tiny house less than fifteen minutes later with a six-pack of beer.

"I don't ... I just ..." Nix had both hands fisted in his hair, and he seemed to have lost the power of coherent speech. "I don't know what I was thinking."

They were sitting in a couple of Adirondack chairs on the porch, the big sycamore swishing its branches overhead.

"Yeah. Not gonna say the whole 'when can you vacate' thing was your finest moment."

"Okay. It wasn't. I can admit that. But was that bad enough that it's worth throwing away a whole relationship? I mean ... it's not like I cheated on her or something."

"No, you just asked her how soon she could get her ass out of your house." She pointed her beer bottle at him for emphasis.

"But ... I didn't mean she should leave town! I didn't even ... God. I didn't even want her to leave the house. I just was upset and angry and hurt, and I acted like a fool."

"No argument."

"But I can't tell her any of that if she won't take my calls, can I? Or if I don't even know where she is."

Louise took a swig of her beer and gave Nix a side-eyed glance. "You know where she is."

"No, I don't! She didn't tell me! She didn't leave a note, or an address, or—"

"You know her best friend. Don't tell me you can't find her if you want to."

"Oh."

Nix hadn't thought about that, but Louise was right. Once when Amber was visiting, Joy had texted him from Amber's phone because her own had been out of battery power.

He had Amber's number. And even if Amber wasn't with Joy, she surely knew where she was and what she was planning.

~

JOY WENT to Amber's place, because she didn't know where else to go and because Amber had offered. The fact that it was more than two hundred miles away from Nix was a bonus.

"It's so good to have you back home." Amber gave Joy a good, hearty hug. "I missed you, you know."

"I know. I missed you, too." Joy stood just inside Amber's front door with two suitcases at her feet, tired from the drive and heartsick over Nix.

"Let's get your stuff into the guest bedroom, then we can get some dinner," Amber said. "And if you want to talk—"

"I don't. Not really. Maybe later."

"Okay." Amber gave Joy one more squeeze. "What do you want to eat? I can order a pizza."

~

NIX THOUGHT ABOUT TEXTING AMBER, but he decided to call her instead. This type of thing seemed urgent enough to merit a real-time conversation.

He wasn't sure whether she'd pick up—the whole sisterhood thing might prohibit it—then was pleased when she did.

It was the morning after Joy's departure, and Nix had barely slept. He was back in the tiny house, and he'd thought that might help. But he could still feel Joy's presence there. He could, even more acutely, feel her absence.

"Nix," she said.

"Hi, Amber. Is Joy with you?" He endured a long silence, presumably while she considered the pros and cons of answering him.

"Look," he said. "I just want to know if she's okay. That's all."

"Yes, she's with me. And she's fine."

"Good. That's ... good." That wasn't all he wanted to know, though, was it? He wanted to know if she was coming back. If she missed him. If she was angry or hurt. If she loved him.

"I don't suppose you'll let me talk to her," he tried.

"No. She doesn't want to."

"I get that. I do. But I want to make things right, and I can't do that if I can't talk to her."

"That's a dilemma for you, all right."

He wanted to reach through the phone and find Joy, pull her away from wherever she was hiding, and bring her to him, kiss her, apologize for every misstep, and make all of this stop. But right now, Amber had all the power.

"Did she tell you what happened?"

"Some of it. She said you proposed and when she didn't jump into your arms, you acted like an asshole."

He wanted to protest that her characterization was unfair, but it wasn't.

"That's … not entirely wrong."

"Well, I admire that you're big enough to admit it," she said.

That gave him some hope. "Do you admire it enough that you'll let me talk to her?"

"Not that much, no."

So what could he do, then? Walk away? Forget he'd ever known her?

Impossible.

"Look. I just … I know you don't owe me anything, but … am I wasting my time? If she doesn't love me, then I can deal with that. It's going to suck, but I'll survive. But if she does, I don't want to let this thing slip through my fingers. I need to try."

"Nix …"

"Just let me know if I'm wasting my time. That's all I'm asking."

Amber was silent for a while, then she let out a puff of air. "You're not entirely wasting your time, no."

A surge of hope blossomed in his chest.

"That's … great. That's really great."

"But you can't force her to talk to you before she's ready."

"Okay. I get that."

"She's got issues, Nix. Some of them have to do with you, and some of them don't. But she needs to deal with them in her own time."

"That's fair." Still, he had to try. "Will you at least tell her that I called? I don't want her to think I didn't care enough to call."

She sighed. "I'll tell her."

~

Joy had a lot of things to deal with now that she was back in Los Angeles.

She had to find a place to live—somewhere much less expensive than her condo had been. She needed to get her stuff from the storage unit in Cambria. And she had to actually write the book she'd signed a contract to write.

But first, before any of that, she had to do a certain amount of wallowing.

Every day while Amber went to work, Joy lay on the sofa in her pajamas, watching daytime TV and trying not to think.

She didn't tell her mother that she was back in town, because talking to Delores certainly wouldn't help anything.

Occasionally, she scanned online ads for apartments and even for jobs, since her career as an influencer wasn't going to last forever—or even for much longer.

But mostly, she spent the wallowing time yearning for Nix.

She'd wanted to say yes when he proposed. God, she'd wanted that. But the fear was stronger than the wanting, and his reaction hadn't helped things. Then, he'd basically told her to get out of his house.

He'd called her and texted her, and he'd called Amber, so he clearly felt some remorse for the way he'd acted. And that was fine. He was hurt—she got that. But what was the point in seeing him when she didn't even know what she wanted? When she still didn't even know who she was?

She needed space and time, that was all. But needing those things didn't stop her from thinking about him. And she thought about him constantly. The sound of his voice, the feel of his skin. The way his hair felt when it was wrapped around her fingers.

She cried sometimes, but she tried not to do it when Amber was home. Amber would try to fix things, and if anything needed to be fixed, Joy had to be the one to do it.

She just didn't quite know how.

CHAPTER 31

Nix knew he should return the ring, given everything that had happened. If Joy didn't want it, he had no use for it. Having the money in his bank account made more sense than having the ring in his sock drawer.

But somehow, the irrationally optimistic part of him couldn't seem to do it.

Just because she didn't want it now didn't mean she never would. Just because things were crap between them now didn't mean he wouldn't be able to win her back.

He'd taken to carrying the thing around, even though he knew that was stupid. He had it in his jeans pocket as he showed Evan what he'd done to Otter Bluff.

"This is ceramic tile, and I've got a spare box of tiles in the garage in case you need to replace one due to breakage." He pointed at the floor in the master bathroom as Evan looked on. "I considered porcelain, but it's more expensive, and I wanted to stay under budget."

"Looks good. I like the color."

Nix nodded. "It's a nice neutral, so it'll work if you want to change the wall color someday."

They went through the house room by room as Nix pointed out what he'd done, why he'd made the choices he had, and what Evan might need to know about each new feature.

Evan, who was two inches taller than Nix and forty pounds heavier, giving him the appearance of a man-shaped wall, looked around with his eyebrows raised. "It looks good, Nix. Damned good."

"You sound surprised."

"I'm not. I'm just ... Well, maybe I'm a little surprised."

"Asshole," Nix said mildly.

The last thing Nix had done was replace some of the more well-worn furniture, so the place was ready for occupancy by vacationers or short-term residents. The property management company would be sending someone over later in the day to photograph the place for its website.

Nix had logged his hours working on the place, and Evan had paid him the rate they'd agreed on. Between that and the rent he'd gotten from Joy for the tiny house, Nix's finances were more flush than they'd been in a long time.

"Thank you for doing this." Evan extended his hand, and Nix shook it. "This worked out better than I could have hoped."

"It was kind of fun," Nix admitted.

"Then why do you look miserable?" Evan regarded him with a hint of a smile, his hands shoved into his jeans pockets.

"Just tired, I guess."

"Tired, my ass. There's something going on."

Nix thought to deny it, but what for? It might even help to talk about it to someone who wasn't Louise. Get a guy's perspective.

"Well ... that woman I told you about? Joy? I kind of broke up with her. Or she broke up with me. It's hard to tell. Whoever did it, it really sucks." He raked a hand through his hair. "To be honest, I'm kind of messed up about it."

Evan smacked Nix on the shoulder with his hand. "Let's go get a beer."

"It's nine a.m."

"Oh, shit. Is it? Then let's get breakfast. I'm starving."

~

"So what happened?"

Evan and Nix had gotten settled in at a table at the Redwood Café, ceramic mugs of coffee in front of them.

Nix sighed, took a sip of his coffee, then took the ring out of his pocket and put it on the table between them in its small velvet box.

Evan put his hands up, palms out. "Hey, man. You know I like you and everything. But I always thought our relationship was more platonic."

Nix balled up his napkin and threw it at Evan, striking him on the left shoulder.

"Don't be an asshole. I'm trying to tell you what happened."

"Sorry. Sorry." Evan stopped smiling at his own joke and leaned forward to listen, his forearms on the table. "But, I mean … you proposed? I had no idea."

"Yeah, I did. And she said no. And now … is there some kind of rule about what happens if you propose to someone and they turn you down? Are you supposed to break up, or can you just … I don't know. Dial it back and try again later?"

"I'm not sure there's an actual rule book, dude."

Of course there wasn't, but it would be so much easier if there were. He could look at Chapter Six: Failed Proposals for step-by-step instructions on what to do now. Failing that, he had to make it up as he went along.

He gave Evan the summary: how he'd proposed, what she'd said, and how he'd reacted. And, finally, how she'd gone back to Los Angeles, maybe forever.

Evan's expression indicated he was either impressed or horrified by the sheer magnitude of Nix's mishandling of the situation.

"I assume you've called her."

"She doesn't pick up."

"Then you called her friend."

"Yes."

Evan filled his cheeks with air, then blew it out slowly. "The question is, did her *no* mean she's not ready right now, or that she wouldn't be ready if you and she were one of the last surviving male-female pairs on a post-apocalyptic planet and it was dependent on you to repopulate the species."

"Colorfully put, but basically ... yes."

"Did you ask her?"

"Like I said, she doesn't pick up when I call her. But her friend said I'm not necessarily wasting my time, for what that's worth."

The waitress brought plates of eggs, bacon, and pancakes and set them on the table. Then she set down a pitcher of maple syrup and a little plate of butter pats.

When she was gone, Nix poured syrup on his pancakes and sighed. "I just don't know what to do, man."

"You kept the ring," Evan pointed out.

"Yeah."

"You know what you're going to do, then. You just have to summon up the balls to do it."

"I guess."

They ate for a while, thinking about that.

Finally, Nix asked, "So, how much space do I give her before I go down there and apologize for being an ass and ask her to take me back?"

"I don't know, man. But if she's not taking your calls, I'd say she needs more."

He was right. If Nix went down there demanding to see her when she wasn't ready for that, then it was only going to make things worse. He was perfectly willing to grovel and beg, but he didn't want to do it until he was reasonably confident it might work.

"Women are a mystery," Evan declared, a piece of bacon held between his fingers.

"How would you know?" Nix said. "It's been, what, six months since you've had a date?"

"That's why I haven't had a date in six months." Evan pointed the bacon slice at Nix. "Because the ways of women are dark and unfathomable."

It occurred to Nix that he might have asked the wrong guy for advice.

CHAPTER 32

Joy was out of Amber's place within two weeks.

She found a studio apartment over someone's garage in Ventura, at a rent that was roughly the same as what she'd paid Nix. It was a fraction of the size of her condo, so she'd only have to get a few key items of furniture from storage: her bed, the kitchen table and chairs, a sofa, some side tables and lamps.

She'd looked halfheartedly for a place in Los Angeles, but the more she looked at photos of apartments and maps of neighborhoods, the more she knew she didn't want to live there anymore. She'd fallen in love with the Central Coast, and Ventura was closer to that feeling—that vibe—than L.A. was, while also being reasonably close to Amber. It was also closer to Nix than L.A. was, though she told herself that wasn't a factor.

The apartment was nice enough—the main house was an old Victorian on Main Street, and the garage and apartment had been added later—with high ceilings and big windows that let in lots of light. The kitchenette was tiny, but it had been recently renovated, with granite countertops and new compact appliances.

Still, she couldn't help comparing it to Nix's tiny house. Nix had built the house with love, something she hadn't appreciated when she'd moved in but which she did now. Her new place had been constructed by some anonymous crew, no doubt, while the tiny house had been put together piece by piece like an inhabitable work of art.

Also, she had to admit that missing his place was about more than just the craftsmanship. The tiny house was so infused with Nix's personality—was so *him*—that she could feel him in every corner, every space, even when he wasn't there.

The apartment was just a place to live. Nix's house had been an extension of his personality.

But there was no point in looking back, Joy reminded herself. The new place would be fine for now. It wasn't long-term; it was just until she figured out what she wanted to do with the rest of her life.

One thing it did have that reminded her of Nix's place was the coziness of a small space. Before the past year, she'd always thought bigger was better. Now she knew that bigger was just ... bigger.

More space had always made her feel that she had to fill it with more stuff, and before she'd known it, she'd been serving her belongings more than they were serving her.

Getting out of that cycle had been a change she wanted to maintain in her life regardless of what she might do next.

Joy hired movers to bring her things down from Cambria and put some of them in the apartment and the rest in a storage unit close to her new place.

She decorated the apartment with a few favorite things, choosing the look of her surroundings based on what she liked, not what would look good on Instagram.

That was a start.

She'd set up a small desk and chair in a corner of the tiny apartment, and she gave herself a daily writing schedule. Every day, she worked on her book and on her blog, and the regularity of that—the routine of it—helped to structure her day and make her feel less unmoored.

She visited Amber, and sometimes Amber visited her. She walked on the beach or on Main Street, took drives into the hills of Ventura County, took daily runs on the streets surrounding her new home, and tried not to shop.

Sometimes, she took her laptop to a funky coffeehouse in the city's historic downtown to work there. She sipped and typed and took in the people-watching and the gritty but interesting downtown vibe.

She was doing okay, she really was. Even if she missed Nix so much it felt like sharp claws ripping at her heart.

Joy knew she could call him. He'd tried to call her, after all, so that meant he wanted to see her. She could so easily pick up where they'd left off, falling into his arms and forgetting their breakup had ever happened.

But that would leave her right back where she'd started—unsure about what she wanted from her future and from him.

And it wouldn't change how impatient he'd been—how angry and harsh—when she'd needed more time to decide. If he couldn't wait for her to be sure, then there was no future for them, anyway.

Much of the time, she was just existing: eating, sleeping, writing, going through the motions of living but not feeling any of it. Even so, she knew it was in service of something greater, something more.

Joy couldn't have continued the way she'd been going, so taking her life in a different direction had been necessary, essential.

Change was never easy. Hers certainly hadn't been, and it wasn't now.

This part of it—this phase of her becoming—was unavoidable and hard. She was no longer who she had been, but she wasn't yet who she was going to be.

She was still waiting. And right now, she wanted nothing more than for Nix to wait with her.

If he couldn't—or wouldn't—then she'd just have to do this essential, difficult work herself.

~

When Nix had been back in his tiny house for a month, things had gone back to normal—mostly.

He worked at the market, tended his organic garden, saw friends, and, more exciting, worked on plans for a tiny house for someone who had seen his on Joy's blog and had contacted him wanting one of their own.

He'd always dreamed of having his own business designing tiny houses, and now it seemed like he had a start on it—thanks to Joy.

But it was hard to think of Joy without reliving the searing pain of her absence.

He still had the ring, and he still hadn't given up on her.

He knew she needed space, so he was waiting.

The problem was, there wouldn't be some sort of divine signal when she was ready to see him again, so how would he know? It wasn't like there'd be skywriting. It wasn't like it would come to him in a dream.

A couple of weeks after she left, he'd texted her.

I don't want this to be over between us. I know you need time, so take it. When you're ready to talk, I'll be waiting.

He was still waiting.

"Heard from Joy yet?" Louise asked him every now and then at the market, when they were both in the break room or when they passed each other in the cereal aisle.

"Not yet." He tried to keep his tone upbeat. Tried not to sound like a man on the edge of despair.

"You think it's time to go down there and find her?" Louise asked, her eyes wide, eyebrows raised.

She was assuming that at some point, he would do just that.

Every time he had a day off, every time he had some time on his hands, he fought with himself.

Go down there? Amber's home address was listed online, and Nix assumed Joy was still staying with her.

If not, Amber would know where she was, and he was pretty sure he could persuade her to tell him.

Stay here and keep waiting?

Wasn't it true that people who failed to take decisive action often ended up regretting their passivity for the rest of their lives?

Whatever was best for Joy, he was willing to do it. But how could he know what that was if she wouldn't talk to him? If she wouldn't tell him?

~

When Joy had been gone for two months, Nix started dating again.

He didn't want to, not particularly. But he was proving to himself that he could move on. Proving that his life wasn't over just because Joy had left.

One warm Saturday evening, he went to dinner with a woman he'd met at the market. He picked her up at her house on Lodge Hill and took her to a restaurant with an ocean view.

They sat and talked and sipped wine and ate, and the whole time, Nix kept comparing her to Joy.

Through the entire date, he felt an unpleasant tug in his chest, a gnawing ache, because he was here with the wrong woman, and she would never be the right one, no matter how lovely and kind she might be, no matter how funny and smart.

There was only one right one, and she wasn't here.

It felt like a death, really. He'd been in mourning before, and it was a lot like this. Just breathing in and out and going through the motions in the hope that one day you might feel better.

Even though you were certain that such a thing was not possible and never would be again.

~

Joy finished her manuscript after two months of sustained work at her desk in her new home.

She sent it to Paula Green, her editor, along with the photos she planned to use—some were images she'd used on Instagram, and some were photos she'd held back for the book.

Paula got back to her a few days later and told her they'd need Nix to sign a release so they could use the photos that included him or his property. He himself was only in a couple of the images, but his house was in many, many more.

Somehow, Joy hadn't anticipated that, and she froze, speechless.

"But … is that really necessary? I mean, it's just a precaution, right?"

"Well, no. It's required. We can't publish the photos of him or his property without his signature."

"Oh."

"Is there a problem?" Paula sounded distracted, and Joy could hear the sound of typing on the other end of the line.

"No. No problem. It's just … we didn't exactly leave things on good terms, so …"

"Nasty breakup?"

Joy hadn't told Paula that she'd been seeing Nix in the first place, so she hedged.

"That's not … I didn't …"

"I can send him a letter with the forms if you'd like. Nice and informal, so you won't have to talk to him."

But that would be like a slap in the face, and she knew it. Joy didn't want to be a coward.

"No. No, it's fine. E-mail me the forms and I'll … I'll talk to him. I'll ask him to sign them."

Joy heard the tap-tap-tap of Paula's keyboard. "Done. They should be in your inbox now."

"Okay."

"I don't want to alarm you, Joy, but if he doesn't sign, we've got a problem."

"No, I get it. I'll take care of it."

For a good half hour after she got off the phone, Joy went back and forth with herself on whether she should take him the forms in person or deal with it all through e-mail.

She reminded herself that she didn't want to be a coward.

On the other hand, there was something to be said for caution.

She composed an e-mail—a careful, professional one—and sent him the forms.

Surely he wouldn't stand in the way of her getting her book published.

Nix would never do that.

CHAPTER 33

When Nix saw a message from Joy in his e-mail inbox, his heart nearly stopped. Or, it probably didn't, but it felt that way.

He hadn't opened it yet. He was afraid to. What if she was saying she wanted to end things with him for good? What if this was her definitive statement that she didn't want him?

It could be good news, though. Maybe she was ready to talk to him. Maybe she was even ready to see him.

He got up from his little kitchen table where he'd been looking at his laptop and paced the length of his tiny house, his hands on top of his head, fingers entangled in his hair.

Calm down. You're just going to read it, and you're not going to lose your shit.

He was so prepared for it to be either a breakup letter or a reconciliation letter that he was taken off guard when it turned out to be a business letter.

Photos of him and his house—legal release forms.

He felt so let down that at first, he didn't see it for the opportunity it was.

Sign it or don't sign it. Those were his choices.

Then, he realized he had another option.

I'll sign the forms, but only in person, he wrote to her after lengthy deliberation. *You can bring them here or I can come to you. But we're doing this face to face.*

He sent the e-mail feeling satisfied with himself. Seeing Joy was no guarantee that she'd want to get back together with him, but it was an open door. Now he just had to see if he could get her to walk through it.

~

In person?

Joy read Nix's e-mail with her eyebrows drawn together, her mouth slightly open in either fear or surprise.

Or maybe it was excitement.

She didn't know. She didn't even understand her own mind.

Was she angry that he was backing her into a corner? A little, yes. Maybe. But she'd effectively shut him out for months, and she couldn't blame him if he wanted some closure.

And maybe, a voice inside her whispered, *it isn't closure. Maybe it's a new beginning.*

And maybe I'm an idiot for expecting anything but his signature.

Joy might not know yet who she wanted to be or what she wanted her future to look like. But she did know that over the past year she'd become strong enough to face the unfinished things in her life.

At least she could do that.

I'll come to Cambria, she wrote to Nix, her fingers shaking a little on the keyboard. *What's a good day for you?*

~

Nix had a hard time concentrating on anything in the twenty-four hours before Joy was scheduled to visit.

He did his shift at the market, where he dropped a box full of glass jars of pasta sauce, creating a mess that looked like a crime scene.

He tried to work on the tiny house design for his new client but found that he'd accidentally placed the floor of the sleeping loft two feet below the ceiling.

Finally, he gave up. He went into the loft, stretched out on his bed, and looked at the sky through the skylight, examining his options.

One: he could ask her to give him another chance. Two: he could beg her to give him another chance. And three: well, there was no three.

Maybe he'd change his mind once he saw her. Maybe he'd realize that the Joy he'd constructed in his mind since she'd left wasn't the same as the real one. Maybe he'd realize he'd been longing for a lie. Then he could just let go and get on with his life.

Not likely, but it was possible.

He just hoped he'd be able to conduct himself like a man when he saw her. He hoped he would maintain his dignity instead of throwing himself at her feet.

Though, if throwing himself at her feet would work, he was willing to try it.

~

SHE'D SAID she would meet him for lunch at a restaurant on Main Street. She got there early and slid into a booth, the papers she needed him to sign tucked into her purse.

She had a mug of coffee in front of her, though she was only sipping at it halfheartedly. Her nerves were already jittery as it was.

Her eyes locked onto his the moment he came in the door. He froze when he saw her, then she watched him gather himself and put on a neutral expression before he walked over to her.

He sat across from her, the vinyl upholstery of the seat crackling a little under his weight.

"Hi." He tried on a smile, but it was a fragile thing, wobbling at the edges.

"Hi, Nix."

They made small talk for a few minutes about what she was doing these days, how his job was, how things were in Cambria. The waitress brought him coffee, and he added cream and sugar.

"I'm sorry about this," she said once the introductory niceties were over. "It's a hassle, I know. But my publisher says I can't use the photos without your signature."

"It's not that big a hassle. It's lunch and a few signatures."

"Still."

"Congratulations on the book deal." He picked up his coffee mug, then put it down again without drinking. "I mean it. That's great news. I know it's what you wanted, so ..."

"Thanks." She pulled the papers out of her bag and slid them across the table to him with a pen.

He looked at them and hesitated.

"How about we eat first? There's time for business afterward."

"Nix ..."

"Please?"

She nodded. They picked up their menus, perused them, then gave the waitress their orders.

OKAY, yes. Nix was holding the papers hostage. He didn't want her to be able to get up and walk away without at least talking to him first, about things other than the weather and the price of Granny Smith apples at the market.

So they picked at their meals in awkward silence, with the occasional attempt at polite small talk. Then, about a quarter of the way through his pasta, Nix put down his fork and propped his elbows on the table.

"Look, Joy. I'll sign your papers. I'm happy for you about the book deal. Really. But I have a lot I want to say to you, if you'll listen."

She shoved her plate aside and nodded, avoiding his gaze.

Now that he had her attention, he didn't know what to say or where to start. When he'd told Evan what was going on, he'd used the ring as his opening gambit. If it worked once ...

"I still have the ring," he said.

Her eyes widened. "You do? Why?"

"Because I thought … I hope … I want to offer it to you again someday, when you're ready. And I know that might not be soon, and it might not be ever. But if you think there's a chance, any chance at all, I don't mind waiting."

"Nix, I—"

"And," he went on, "I want to apologize for the way I acted. The way I stormed off that day in San Simeon, and … every time I think about *when can you vacate,* I want to punch myself in the face. I was hurt, and I reacted badly. I hope you can forgive me."

~

JOY DIDN'T SAY anything at first. She just stared at him, her trembling fingers touched to her lips.

She hadn't known what he would say when she saw him, but part of her had hoped it would be this. Now that he'd said it, she didn't know how to respond or what to do. As much as she wanted to throw herself into his arms and stay there until stars died and worlds ended, she knew they still had so many questions that hadn't been answered.

"You kept the ring," she said.

He reached out his hand and laid it palm-up on the table. She put her own hand in his.

"I did," he said.

She took a deep breath and closed her eyes.

"Nix, I wanted to say yes that day. I really did. I wanted it so much it hurt. But … I didn't want to make a rash decision. I didn't want to do something I wasn't ready for, because we'd both just get hurt later. I needed time. Just … time. But the way you reacted …"

"You wanted to say yes?"

She nodded and squeezed his hand.

"And I acted like an ass," he said.

"Well. You did kind of make it seem like it was then or never. And I just … I didn't want to make a mistake. I didn't want to say yes until I knew for sure. You … us … it's all too important for me to do it wrong, Nix. I just wanted to think."

"Jesus." He let go of her and scrubbed at his face with both hands. "I really fucked that up."

"My life's gone through so many changes over the past year," she went on. "And marriage … that would be the biggest change of all, so soon after everything else. It's like when you're a kid and you spin around and around, and even after you stop, you're still dizzy. I'm still dizzy, Nix. I just need to be still for a while to see where I am."

"That makes sense," he said.

"It does?"

"Yeah. It really does." He folded his arms on the table and looked at her. "So the question is, can we start seeing each other again while you're waiting? Or would that be too much … you know. Spinning?"

It was a good question, one Joy didn't know how to answer.

"Can I think about it?"

His lips pressed into a grim line—it clearly hadn't been what he'd hoped to hear—but he nodded.

~

THE NOD—IT wasn't how Nix had wanted to respond. He'd wanted to protest that they'd had months away from each other, and wasn't that enough time to think? Didn't she know by now that they were both miserable apart?

But that would have been a repeat of the mistakes he'd already made, and he had to be better this time. He had to be smarter.

He reached over to where the papers sat on the edge of the table along with the pen Joy had brought. He signed where the little arrow-shaped sticky tabs told him to sign, then he gave the papers back to Joy.

"Here you go. I hope everything goes well with your book."

"Thank you." She tucked the papers back into her purse.

"I don't really know where this leaves us," he said. "I tried going out with someone else, but … she wasn't you."

Her eyes got shiny and wet as tears shimmered in them, and that wasn't what he'd wanted at all. He hadn't meant to make her cry.

"I love you," he said. "That hasn't changed. I just wanted you to know that."

I LOVE YOU, too.

Joy knew that was what she was supposed to say—that was what he wanted to hear. And it was true. It was so thoroughly true.

She loved him, but she didn't trust him to keep loving her.

She'd gained another few pounds since she saw him last, for one thing, and what if it was more? What if it kept happening, and her mother was right, and a woman with some extra weight wasn't worth loving?

Even as she thought all of those things, she knew this was her problem, not his. This was the result of the messages she'd been given by other people, not by him. This wasn't a problem he'd created, so it wasn't one he could fix.

"I love you, too." There. She'd said it, finally. Because surely telling the truth about things was part of what would heal her.

"You do?"

"Yes. I … God, yes."

"Then there's hope for us."

"There's hope."

He smiled—really smiled—for the first time since she'd arrived.

CHAPTER 34

Nix was a mess of mixed emotions as he and Joy walked out of the restaurant after their lunch.

She hadn't said she would see him again—she'd only said she would think about it.

But she'd said she loved him, which was, frankly, more than he'd hoped for.

He walked her to her car because he wanted to be a gentleman, but once they got there, his gentlemanly impulses turned to something much less honorable.

"It was good to see you again," Joy said, standing on the curb next to her car.

"It was good to see you, too." He knew he should just let her get into her car and go, but something desperate in him told him if he didn't take this chance, he might not get another one.

"Can I just ..." He took her hands in his, entwining their fingers together, then leaned in and kissed her. He'd meant it to be a friendly kiss that might remind her of what she was missing when she wasn't with him.

But before he knew what he was doing, he had her back pressed against the car, her hands, still in his, stretched behind her and pinned to the roof, his mouth plundering hers.

He let out an involuntary moan, and she whimpered a little in response.

Time stopped, at least for him. He wasn't aware of anything but the feel and taste of her. He let go of her hands and plunged his fingers into her hair.

When someone passing by on the sidewalk called, "Get a room!" he came back into himself, back into reality.

He pulled away from her with some difficulty, but it took her a while to catch up. After he released her and stepped back, she still stood plastered against the car, her head back, her eyes closed.

She blinked after a moment and stood up straight, looking flustered and lovely.

"I … oh." Her purse had fallen to the sidewalk, and she bent to pick it up. "I should just …" She pointed to the car, then went around to the driver's side and got in.

Feeling satisfied with himself, Nix gave her a little four-fingered wave as she drove away.

~

JOY TRIED to act nonchalant as she got into her car and drove away from Nix. But as soon as she was out of his sight, she had to pull over and pull herself together so she wouldn't run her car into a utility pole.

That kiss.

She'd felt like her bones had turned to some hot, flowing liquid that had surged from her toes to the top of her head before coming to rest in that thrumming, throbbing spot below her belt.

If he'd wanted to shatter her with that kiss, well, he'd accomplished it.

She sat in her idling car at the curb trying to bring her rebellious body into order.

Calm down. Just calm the hell down.

How was she supposed to make smart choices about her life when he made her body feel that way? When he made her feel like pure molten pleasure was surging through her veins?

Thinking like that made her wonder what the harm would be in sleeping with him a few times. Or more than a few times.

But that wasn't the answer. She needed to clear her head. Damn it, she just needed to think.

Once she'd gotten herself under control, she drove the 150 miles to Ventura trying to distract herself with music, a fancy coffee drink, and personal pep talks. But she arrived back at her apartment just as conflicted as before.

I saw him. He signed the papers, she texted to Amber once she was settled in on her sofa, dressed in sweatpants and a T-shirt and sipping a mug of tea.

That's good, Amber answered. *How was it seeing him again?*

How to answer that? It was good. Hard. Frustrating. Confusing. Mostly, it had filled her with an all-consuming longing, a desire so hot and commanding that more than a few times, she'd almost turned the car around and gone back to him.

It was probably a mistake, she texted. *Because now I can't stop thinking about him.*

Amber: *!!!!*

I wish my goddamned heart would just shut up about him, Joy wrote.

Or, Amber texted, *you could just try listening to it for a change.*

~

JOY HAD LEFT. Despite what he'd said about still loving her, despite the kiss, despite the way he'd apologized and then pleaded for her to give him another chance, she'd just gotten into her car and left.

Nix had given it his best, and it still hadn't persuaded her to stay.

She'd said she would think about it, but what had she been doing for the past months except thinking about it? If she hadn't thought enough by now, it was possible he was wasting his time.

By the time Nix got home, his optimism about Joy—the way she'd admitted she loved him and the way she'd reacted to his kiss—had fallen away, replaced by a sense of doom.

He went to his house, got a beer out of the refrigerator, and sat on an Adirondack chair on his porch, drinking and feeling sorry for himself.

Shit. If only he'd ... what? What else could he have done?

He was on his third beer and starting to feel a little tipsy when Louise's car made its way up the dirt road to his house. She parked, got out, and stood at the bottom of the stairs to the porch, looking at him with pity.

"I knew you were seeing Joy today, and then you didn't answer your texts," she said. "I figured that either meant you were still with her, or she shot you down and you were feeling like shit."

"What if it had been the first one?"

She shrugged. "If I saw her car, I was going to turn around and go home. But I didn't see her car. And here you are."

"Here I am."

She climbed the stairs to the porch and took the seat beside him.

"There's beer in the fridge. Help yourself." He gestured vaguely toward the house.

She went inside and came back with a cold longneck bottle. She sat down, took a deep drink, and gazed out at the grass and the trees.

"You want to tell me how it went, or do you want to just sit here and drink?"

"I want to just sit here and drink."

"You want me to leave?"

"No."

So they sat there together, drinking and taking in the view of Nix's property. The day was cool, and birds tittered in the trees.

It did make him feel better to have Louise here, even if they weren't talking about anything. Even if she couldn't help him.

"Clara and I broke up one time. Did I ever tell you about that?" she said after a while.

"No. When did that happen?"

"A couple of years ago." She shrugged. "She'd been seeing someone else. Then she moved out. I was a mess."

"Clara cheated?" Nix turned to face her, shocked. Louise and Clara were Nix's aspirational couple, the two people, along with his parents, who most embodied enduring love to him.

"She did. It was right after her mother died, so … I think she was just hurting so much she needed something to distract her from it, you know?"

"So, what happened? How did you get her back?"

"I didn't *get* her back. I waited for her to come to her senses, and she *came* back."

They both sat with that.

"If you love something, set it free …" Louise began.

Nix scoffed. "Don't you dare finish that. If I have to come over there …"

"I'm just saying. She's gotta want it, Nix."

He knew that. Shit, he knew it. But the waiting was excruciating.

"I thought I said I didn't want to talk about me and Joy," he reminded her.

"We weren't. We were talking about me and Clara."

Nix sighed and sank deeper into his chair. "I feel like shit."

"Yeah. That'll happen." She took another swallow of her beer.

CHAPTER 35

Joy needed to visit her mother.

It had been months since she'd seen her, and it couldn't be put off any longer, especially now that Joy was a mere hour and a half away from Delores's house.

The key, Joy had found, was to manufacture some other reason for being in Los Angeles so she could drop in on her mother and then, after an hour or so of uncomfortable conversation, claim that she had to run because she was late for whatever that other thing might be.

She bought tickets to a musical at the Ahmanson Theater for herself and Amber—a Sunday matinee, which would allow her to make a lunchtime visit to her mother and then flee in time for the two p.m. curtain.

Her stomach was in knots as she drove to her mom's place. She always felt that way in the run-up to a visit with Delores.

Joy told herself she wouldn't be affected by anything her mom had to say to her. Insults and criticism would just bounce off, as though she were made of Kevlar.

That same internal pep talk had never worked before, but who knew? Maybe she'd have better luck with her own resilience this time.

She arrived at her mother's place with takeout from Delores's favorite restaurant. She brought a salad for Delores and a BLT for herself.

Delores launched in as soon as she saw Joy's lunch.

"Oh, honey. Should you be eating that?"

"What else should I do with it, Mom? Apply it to my skin?" She tried to keep her tone light, as though the whole thing were merely humorous banter.

"Don't be smart with me." Delores frowned, looking into the Styrofoam box in front of Joy. "It's just that, my goodness, you've gained so much weight over the past year. . . ."

"Just under ten pounds," Joy said mildly. "Which still puts my BMI in the normal, healthy range, for your information."

"Well, *health*." Delores spat out the word as though it were an obscenity. "That's one thing, I suppose. But, Joy, you just looked so much *better* before."

All at once, Joy felt her body and her soul flood with shame. Just as it always had under her mother's scrutiny. Just as it had every time she'd felt as though she were not good enough to deserve whatever it was she wanted.

"Mom . . ."

"After all, you were dating a nice young man, and now you're not." She tsked, shaking her head. "Surely if you just lost the weight . . ."

"Mom."

"I know it's not easy, but all it takes is a little discipline."

"Mother, that is enough!" Joy smacked the top of the table hard with her palm, fury clouding her vision.

"Joy Rebecca Maxwell, don't you take that tone with me."

Joy stood up from her seat. Having a showdown with her mother seemed like the sort of thing one should be upright for.

"I'll take whatever tone I want, Mother. And I won't stand here and let you insult me."

Delores rolled her eyes. "You've always been so overly sensitive."

"I am not overly sensitive, I am not fat, and I am not going to listen to you anymore." She abandoned her lunch, picked up her purse, and walked toward the door.

"Where are you going?" Delores demanded.

"Anywhere but here."

Delores jumped up from her chair and followed Joy, her voice becoming loud and shrill. "Do not walk away from me, Joy. Stop. *I told you to stop and listen to me!*"

Joy kept walking, but she paused when she got to the door, her hand on the knob.

"I suppose I should expect this of you," Delores said. "Walking away. Or, running away, I should say. It's what you do, isn't it, Joy? I don't know how I raised a daughter who's such a coward."

Joy turned around slowly. "What did you just say to me?"

"Oh, don't take that wounded tone. You're a coward, and you know it. You ran away from Los Angeles, ran away from that man you were dating. You're running away from your weight problem, and now you're running away from me."

In that moment, Joy might have raged, and she might have fallen apart. Instead, a sense of calm came over her. For the first time, she could see her mother for what she was—a flawed, scared woman who'd tried to love her daughter but didn't know how.

Joy didn't feel anger in that moment. She felt pity.

"I know you did your best, Mom. I know that."

"Joy—"

"But your best isn't good enough for me if you can't accept me the way I am. It's just not."

She opened the door, walked through it, and didn't look back.

~

AS JOY DROVE from her mother's place to Amber's, she ran over the entire exchange in her head.

Her mother was wrong about so much, but she'd been right about one thing: Joy was a coward. She really had run away from L.A., and she really had run away from Nix. She'd fled one life, created another for herself, and then fled that, too.

At some point, she had to stop running, didn't she?

At some point, she had to trust someone. Trust Nix, trust herself.

If she couldn't find it in herself to take some kind of leap of faith, she was going to end up alone. Not because of what she weighed or how she dressed or how she looked, and not because she wasn't worthy of love. She was. But because she was too scared to accept all of the things life was offering her.

She went to Amber's and didn't talk about any of it. They ate lunch together because Joy hadn't eaten at her mother's house, and they went to the theater.

She was quiet, and Amber asked her if she was okay. She assured her friend that she was.

It wasn't until halfway through the show that she broke.

THE SHOW WAS *WICKED*, and the song was "Defying Gravity." Okay, so it was a song about a witch deciding to unleash her evil powers on the world. Joy wouldn't have thought it would apply to her.

But as Elphaba threw off the restrictions of trying to be what everyone else wanted her to be, as the music swelled with her revelation that she had to be fully herself despite the expectations and judgments of others, Joy felt it like a bolt of lightning, like an earthquake.

The song spoke of the pain of trying to conform to someone else's standards in an attempt to attain love, and how the cost of that was far too high.

First Joy's eyes started to sting, then her tears began to fall. And then her shoulders shook and she began dragging in deep, shuddering breaths.

"Are you okay?" Amber whispered, her hand on Joy's arm.

"I … I …" Joy couldn't even get out more than the one syllable, and a deep, animal wail started to come out of her. She got up from her seat and scooted out past the knees of other audience members.

It wasn't until she'd burst into the lobby that she realized Amber had followed her.

"Hey. Hey, hey. It's okay." Amber uttered comforting words and rubbed her friend's back.

"It's ... I ..." Joy was crying too hard to speak.

"Come on. In here." Amber took Joy's hand and led her into the ladies' room.

They realized their mistake when the theater let out for intermission and the ladies' room was flooded with audience members who'd been holding their bladders for three numbers.

"Let's find somewhere more private," Amber said.

"Can we ... can we just ... go?" Joy managed in between heaving sobs.

"Yes. Of course we can."

"But ... you've been ... wanting ... to see this ... show ... forever."

"That's true. But you're more important, Joy. Let's just go."

~

BY THE TIME they got to Amber's car, Joy had mostly gotten hold of herself. Who'd have thought she would be so affected by a song about being yourself even if it meant unleashing flying monkeys on an unsuspecting populace?

"I'm sorry," she told Amber. "Not for ... you know. The crying. But for making you miss the rest of the show. You should have been able to enjoy it."

"That doesn't matter." Amber sat in the driver's seat in the parking lot, rubbing Joy's arm. "You're what matters."

"I love you," Joy said.

"I know."

They didn't talk about what she was feeling, because it was too big for that. Too big for discussion or description. Her feelings were immense, uncontrollable.

And necessary.

What kind of power might Joy have if she were to let herself be who she wanted to be? What kind of life might she have if she let the ... okay, the flying monkeys ... run loose? She'd never know if she continued to be scared. If she continued to be a coward, like her mother had said.

"I need to see Nix," she said.

"Oh, boy."

"I need to go now. Can you take me back to your place so I can get my car?"

Amber assessed her friend. "I'll take you to your car, but I'm driving you to Cambria. You're too upset to make that trip on your own. Besides, I want to see what happens."

THEY WENT to Amber's place, grabbed Joy's overnight bag, and got on the road immediately after.

Since it was already late afternoon, they figured they wouldn't get to Cambria until eight p.m. at the earliest—that was if they didn't make any stops and if the Los Angeles traffic was good to them, which it almost certainly wouldn't be.

Their progress was slowed further when Joy announced that she had to make a stop on the way.

"What? Where?" Amber asked.

When Joy told her, Amber let out a squeal of excitement. "Oh, boy. Oh boy oh boy oh boy!" She wiggled in her seat like her butt was doing a happy dance.

"I'm probably crazy," Joy said.

"Probably. But I'm here for it."

CHAPTER 36

Nix had waited long enough.

He didn't want to be lonely anymore, and he didn't want to be sad. It was time to get out there and meet someone else if Joy didn't want him.

It had been more than a month since he'd signed the papers—a month since the kiss—and she hadn't called him yet. Enough was enough. He loved her. He wanted her. But if she didn't want him, there wasn't much he could do about it.

Determined to move on with his life, he'd started flirting with a pretty barista at his favorite coffee place. Then, when the flirting had gone well, he'd asked her out.

He didn't expect it to amount to anything, but it was a step, and that was something.

Another step would be to return the engagement ring he'd bought for Joy, but he couldn't quite bring himself to do that yet. He'd tried a couple of times, going so far as to drive to the jewelry store with the ring in his pocket, but he hadn't been able to make himself go inside.

One step at a time. First his date, then the ring.

The woman, whose name was Vanessa, was a single mother who'd moved to Cambria a couple of years before. Nix wasn't sure he could overcome the challenges of dating a single mother, but he'd never tried it, so maybe he could.

He took her to Robin's, and they were seated on the patio under a string of fairy lights.

"This is pretty." Vanessa looked around as she opened her menu. "I don't get out that often, with Charlie and everything." Charlie was her son, a seven-year-old with blond hair and a spray of freckles across his nose. Nix had seen Vanessa and the kid around town a few times.

They talked about the menu, what she was going to order, what he was going to order, and what wine they should get, and the whole time, Nix kept wishing a different woman were sitting across from him.

That wasn't fair—it wasn't fair at all. Vanessa was lovely, and she deserved his full attention. He applied himself to the task of giving it to her.

It wasn't as though he was using Vanessa to get his mind off Joy. It was more ... practice. He needed dating practice if he was going to get back out there now that Joy was gone. He needed to normalize the idea of moving on.

And he needed to return the damned ring—though that was a matter for another day.

"Are you okay?" Vanessa looked at him with concern, her eyes big and dark and warm, and Nix realized he'd been conspicuously silent for the last several minutes.

"Yes. Yeah. I'm fine. Of course." He shut his mouth before he could throw in an extraneous *absolutely*.

"Is there something on your mind?" she asked.

The waitress brought their wine, and Nix grasped at his as though it were a life preserver.

He was not going to talk about Joy. He wouldn't do it even if she, by some miracle, were to appear as an apparition in the middle of their table.

He gave Vanessa what he hoped was a winning smile. "I am completely fine, and there's nothing on my mind but you."

Her smile told him he'd been convincing, so that was good.

~

JOY AND AMBER rolled into Cambria at around eight thirty, and Joy felt so hopped up on adrenaline and hope that she was nearly jumping out of her seat.

"Please be home. Please be home." She chanted it as Amber maneuvered her car down the dirt road that led to Nix's place.

When they got there, the tiny house was dark and Nix's car was nowhere to be seen.

"Shit. Shit!" Joy smacked the dashboard with her palm.

"Where else do you think he might be?" Amber asked.

"I don't know. The market's closed. He could be anywhere."

"What do you say we get something to eat and then try coming here again after?" Amber suggested. "I'm starving."

"I'm too nervous," Joy said. "I can't eat."

"Well, I can. We haven't had anything but that bag of chips back in Goleta. Have pity on a girl."

~

THE PROBLEM with getting something to eat at that time of night was that very little was open in Cambria. They tried the Main Street Grill, but it was closed. Linn's was, too. They struck out on their third swing when they tried Robin's on Burton Drive and found that they were no longer seating new parties, and just a few people were left scattered on the back patio, finishing their meals.

"Damn it. I'm going to die. I'm going to starve to death and die," Amber complained.

"Well … the minimart at the Shell station is open until midnight. We can get some granola bars or something," Joy said. "I'm sorry I didn't let you eat."

"It's okay."

They were standing, dejected, in front of Robin's, as though if they stood there long enough, the sheer force of their will might cause the closing hours to change so they could get some nourishment.

If Amber was crazy with hunger, Joy was crazy with anxiety and longing. So much so that she was hearing things that weren't there. She was certain she could hear Nix's voice somewhere in the distance even as they stood there formulating their plan.

"It's the oddest thing," Joy told her friend. "I can hear his voice."

"So can I," Amber said. "Because he's right there." She pointed behind Joy to the restaurant's entrance. Joy spun around and saw Nix coming out with a dark-haired woman, both of them laughing and smiling.

Oh, shit. Oh, shit.

The two words kept repeating in Joy's brain, her heart pounding, a weird buzzing in her ears.

Oh, shit.

"He's ... Who is ... Oh, my God. Nix ..." She wasn't making sense, but Amber understood her easily enough.

"It looks like he's on a date. Come here!" Amber, whispering fiercely, grabbed Joy's arm and yanked her behind a hedge so he wouldn't see them.

A date?! No. No no no no no.

Noooooo.

Surely it wasn't how it looked. Surely she was his sister or his ... accountant. Anything other than his date.

As Joy peeked through the hedge, the woman took Nix's hand in hers and smiled up at him, then leaned her head against his arm.

Oh, shit.

"I'm too late." Joy wanted to wail it to the heavens, but Nix would hear her if she did that, so she whispered in misery. "I'm too late, Amber."

"We don't know that."

"He's on a date."

"But ... that doesn't mean anything. Maybe it didn't go well. Maybe he doesn't like her."

"Well, she likes him. Look at her. She's beaming."

Amber peeked out from the hedge to look. "Okay, she is. She's beaming."

"See? Oh, God. I blew it. I waited too long, and now he's with someone else."

"Just because he's with her right now doesn't mean he's … you know. *With* her."

Nix and the woman were headed down the sidewalk toward where Joy and Amber were hiding, and Joy scrambled to decide what to do. Say hello and act casual? Say hello and throw herself at his feet? Squeeze deeper into her hiding place so he wouldn't see her?

"He's coming. What do I do? What do I do?" she pleaded to Amber.

"Shove over!" Amber nudged Joy farther into the hedge.

Apparently, they were going with Plan C.

Nix and the woman walked hand in hand, focused on each other, and Joy thought she was going to get away without being seen. But just as they passed the hedge where Joy and Amber were hiding, the silk scarf the woman was wearing slipped off. She didn't notice, and it seemed like they still might not be discovered. But then a voice from somewhere a few feet away called, "Ma'am? Ma'am! You dropped your scarf!"

Damn it. Why did there have to be a good Samaritan right here and now?

"Oh!" The woman turned and spotted the scarf. "Thank you!" She walked over, bent down, grabbed the scarf—and then let out an involuntary yelp when she glanced over and realized there were two crazed women hiding in the bushes.

"What's going on? Are you okay?" Suddenly Nix was there, peering into the bushes. His eyes widened when he saw Joy.

"Ah … hi, Nix." Joy waved weakly with her fingers.

"Hi," Amber put in.

"What are you doing in the bushes?" he asked.

"We were just … we wanted to get something to eat," Joy said.

"In the bushes? Were you foraging for acorns?"

"I … just … I can explain," she said.

"Nix? Are you going to introduce me?" the woman asked.

Joy tried to will herself to vaporize, but it didn't work. She was still here. And so was Nix, looking as gorgeous as she'd ever seen him.

He also looked baffled as hell.

Nix wasn't sure what to do or say in that moment. He didn't know how to feel, and he was pretty certain that whatever he did feel was wrong. If he was thrilled and excited to see Joy—which, he could admit, he was—then it was unkind to Vanessa. If he pretended not to be thrilled and excited to see Joy, it would be a betrayal of everything that combined to make Nix who he was.

In the middle of all that, he found his voice.

"Ah … Joy Maxwell, this is Vanessa Carr. Vanessa, this is Joy."

"Hello." Vanessa offered her hand, and Joy, with obvious reluctance, took it.

"I'm Amber." Amber, whom everyone had forgotten about, offered her hand as well.

"And how do you and Nix know each other?" Vanessa was looking back and forth between Nix and the women. From the look on her face, she was trying to keep an open mind but having limited success at it.

"I … ah … was his tenant," Joy offered. "I rented his house for a while. And now I'm just … visiting. As a tourist. With my friend." Joy pointed at Amber to illustrate.

Okay, that was fine. Telling Vanessa she was a tenant was fine. He could walk away and pretend this was nothing.

Only, it wasn't nothing.

It was clearly something.

Had she come back for him? The thought of it made his heart speed up and his body tingle. Had she come back for him after all this time?

Nix wanted to grab Joy and pull her into his arms, but he liked to think of himself as a gentleman, and he was with a date who had nothing to do with any of this and who wasn't to blame for any conflicted feelings he might be having.

"Well … it was good to see you." Nix gave Joy a smile he hoped would communicate more than mere courtesy. He turned to Vanessa. "You ready to go?"

As they walked away, Nix's hand on the small of Vanessa's back, he looked back at Joy, and their eyes met. Then he turned away and walked his date to his car.

~

NEITHER NIX nor Vanessa said much at first on the drive back to her place. Mostly because Nix's brain was too overloaded to accommodate speech.

Had Joy come for him?

No, she couldn't have. If she had, surely she'd have called him or texted him, and she hadn't. If she'd come to see him, she wouldn't have dived into a hedge when she saw him coming. She'd have simply spoken to him.

Wouldn't she?

Shit. She'd been hiding from him, and when you hid from someone, it was because you didn't want to see them, and you didn't want them to see you. You hid from someone when you wanted to avoid them.

Why was she here, then?

It didn't matter. If she wasn't here for him—if seeing him was such a negative prospect that she had to hide from him—then the rest of the story was irrelevant.

He didn't even realize how awkwardly silent he'd been on the drive until Vanessa spoke up.

"So, I figure she's either an ex, or you're still seeing her and you got caught with someone else."

Nix glanced at her as he drove, feeling like shit on so many levels that he could hardly enumerate them.

"My ex," he said.

"Ah."

They drove a little farther without saying anything.

"And you're still hung up on her," Vanessa said. It wasn't a question.

"I … yeah. Yes."

"So this date was, what? Revenge?"

"No. Not at all. It was just … It was me trying to see if I was ready to be over her."

"And you're not."

"Apparently, I'm not."

"Okay."

He shot her a look. "You're not mad?"

She shrugged and let out a breath. "It's a first date, Nix. I didn't exactly have time to get attached."

"Right. Okay. Good."

"Plus, it'll make a good story tomorrow when I'm telling my friends," she added. "We're coming out of the restaurant and the ex pops out of the bushes? Priceless." She laughed.

He couldn't help smiling at that, even though he felt the misery of the brokenhearted. "You're really being a good sport about this."

"Oh, God. The stories I could tell you about my first dates gone wrong." Then she began to tell them, and they were good stories. Nix started to feel a little better.

CHAPTER 37

"Holy shit. What do I do now?" Joy stood with Amber on the sidewalk outside Robin's, still in shock over what had happened.

"You go ahead with the plan," Amber said. "You do what you came to do. Only, you wait until tomorrow."

"I can't do it now! What if he and she are a thing? What if she's back at his place getting naked right now? Oh, God." Joy covered her face with her hands, then slid her hands into her hair and pulled at it. "Shit. I've lost him. It's over."

"Maybe it isn't. . . ."

"It can't be over. It can't." Joy went on as though Amber hadn't spoken. "I can't lose him, Amber. Not now that I know I love him."

"Come on." Amber took Joy by the arm and led her toward the car. "Let's get some sleep, then we can regroup in the morning."

THEY HADN'T BOOKED a room ahead of time, and most of the hotels in Cambria stopped staffing the reception desk at eight p.m. So they drove up to San Simeon and checked in at the Motel 6.

It was everything you'd expect from a Motel 6—relatively cheap and available and strangely orange—and they flopped onto the two double beds as soon as they got inside their room.

"You didn't get to eat," Joy said. "You must be starving. Amber—"

"Don't worry about it." Amber was spread out like a starfish on her bed. "I'm too exhausted to eat now, anyway."

Joy was certain she wouldn't be able to sleep, and she was right—she didn't. She took a hot shower to relax, but that didn't help, and afterward, she lay in bed in the dark listening to Amber's soft breathing and pondering whether to text Nix.

If she did text him, what would she say?

Sorry I interrupted your date. Hope you still got laid.

Obviously, that was out.

The idea of him with that woman, possibly in bed, his hands on her body, made her stomach hurt and her chest burn.

When she started to cry, she tried to keep quiet about it so she wouldn't wake Amber. It was all her fault, anyway, so she deserved to suffer alone and in silence.

NIX WAS NOT GOING to text Joy. He was *not* going to text Joy.

He reminded himself of this fact many times over the long sleepless night as he lay in his bed looking out the skylight at the vast, unknowable universe.

If she'd come for him, she would get in touch. And if she hadn't, then there was no point anyway.

But what if she *had* come for him, and she'd abandoned her plan to approach him when she'd seen Vanessa? That seemed like a distinct possibility.

Still, he was not going to text her.

After a long and fruitless time trying to sleep, he got up, went downstairs, and paced the length of his house, scrubbing at his face with his hands and raking his fingers through his hair.

He could text her.

Why shouldn't he text her?

He grabbed his phone off the coffee table and composed a message.

It was our first date. I took her home right after, and then I came back to my place. Alone.

Once the message had been written, he stared at it for a long time, deciding what to do. Send? Don't send?

"Fuck it," he said out loud, to no one, and hit SEND.

~

JOY GASPED when her phone pinged with a text. Because, who else could it be but Nix? She checked the clock—just after two a.m. He'd had time to sleep with his girlfriend, surely. Maybe he was letting Joy know he'd moved on. Maybe the woman—Vanessa—was lying beside him, naked, right now.

The idea swirled around inside her like an illness.

Stop torturing yourself. Just read it.

First date. No sex. She processed all of it as she read. She should have been happy about the no-sex part—and she was—but the fact that there had been a date in the first place showed that Joy had very nearly been too late.

But she wasn't too late—she wasn't—because he wanted her to know there'd been no sex. He wanted her to know that woman wasn't his girlfriend.

Not yet, anyway.

You're dating, she wrote to him. *You're moving on.*

Trying to, he responded. *Unless there's a reason I shouldn't move on.*

Her heart pounded, and her palms were getting sweaty. Tears sprang to her eyes, and she wiped them away with her fingertips.

You're at home, then? she texted.

Yes.

Joy hesitated only a moment. *Don't move. I'm on my way.*

~

SHE SCRAMBLED to get dressed in the dark without waking Amber. She grabbed the first clothes she could find in her bag—a pair of sweatpants and a hoodie. She crammed her feet into her shoes, grabbed her purse and Amber's keys off of the dresser, and left, an adrenaline rush vibrating through her and annihilating the tiredness she'd felt.

This is crazy. It's the middle of the night. I'm crazy.

What if she got there and said what she had to say, and he rejected her? What then?

She couldn't think about that. She just couldn't. She had to have courage. She had to ... well, yes. Defy gravity. It was time to unleash the flying monkeys.

~

HOLY SHIT. She was coming over. She was coming over now.

Nix didn't know what to do. Should he be ... preparing somehow? Should he be planning what he was going to say?

But it wasn't his turn to say anything, really. He'd declared his love, and now that fact was out there. The ball was in her court. It was her turn to either return it or end the game.

When he heard her car pulling up in front of the house, he felt sick with nerves. It wouldn't do to show it, though. He took a deep breath, let it out with his eyes closed, then walked out onto the porch to meet her.

~

THE THING WAS, the moment Joy parked the car and saw Nix standing under the porch light, she was pretty sure she didn't deserve him.

God, just look at him, his shoulder leaning against the doorjamb, his hands tucked into his pockets like he was waiting for the mailman or the Amazon delivery guy. So casual, like none of this mattered. But even from here, even this far away, she could see that it did matter. She could read it in the way he shifted from one foot to the other, the way he rubbed his mouth with one hand before returning the hand to his pocket.

She'd been wanting him for so long that the wanting had become a part of her, a standard piece that couldn't be removed from the rest without the entire structure of her life falling to the ground.

Her hands trembling, Joy unlocked the car door, opened it, and got out.

She didn't walk to him at first. She just stood there next to the car, waiting for him to make the next move, waiting for his words or his body language to tell her what to do.

It wasn't until that moment that she realized she must look awful. Sweatpants, a hoodie, no makeup, her hair a disheveled mess. She should have planned this out more. She should have—

"You look beautiful." He said it as though he were reading her mind. And then he was coming down the stairs from the porch, coming to her.

She laughed at that, at the ridiculousness of it. "I don't."

"You really do." And now he was standing in front of her, so close she could smell his scent. He reached out to brush the hair away from her forehead. "You're the most beautiful thing I've ever seen."

She'd stopped breathing, and she willed herself to start again.

"Nix."

"She was just … a date. That's all. Just a date. I went out with her to try to forget about you."

"Did it work?" Her voice was a ragged whisper.

"No." He pulled her to him, tangled her hair in his hands, and kissed her.

~

Joy clung to Nix with all of the intensity of months of unresolved longing. She opened her mouth to him, letting him devour her, giving everything back to him as her body filled with heat.

She staggered back and bumped into the car with Nix still on her, and she recalled dimly that this was the second time she'd been pressed against her car in a kiss.

She wouldn't mind it happening again and again.

Her hands lay against his cheeks and then moved down to his throat, feeling him, wanting his skin beneath her palms.

"I..." She gasped as he moved his mouth to her jawline, tasting her. "I thought I was too late."

"You're exactly on time."

She squealed as he picked her up in his arms and carried her up the stairs and into the house.

CHAPTER 38

Nix still didn't trust what was happening. He wanted to, but some little voice in his brain said it could all end in a second if he made the wrong move.

So he just wouldn't make any wrong moves.

He felt like a happy caveman, carrying a woman to his bed. Or, he did until they got to the ladder that led to the sleeping loft.

"I don't think I can manage to carry you up the ladder." He set her down on her feet. "It would kind of ruin the moment if I drop you on the floor."

She giggled and smiled at him in a way that lit up her whole face. Hell, it lit up the room and, beyond that, his entire world.

Joy scrambled up the ladder into the loft, and he was right behind her, enjoying the view.

When they got up there, they turned to each other, on their knees in the low space, and kissed more tentatively, more slowly, because they had time to do this right. He rubbed his hands over her back.

"Are you sure this is what you want?" He was afraid to even ask it, his voice breaking, because what if she said no?

"Yes." She nodded. "Yes. I'm sure."

"Thank God." He took her face in his hands and tasted her mouth, her cheek, the line of her jaw. Then he took her hoodie by the hem and lifted it over her head, tossing it aside onto the bed. He wanted to go for her T-shirt next, but he hesitated. "I can turn the lights out if you want."

"No. Leave them on."

"Really?"

"If you want to."

"I do. I really do. God, I want to see you." The idea of it—of her letting him undress her and see her body—made him even more painfully hard than he already was.

He saw something in her face—something brave and determined—and she took off her shirt, kneeling before him in sweatpants and a bra.

Her skin was pale and smooth, and he couldn't believe it was his to touch.

"You're gorgeous." He ran his hands over her shoulders, everything he'd ever wanted right here within arm's reach. "You're absolutely … you're an angel."

He undressed her the rest of the way, and he spent the rest of the night exploring—and pleasuring—every part of her.

As it happened, nobody needed a blindfold.

~

IN THE MORNING, Joy woke to find herself wrapped around Nix, both of them warm and naked in the morning sun coming through the skylight. She'd never thought she could be this happy. Or, if she could, she'd never thought it would last. But now? She was ready for this.

She was ready for forever.

She lay there and breathed in Nix's warm morning scent, and she couldn't wait to tell Amber.

Oh, crap. Amber.

Joy had sneaked out in the dead of night without even leaving a note. Plus, she had Amber's car.

She got out of bed, careful not to wake Nix, and scrambled into her clothes. Then she went downstairs, hunted up Amber's keys, and went to the car where she'd left her bag.

She brought her purse into the house, dug her phone out of it, and saw that Amber had texted her several times in the last hour.

Joy, where are you?

Where's my car?

You're at Nix's, aren't you? :D

But seriously, I need my car.

Joy composed a text: *Sorry! Yes, I'm at Nix's place. Your car is safe. Will bring it to you before check-out time.*

Forget the logistics. How did things go?! Did you do it yet?

Depends on what "it" you mean.

You know what I mean! Did you give it to him?

Not yet.

She'd gotten so wrapped up in the events of last night, she'd almost forgotten the thing she'd come to Cambria to do.

Nix handed her the perfect opportunity when he came downstairs a couple of minutes later, looking delicious in nothing but a pair of jeans, his feet bare, his hair down and brushing his shoulders.

~

"Everything okay?" he asked.

"I was just texting Amber." She held up her phone to illustrate. "I left the motel last night without telling her, and I thought I'd better check in."

He nodded, then grinned and gave her a long, deep kiss. Still holding her in his arms, he said, "Coffee?"

"Yes, please."

He went into the kitchen, set up the coffeemaker, pushed the ON button, then turned to her, leaning his butt against the countertop. "Come here." He opened his arms to her, and she stepped into them. "Is this ... I don't want to be that guy who has to talk about what it all means, but ... I need to know what this is. I want ... I want this every day for the rest of my life. You, here, with me. If that's not what this is, then I need to know."

She leaned into him and gave him a tentative, shy smile. "That's what you want? Every day, forever?"

"That's what I want." He rubbed her back with both hands. "I still have the ring. I can hold onto it until you're ready. I don't need to rush you. But ... just so you know."

"Speaking of that." Joy pushed against his chest to free herself from his grasp, then went to her purse. She rummaged around inside it, then came out with something she had hidden in her hand.

"What's that?" he asked.

"Just give me a second." She took a deep, shuddering breath and let it out. She was trembling. "I have to ... you know. Mentally prepare." She wiggled from one foot to the other, stretching her neck as though she were getting ready to accomplish some athletic feat.

"Joy, what are you—"

"*Shh.*" She put one finger to his lips to quiet him. Then, incredibly, she got down on one knee and reached for his hand. "Nix, I love you. I couldn't say it before, even though I felt it—God, so much—but I can say it now. I'm ready for this, for you, for all of it." She held out a ring, gold and sparkling in the morning light. "I'm not perfect, and I'm never going to be. But I'll do my best. Will you marry me?"

"You bought me a ring." He stood there, stunned, looking down at her, at the ring in her hand. "Holy shit. You bought me a ring."

"Will you take it? Will you take ... me?"

He dropped down to his knees in front of her and pulled her into his arms. "Of course I will. God. Yes. Of course I will." He kissed her soundly, then took the ring and put it on his finger.

Then he grabbed her, and she squealed as he brought both of them to the floor, his body covering hers.

After that, it was a while before either of them said anything.

~

AFTERWARD, as they lay naked on the floor of his house, somewhere between the kitchen and the sitting area, he rose up on one elbow to look at her. "What do you think about living here, in the tiny house?"

"I just assumed we would."

"Good. But ..."

"But what?"

"But now you're going to have half as much room for your clothes as you did before."

"Oh. That's a good point."

"I had a thought about that," he said.

"You did? When? Between last night and this morning?"

"No. Jeez. I've been thinking about you coming here to live with me for a hell of a lot longer than that."

She trailed her hand down his chest. "So, what's your thought?"

"A dressing shed."

"A dressing shed?"

"Yeah. I could build a ten-by-ten shed next to the house, with hardwood floors and built-in shelving and vanity lighting. It could be like a big walk-in closet for all your things."

Her mouth fell open. "You'd do that for me?"

"Joy, I'd do anything for you. Including moving into a regular house, if that's what you want."

She knew he loved the tiny house, knew it was a part of who he was. And she wanted that for him. She didn't want him to compromise on that or anything else.

"I've never had a dressing shed before. I like it."

"Yeah?" He looked so happy, so proud, that she knew it was right.

"Yes. Yes to that, yes to everything. Yes."

~

NIX WENT ALONG to pick up Amber from the motel, because now that he had Joy back, he didn't want to let her out of his sight.

When they got to the room, Joy unlocked the door, knocked tentatively, and called, "Amber? Are you decent? Nix is with me."

"He is? Come in! Come in! Tell me what happened!"

They came into the room to find Amber fully dressed and in the final stages of packing her bag.

Nix grinned and waved to her from the doorway.

"It went pretty well, I think," Joy said. "But … there's something I have to ask you."

"Uh oh. What?" Amber propped a fist on her hip and faced them.

"How do feel about being a maid of honor?"

Amber's eyes widened, and she squealed and jumped up and down. "Really? Oh, God. That's great. Yes! Of course. Even if you make me wear an ugly-ass dress, I'll do it. I'm so excited. Oh, my God. Nix, come here!" She ran over to him and grabbed him in a bear hug, then moved on to Joy and hugged her, too. "I'm so happy I'm not even going to mention the fact that you stole my car."

"It was for a good cause," Joy said.

"Yeah, it was. Meanwhile, I haven't eaten since yesterday at lunch. You can make up the whole car theft thing to me by taking me out to breakfast."

EPILOGUE

Joy stood in the middle of her dressing shed, her hands on her hips, appraising Nix's work.

"Maybe if we put the rods for long hanging items over here, we can use this area over here for shelves." She pointed to the wall to the right of her.

"Right." He rubbed the stubble on his chin while he thought about it. "You want the shelves big enough for storage boxes, or . . ."

"Shoes," Joy said.

"Shoes."

"Yep."

"And how many shoes are we talking about? You know. Just for planning purposes."

She winced apologetically. "I don't have an exact number, but it's a lot of shoes."

Most of her clothes were still in storage until the shed could be completed, but once she retrieved everything, there would be shoes.

"Are we talking, a dozen pairs? A hundred? Just give me a ballpark figure so I'll know what we're looking at here."

"More than a dozen, less than a hundred."

Since Joy had come to live with Nix, she'd had more time to figure out who she was and what she wanted. And while the new Joy knew there was more to life than looking good—knew there was so much more about her to value—she still enjoyed shoes. And while that wasn't necessarily a thing Nix could understand, he was doing his best to accommodate her.

"Okay. Shoe shelves over here, rods over here, maybe some drawers here for scarves and accessories and whatnot, and a full-length three-way mirror over here." He walked around the room, pointing and gesturing to indicate his plans.

The hardwood floor had already been laid, the walls had been insulated and drywalled, and the place had been wired for electricity. Nix had installed the lighting to Joy's specifications, and it was designed to flatter, not to make her look three times her actual size the way so many department store dressing rooms did.

Not that she was willing to make her size an issue.

She'd gained a little more weight, and then things had leveled off. She'd ended up as a size ten, with the happy benefit that her boobs were bigger and more lush than they'd ever been.

If someone had asked her now, after the fact, she wouldn't have been able to say what she'd been so afraid of. Her body was fine. Her health was fine. She still ran, and she ate food she enjoyed.

And, far from being put off by the extra weight, Nix seemed more attracted to her than ever.

"Maybe we could fit a couch in here," he said, grabbing her around the waist and pulling her to him. "You know, for relaxing. Or … whatever." He began nuzzling her neck with his nose.

"A couch for whatever." She giggled as his breath on her throat tickled her. "Add that to the list."

"Will do." He ran a hand down to her ass—an ass he never ceased to delight in, especially since it had become more *there*. "And while we're adding things to the list …"

"Mmm?" Her eyes had slid closed, and she'd slipped into a reverie of pleasure. Her response came up through the fog of her growing desire.

"You need to meet my parents."

At that, her eyes flew open. "You're right. I do. And, oh, God, you need to meet my mother. I just hope you still love me after that."

"I will. I do."

Nix had told Joy about his parents, of course. She knew they'd raised him in Cambria in a farmhouse not far from where they lived now. She knew they'd lived a life not too different from Nix's—he'd grown up with organic farming and sustainable use of the land, with chickens and a couple of cows. Joy and Nix didn't have any livestock now, but they were planning to build a coop and get some chickens in the next month or so.

But he hadn't visited them in the time she'd known him, as far as she knew, and she didn't know where they lived. That was a big gap in her knowledge of him—one she set about rectifying.

"I can't believe I don't know this, but ... where are they? Your parents?"

"Right now?" He did the chin-rub again as he considered the question. "Hard to say. Maybe South Africa?"

She gaped at him. "South Africa? Maybe?"

"It's hard to keep track of the itinerary."

At her blank look, he said, "They're cruisers."

"Cruisers?"

"They live on a cruise ship. Which, right now, is probably somewhere around Cape Town."

Joy blinked at him. "How have you never told me that?"

He shrugged. "It's embarrassing. I don't tell anybody, if I can avoid it. That kind of hedonism, that kind of consumerism ... it's appalling. And the environmental impact ..."

"But ... how did they go from ... from sustainable farming to deck chairs and all-night buffets?"

He sighed and put his hands on his hips, resigned to telling the story. "They were planning to retire in Cambria, live here for the rest of their lives. Then my aunt Bridgette gave them a cruise for their thirtieth anniversary. It was like a religious conversion. They sold the house, put all their stuff in storage, bought a cruise residence, and they've been out there ever since."

This information was so shocking that Joy simply gaped at him, her jaw slack. "Holy shit."

"Yeah."

"So ... do you ever see them, then?"

"Oh, sure. Sometimes their ship docks in San Pedro or San Francisco and we get together for dinner or something."

"So we'll do that." She wrapped her arms around him and pressed a kiss to his chin. "The next time they dock in California, we'll go see them."

"I've got a better idea." He grinned.

"What's that?"

"Their ship is heading to the Caribbean in June. It's a seven-day cruise. I thought maybe we'd take a little trip. If you want to."

Joy stared at him, speechless, for a long moment, then she said, "Yes! Oh my God. Are you serious? I can't wait! I'll need a new bathing suit, and, oh, jeez, the dinners are usually formal dress, right? That's okay, I've got some stuff that'll work, so I won't really need to buy anything else. Oh, Nix! I've never been on a cruise. I can't wait! Amber's going to be so jealous."

"I kind of thought we might bring her along."

"Really?" That part didn't make sense, but she went with it.

"Sure. Also, Louise and Clara. And maybe your mother."

The part about her mother really didn't make sense. She stopped bouncing and looked hard at him, trying to imagine why in the world he'd want such a thing.

"And, the part about not buying anything else? Maybe just one dress."

"One dress?"

"Sure, unless you want to get married in something you already have. But I figured you'd want a wedding dress."

"A ... I ..." She seemed to be stammering vowels.

"There's a wedding chapel on the ship, so I thought ..." He shrugged. "But if you want a big wedding somewhere around here, we could do that instead."

"I ... no. No. A cruise ship wedding sounds perfect." And it did.

Even if the idea of seven straight days on board with her mother sounded less perfect. Ah, well. Maybe her mother would find some activities she enjoyed. Bingo, maybe, or napkin folding.

"I'm glad." He kissed her, a long, leisurely kiss that spoke of their equally long and leisurely future together.

"I love you," she said. "But what about all of that stuff you said about consumerism and the environmental impact of cruise ships? If this isn't what you want …"

"I want you," he said. "And I've got to be honest, my parents have made the whole cruise ship thing sound pretty cool. With the tiny house commissions I've gotten since your book came out, we can afford it, so why not?"

"A June wedding," she said.

"Yep. A June wedding. I just hope you don't get seasick."

"Oh, jeez. I hadn't thought of that. Do you?"

"I guess we'll find out."

In the meantime, they discovered that they didn't really need a couch in the shed in order to do … whatever. The floor worked just fine.

Made in the USA
Columbia, SC
01 July 2021

41124463R00155